PRAISE FOR TH

MYSTE... _

**2020 Next Generation Indie Book Awards
Finalist in Mystery**

**2019 Best Book Awards Finalist in Fiction
(Mystery/Suspense)**

"A solid series entry."

—BOOKLIST

"Dark and gripping with plenty of twists and good solid characters
that you actually cared about . . . the premise was original and
gritty."

—THE INTERNATIONAL REVIEW OF BOOKS

"Doucette's fluid prose and deft feel for the revealing detail will
draw you into her beguiling tale of a triple murder. You'll love
how Dr. Pepper Hunt and her brooding partner, Detective
Beau Antelope, plunge without fear into the dark forest of
the human heart."

—BRYAN GRULEY, author of *Bleak House*, and the
    Starvation Lake trilogy

"Filled with shocking twists and turns, J.L. Doucette, masterfully
weaves a gripping, suspenseful tale of duplicity, secrecy, and
murder."

—GLEDE BROWN KABONGO, Amazon #1 best-selling author
    of the Fearless Series

"Doucette carefully crafts the connection between personal relationships and mental health and the kinds of secrets people keep to protect themselves and sometimes others . . . but those secrets often come with unexpected costs."

—READERS' FAVORITE

"A missing person tale with a strong setting and cast of characters. . . . Doucette's auspicious first novel puts a welcome focus on the players instead of transgressive twists."

—KIRKUS REVIEWS

"Readers will devour this page-turning mystery, full of enthralling characters, sinister plots, and an ending that you won't expect."

—BUZZFEED

"Compelling and intense. . . . a sensational murder mystery that engages the reader from the first page."

—READERS' FAVORITE

UNKNOWN ASSAILANT

UNKNOWN ASSAILANT

A DR. PEPPER HUNT MYSTERY

J.L. DOUCETTE

SHE WRITES PRESS

UNKNOWN ASSAILANT

Book Three in the Dr. Pepper Hunt Mystery Series

J.L. DOUCETTE

Published 2021
Printed in the United States of America
Print ISBN: 978-1-64742-219-6
E-ISBN: 978-1-64742-220-2

Library of Congress Control Number: 2021914650
For information, address:
She Writes Press
1569 Solano Ave #546
Berkeley, CA 94707

Interior design by Tabitha Lahr

She Writes Press is a division of SparkPoint Studio, LLC.

All company and/or product names may be trade names, logos, trademarks, and/or registered trademarks and are the property of their respective owners.

This is a work of fiction. Names, characters, places, and incidents either are the product of the author's imagination or are used fictitiously. Any resemblance to actual persons, living or dead, is entirely coincidental.

In memory of Michael Caviasca,

who told me his stories

Separation

By W. S. Merwin

Your absence has gone through me
Like thread through a needle
Everything I do is stitched with its color.

PROLOGUE

Like many people referred to me for psychological evaluation, Bella Sanderson didn't want to be there.

I'm a forensic psychologist in Sweetwater County, Wyoming, where I have a private practice and consult with the Sheriff's Department on murder cases that require psychological insight.

An attorney from Green River asked if I would do a competency evaluation on an elderly female client who hired him to revise her will. After meeting with her, he began to think there was something off about her thought process. He wanted an expert opinion on her competence to make legal and financial decisions regarding her estate to avoid challenges to the document later.

The woman in my waiting room didn't fit the image I'd created from the attorney's description of his sixty-six-year-old client. She sat tall, with a dancer's graceful posture, on the edge of a chair closest to the door, her folded hands resting on her knees, long legs crossed at the ankles.

She clearly cared about fashion: light denim jacket, white summer dress, boots of caramel suede, soft and expensive, a heavy turquoise pendant that matched her eye color, and a long silver braid, the single indicator of her age.

Regal and elegant—those were the words that came to mind on first impression. A second later, a hint of something else, in spite of her effort to conceal it, the bedrock core of her—feral and ruthless.

I introduced myself and offered my hand. She remained seated, tilted her head, and took her time assessing me.

After a while, the standoff began to feel uncomfortable.

"Why don't you come into my office, and we can get started, Mrs. Sanderson," I said.

I opened the door and motioned her into my consulting room. A tall woman, almost six feet, she moved with an easy grace. I pointed to the large desk set under the wide windows that looked out on White Mountain, glowing like a white-hot coal in the bright summer sun.

"That's a nice view you have. I'm partial to mountain views. I can see the Wind River Mountains from my kitchen."

A girlish voice, soft and high, unexpected because it didn't align with the strength of her physical presence. I made a mental note—watch for other contradictions.

"That sounds lovely."

"I apologize for my rudeness out there, Doctor. I didn't want to come here. My lawyer needs proof I'm not losing my mind, and my son agreed with him, so here I am."

She smiled and held out her hand. "Call me Bella."

We sat at the desk where I set out the testing materials. I handed her the first of the Rorschach Inkblot cards, the gold standard of projective tests designed to reveal the secrets of the unconscious.

I'm always excited at the beginning of the testing process. For me it's an honor and a thrill to be allowed into the mind of another human being. I never know what I will learn, what secrets the tests will reveal.

In the clinical interview the psychologist elicits the individual's life story, which is reliant on memory. Some memories are forgotten, and some stand out more than others. Surprising personal events, called flashbulb memories, are usually recalled in vivid detail. Bella Sanderson had experienced four traumatic events in her life: Mother died in childbirth. Brother accidental death when she was eight, he twelve. Sexual assault/rape senior year UW, age twenty-one. Husband suicide, gunshot, twenty years ago, age forty-six.

Standardized testing indicated no short-term or long-term memory loss and no problems with insight or judgment. In the report I prepared for her attorney, I recommended the court consider her mentally competent at the time of the evaluation.

At some point in our time together that afternoon, I felt the first stirring of sadness. By the time she left my office and for hours after, I was caught in a time warp of the discarded sorrow Bella Sanderson had left behind.

■ ■ ■

Three months later, on a Sunday evening in late November, Detective Beau Antelope called to tell me about the shootings at the Sanderson Ranch. During the investigation into the deaths, I went back to my report and read through the narrative history, the negative experiences in early life, the traumas and losses, to see how they might be connected to the tragic events that had recently unfolded. And as is often the case, I had to consider that there were other important life events that Bella Sanderson had chosen not to disclose.

The main thing I have learned in my work as a psychologist is that the outcome of a life is determined by the balance of two profound and opposing forces—love and trauma. I wanted to understand why the balance tipped for Bella Sanderson. This strong woman had survived so many challenges to her security through determination and self-reliance, yet in the end did not escape tragedy. Some lives are marked by so many sorrows, one following the other in a gathering momentum of pain, surging through the years, unstoppable and unjust, that it makes you ask why?

CHAPTER 1

On the Sunday before Thanksgiving, Detective Beau Antelope
looked forward to watching hours of football on his new seventy-
inch flatscreen, an early Christmas present he'd bought for himself.
He turned on the pregame show and sipped tomato juice and
vodka; liquid relief flowed through his bloodstream. Domino, his
border collie, was asleep on the couch. It would be a good day.

The phone rang and changed those plans. Murder always
took priority.

Murder thrilled him more than football. He shouldn't have
felt that way and would never tell anyone. He had chosen his job
for a bigger reason than keeping the streets safe from petty crim-
inals, just as in hunting where only the big game called to him.
You could keep your rabbits and sage grouse, small-time drug
dealers and vandals; he stalked elk and killers.

Shower, dress, Italian espresso to go. An hour later, he turned
onto the ranch road and parked in front of the crime scene.

The house where two people had died by gunshot sat at
the southeast corner of the Sanderson Ranch. A stand of birch
trees separated the modern log-and-stone structure from dormant
alfalfa fields.

In the distance, the Wind River Mountains formed a granite
boundary the length of the Eden Valley, the western slopes still

dark with shadows. On the other side of the working ranch, cattle sheltered against wooden windbreaks built in the winter corral.

Memory of woodsmoke, sweet and charred, came on a current of biting wind.

The kind of place I'd want to come home to, he thought.

The whole scene was tied up in garish crime scene tape.

As he got closer to the house, he sensed a disturbance in the air, the presence of a new and unwanted energy, recently arrived and settled in.

No signs of forced entry. Like many people in Wyoming, the residents of this house believed they were safe in their own homes and didn't lock their doors at night. For peace of mind and protection from any threat that walked through the door, they slept with firearms close at hand.

So often those weapons, accidentally or intentionally, became an agent of death for a friend or family member.

He pictured the master bedroom and braced himself for the sight of the bodies of the recently dead, sprawled and bleeding. Even with training and experience and his own defenses against feeling too much, the first sight was always a shock.

He walked up the carpeted stairs and stood alone in the hallway as he prepared to meet Dan and Heather Petrangelo.

He entered the large bedroom furnished in heavy dark wood, and in the center a king-sized bed, pillar posts carved with scrolls.

The man lay on his back in the middle of the bed. Mid-forties, stocky build, black hair, white T-shirt, plaid boxers. There was a single bullet hole in the right side of his head. He wore a wide gold wedding ring on his right hand, and a Glock service revolver rested on his open palm.

The woman lay on her back in the doorway between two rooms, her lower body in the bedroom and her upper body in the bathroom. One gunshot wound in her chest. The thick white bath towel on the floor beside her had turned dark with her blood. Same approximate age as the male, tall and slender, long blond hair still wet from a shower, no wedding rings. On the bathroom floor, to the right of her body, was an open suitcase. From where he stood, he could see the contents: lingerie, a make-up case, and a hair dryer.

At first look, it appeared to be a domestic murder-suicide. The coroner would come from Cheyenne in the morning and, after autopsy, prepare a formal statement on the cause of death.

What happened here? How did these two ordinary people arrive at this violent exit from life?

Domestic homicides were often referred to as crimes of passion. Those words conveyed a sense of tortured love that he believed was accurate more often than not. What they didn't convey was the flat-out ugliness and brutality that came from a love obsession gone wild.

A somber mood settled over the house while the technicians worked in silence. The quick, repeating flash of light from the cameras made the scene feel like a special occasion, a wedding or political event. These images would never grace anyone's home or run on the front page of credible print media. They might contribute to a reenactment of the events that occurred in this house in the dark of night.

Paige Petrangelo, the deceased's eighteen-year-old daughter, had discovered the bodies. The girl and her grandmother, Bella Sanderson, who owned the ranch, had been taken by ambulance to Sweetwater County Memorial Hospital to be assessed and treated for shock.

From the responding officer, Antelope learned that Paige had stayed overnight at her boyfriend's place in Rock Springs. He'd dropped her off to spend the day with her parents with the plan that he'd pick her up in the evening. Her car was in for servicing at the Get and Go Gas Station in Reliance.

"Why didn't she call him? The boyfriend, why didn't she call him when she found this mess? Wouldn't that make sense? Call the boyfriend who dropped her off?"

"She tried. He turns his phone off at work."

Pictures of Paige covered one wall of the bedroom. The shining star in her parents' world. Other photos on display: a wedding picture, Heather at a show of her paintings, Dan as he received an honorary award from the Police Academy. Antelope couldn't determine which of her parents Paige resembled. He gave up and focused on the big picture.

"Where does the boyfriend work?" he asked.

"He works two jobs. Engine mechanic out at the airfield, and a part-time gig down in Reliance at the Get and Go."

"Bring him in from wherever he is."

"Yes sir. On my way," the officer said.

"Bring him straight to me. I'll do the interview. Nobody else."

He wanted the first shot at this guy, no pun intended. Sometimes outsiders, having a different perspective, knew more about family dynamics than the family members themselves.

As he left the ranch and got on the road to Rock Springs, the heavy mood of the crime scene lifted. It was still Sunday, and the ease of the day remained, helped by sunshine and snow in the desert.

There was something about the crime scene that bothered him—the position of the bodies.

Was it a straightforward murder-suicide? This kind of case got to him more than any other.

■ ■ ■

Antelope was a thirty-nine-year-old single male, who'd never married or lived with a woman other than his mother. He'd recently figured out why making a commitment in love was something he couldn't do. He was one of those people who didn't think having love was worth the pain of losing love. His fear of abandonment was stronger than his desire for connection.

Domestic murder-suicide cases won the trophy for the worst way to end a relationship. They were the most extreme example of love gone wrong, a reminder that love is a high-stakes game.

This was a case for Dr. Pepper Hunt. He'd call and ask her if she had time to consult on the investigation.

He'd been thinking about calling her anyway. There was something he wanted to talk with her about, but that conversation would have to wait for now.

CHAPTER 2

I sat alone in the dark house. At the windows, moonlight reflected the snow-covered desert. It was an unusually still night, not a hint of wind, peace outside and inside the house. I poured a glass of wine and listened to a Beethoven piano concerto on the stereo.

Something fluttered at the edge of my mind, a sheer slice of memory, a sensory rush popped in from another time when the world had been shiny and good and mine.

It happened more often at the winter holidays. I was sure it was because of the tragedy that occurred in this season.

When you get hit with a big trauma, everything you trusted and believed gets smashed and broken. You are not the same person. The trick is to remake yourself from the tiny, shattered pieces.

These shimmering moments of clarity, they're pieces of me, my original self.

When the music ended, I listened to the room's small sounds—tick of electric heat, flutter of candle flame, the minute hand marking time in small metallic steps.

My cell phone startled me out of the quiet.

"I just left the scene of a domestic homicide in Farson. A husband and wife murder-suicide. I need someone to talk to the family members. I thought of you. It sounds like your kind of thing."

In the two years since I've known Detective Beau Antelope, I've learned he doesn't follow the usual social conventions of conversation, like *hello* and *good-bye*.

"That's so sweet of you to say. In your mind I'm associated with deadly lovers. Not the most wholesome image, but I can see how you got there. What happened in this case?" I asked.

After living in Wyoming for three years, I was still a newcomer. Farson was a small ranching community north of Rock Springs. I only knew one person in the town of Farson.

"I meant that in the most professional sense. Don't take it the wrong way."

"You're lucky. I have both professional experience and personal experience with love and murder. I consider myself a specialist. Tell me about the case."

"A married couple in their forties, recently separated, looks like they tried reconciling, something went wrong, he shot her and then took his own life. He's a local, just moved back to run the family ranch."

As he laid out the demographics, piece by piece, I got a sinking feeling in my stomach. It sounded like the one person I knew in Farson.

"Who are the victims?"

"Dan and Heather Petrangelo."

I tried to speak and couldn't. The shock left me without words as my brain scrambled to make sense of what I heard. Antelope spoke into the silence.

"Pepper, are you there?"

His voice shifted, softened with concern.

"Dan…oh my God…!" I said.

"You know him?"

"I know him. He played cards with my husband—they were friends. He called me when he moved back to Farson. We planned to get together, but it never happened."

"This has got to be tough to hear."

"What happened "

A violent, impulsive act didn't match my picture of Dan Petrangelo. I couldn't believe it. Dan was a former detective, a friend, a man of restraint and judgment.

"The county medical examiner will determine the official cause of death after the autopsies.."

"I can't believe Dan would do that. That's what everyone says, I know. But it's true. I can't imagine it."

"We never see things coming," Antelope said.

"I should know better. I'm a psychologist. I talked to him last week, and he sounded fine. Listen to me. I sound like I'm reading a script."

"It's a lot to take in."

"I don't think I can talk about this anymore tonight."

"Let's check in tomorrow. I'll understand if you decide this case is too close."

"I'll think about it," I said.

Most of the time people are surprised when they learn about someone they know committing suicide. In the same way that neighbors describe a crazed murderer as "a loner" or "a quiet person who never gave anyone any trouble."

It's not normal or healthy to live in isolation and repression. Better to make some noise, make some trouble, have people take notice, claim your place on this earth instead of keeping things bottled up and ready to spring out in full nuclear power destroying everything you've ever loved. And it's sad to think that many people suffer so much psychic pain that they take their own lives, while the people around them, even the people closest to them, didn't know that things had gotten to that desperate state.

Antelope was right. I had to sleep on this one. Maybe it was too close. It's generally not recommended that a psychologist take on a case that is likely to trigger their own issues. I tended to take a different view. I always moved toward the problems of others. It's a question at the borders of morals, values, ethics, and plain being human. When others encounter intense feelings and experiences, I can be a witness to their pain.

Of course, there'd be a price to pay if I got involved with this case.

As always happened when I heard about a violent crime, there was an immediate association to a trauma in my life. I live in Wyoming because I couldn't be at home in the place where my husband was murdered. All the details of that crime—I discovered the bodies in the office we shared, killed by a patient, his lover in his arms, his lover my friend also—compounded the horror.

What pushed Dan to his final tragic action? In men his age, mid-forties and healthy, jealousy or infidelity often showed up as the motivation driving marital murder-suicide. That also didn't fit with what I knew about Dan. But did I know Dan? I knew from my clinical practice and my own marriage that everyone is capable of being unfaithful, even those who protest that they could never do that.

My body shifted into survival mode in response to an unseen threat, my heart pounded in my chest, and adrenaline set every nerve on edge. I wanted to run away from the panic and dread that claimed me. I turned on every light, made all the rooms bright to chase away shadows and the things that hide in them.

I closed the blinds against the night and the eerie blue mist that rose from the snow.

I wouldn't sleep. For the third year in a row, Christmas had brought murder to my door. First Zeke, then my patient Kimi, now Dan and Heather.

CHAPTER 3

Graham was at work at the Get and Go with his head under the hood of a Chevy Tahoe, lost in concentration, when he heard someone call his name. The deputy informed him he needed to report to the Sweetwater County Judicial Complex for questioning in the process of an investigation into a crime.

The first thing Antelope would look for in Graham Douglas was his level of empathy for his girl. Graham Douglas was medium height and had a stocky build. He wore Carhartt coveralls and a black knit cap pulled low over blond curls. The kid was handsome in a feminine way. He could pass for Paige Petrangelo's twin.

Had their similar looks drawn them to each other, each one seeing their mirror image reflected back? They were part of a narcissistic generation, that's for sure.

Graham looked at him without expression, blue eyes focused to the left of him, missing direct contact slightly, making eye contact but not. Someone less skilled in observing human behavior and nonverbal communication might not have picked it up. Graham was nervous. He drummed the table with the fingers of his right hand and stroked the soft woolen fabric of his cap.

Detective Antelope sat directly across from Graham. The two of them faced off, animals in the wild, a wordless face. After a minute, Antelope moved in to turn on the recording device.

"Detective Antelope interviewing Graham Douglas."

The tape whirled like an endless slow snake in the ancient tape recorder.

"How long have you known Paige Petrangelo?"

"This is about Paige? What happened to her?"

"Answer the question. How long have you known her?"

"Me and her have been together less than a year," Graham answered.

"How did you meet?"

"This isn't right. Did something happen to Paige?"

"Paige is fine. Now answer the question. Where did you meet her?"

"I'm friends with her cousin Cody. Is that a crime?"

"Who said anything about a crime? Do you know anything about a crime?"

"You pulled me off my job and read me my rights, what am I supposed to think?"

"Guess you need two jobs with a girlfriend like Paige Petrangelo"

"What do you mean by that?"

"I ask the questions, son. But in case you didn't notice, you don't roll in the Petrangelo league, know what I mean?" He didn't like the kid, wasn't sure why, but he wore arrogance like cologne. It wouldn't do for him to feel too sure of himself.

"Paige's a good girl. She doesn't care about that stuff."

"What stuff would that be?"

"Status, class, all that crap."

"Money, though, I bet she cares about money. Haven't met a woman yet who doesn't."

"Maybe I offer her something money can't buy."

"That's why you're working your tail off to keep up with her, huh?"

"You don't know anything about me. I've been working all my life. Nobody ever made it easy."

"Is that what you wanted with Paige Petrangelo, a sugar mama to make it easy?"

"Don't insult me. It's not like that."

"Tell me, what's it like being the boyfriend of Paige Petrangelo? Another thing that's not easy, I'm guessing."

"It's cool."

"Yeah? Dan Petrangelo, a former detective, was thrilled to have his daughter hooked up with a small-time drug dealer? He did a background check on you and found some things that concerned him. His daughter could do better. That's what he told her. Did she tell you?"

"We talked. She knows I'm done with that. It doesn't matter to her. She wants me. End of story."

"Well, good news for you. It doesn't matter anymore."

"You want to tell me what's going on here?"

"Dan and Heather Petrangelo are dead."

And nothing changed in Graham Douglas's face. He might later claim he was in shock and that's why he didn't respond. Was there something of the psychopath in him, the missing empathy chip that kept us human? He might not be the one who had offed the Petrangelos, but he wouldn't mourn them either.

"I took her home this morning. What happened? What about Paige? Where's Paige?" He moved with such force the chair fell over behind him. On his feet and shouting.

"Sit down," Antelope said. "You're not at the Saddle Lite."

"Tell me!"

The reaction was so immediate and intense, he couldn't determine if it was genuine or an excellent display of psychopathic pretense.

"Paige is unharmed. They were dead when you dropped her off. She found the bodies. She's at Sweetwater Hospital now getting treated for shock."

Graham held his gaze for a long minute. Finally, he righted the chair, and both men returned to their places at the table.

"What time did you and Paige arrive at the Sanderson Ranch this morning?"

"Early, eight o'clock, close to. I start at the airport at nine. How did they die?"

"They were shot."

"Holy shit. Someone shot them? They got murdered."

"We don't know yet if we're dealing with a double homicide or a murder-suicide."

"This is gonna wreck Paige."

"What can you tell me about her parents?"

"I met them, just a few times. Her old man didn't like me. I had no reason to hang around there."

"Was that a problem for you?"

"More of a problem for him. Paige came and stayed with me. Nothing he could do about it."

"Graham, I'm going to be honest with you. You're a person of interest. That's how we'll refer to you when we discuss the case with the media. These domestic murders are crimes of passion. We look at family members and close associates first. That puts you high on the list of suspects in this case. Where were you last night?"

"A lot of places. Depends what time."

"Tell me everything you did from six p.m. to six a.m."

"I got off work at the Get and Go at nine o'clock. I went home, hung out with Paige for a bit, took a shower, met up with my buddy Cody at the Saddle Lite around ten. I stayed there for a while, went home. Paige was there, she'll tell you."

"When was the last time you saw Dan or Heather Petrangelo?"

"It's been a while. Like you said, I'm not their favorite person. Since Paige started staying with me, I have no reason to go out there."

"When did Paige move in with you?"

"It's not official like that."

"When?"

"Two months ago maybe, yeah, at least that. That's when things got crazy there."

"What do you mean by crazy? Be specific."

"Her old man was crazy jealous of her mom. Paige said he had no reason. He wouldn't shut up about it."

"He suspected his wife was cheating on him?"

"That's what Paige told me. She couldn't take them fighting anymore. We decided she'd stay at my place. Looks like that was the right call. Paige is still alive."

CHAPTER 4

The ringing cell phone startled her awake—her niece Paige. A feeling of dread spread through her body, an automatic reaction to the sound of the phone. She let it go to voicemail. *I'll deal with you later, Paige.* But the phone rang again, so she answered.

Paige was hysterical, crying, screaming, "They're dead, they're dead! My parents are dead."

Where was Mark when she needed him? At a legal conference in Casper without her! She wanted to go with him except Cody had come home for the Thanksgiving break, and Mark said she couldn't leave him. And he was right about that. He wanted to win Cody over, and it wouldn't help if she took off with Mark for the weekend the minute he got home from school. Where was Cody? He never came home last night.

Paige was at the hospital with Bella. She had to go to them. She wanted so badly to talk to Mark but he'd already be in the conference, his phone turned off until the break at noon. She texted him anyway, just in case he checked his phone before then.

Sweetwater County Memorial Hospital sat at the top of a ridge overlooking an expanse of high desert. In the dim light of early morning, heavy snow blanketed every surface. She was so tired, and her head throbbed with the beginning of one of her migraines. There'd be no stopping it. She didn't have her medicine with her.

When she got back to emergency reception from the treatment rooms, the place was packed with sick and injured patients. People waited at the triage counters, stood in the hallway, took up all the good seats near the televisions.

When Nicole first came in, a few people were waiting to be seen. She gave her name, and a nurse pointed the way to Bella and Paige's treatment rooms, where she learned of her mother-in-law's admission. She found Paige, finally silent, stoned on Xanax, half asleep, and left her to rest. She returned to the waiting room, more crowded than when she first arrived, and found a private seat near the window to wait for the results of Bella's diagnostic tests.

She got a coffee from the vending machine, weak and burned to bitter. Cold seeped in through the large windows. She zipped the quilted vest to her chin and longed for her puffy jacket.

She hated hospitals, resented the trap of obligation, wanted free of this family. She looked for an escape, found torn magazines slick with germs, a sports channel muted on the giant flatscreen. Dan and Heather dead—and nothing new from Mark on her phone.

Bella was in shock. And Paige so hysterical no one could calm her. She couldn't stop sobbing to answer any of their questions.

Paige was weak. Taller than her boy Cody; did that help or hurt her? It gave the wrong impression, made her appear stronger. Nicole knew the truth. Bella favored Paige because she looked like her, and both of them were self-centered. Who would take care of Paige now? Nicole hoped she wouldn't get stuck with her. Plenty of money, that's for sure; Paige wouldn't need them for that. Thank God she had turned eighteen last summer. Nicole wouldn't have to be responsible for anything, Paige could make her own decisions. Cody had struggled at the University of Wyoming, always the black sheep, while Paige had inherited her princess status from her father. Could Paige hold her own without her parents?

Mark would judge her, call her petty, especially now. She wouldn't tell him, no need for him to know every little thing that came into her head. She didn't plan on screwing things up with Mark. She'd learned from being married to be careful what she said, how much she said. Marriage, not the close and trusting relationship people made it out to be, but rather a small-scale war of survival of the fittest that she intended to survive. So different, the two men in her life. Never again would she stay in a bad situation.

She remembered Jack's rare sudden explosions—a slap, a push, his fist slammed on the table, all followed by retreat into days of sullen silence, more than a few times over the years. It had made her hone her skillful indirection and subtle maneuvers. They never talked about it. This restored the power balance in the relationship. Yes, she'd endured his temper tantrums. He sometimes joked when people asked him how he got such a pretty woman to be his wife, "I came with the ranch." That pretty much summed it up, and he didn't push it too far.

Why was she thinking about Jack? Would she ever be free of him and his family? She still hadn't heard from Cody. He wasn't answering her calls or texts.

She'd set her phone to vibrate in accordance with the hospital rules to silence cell phones. It buzzed in her pocket and she pulled it out quickly. The Caller ID read Sweetwater County Jail.

CHAPTER 5

When Cody walked out of jail, he saw his mother waiting for him. She came when he called her and paid his bail. She was the only reason he was free, but he didn't want to see her or hear what she had to say. He gave her a look that he hoped carried the full force of his fury and quickly turned away, walking in the direction of the Saddle Lite.

■ ■ ■

She was a big part of the reason he freaked out and drank himself into oblivion periodically. Let her pay some dues, that was how he looked at it.

She called his name, and he ignored her.

"Cody, you come here."

Like a runaway dog, he kept walking. He heard her SUV start up and was ready when she pulled up beside him. He didn't even turn to look at her, just kept walking.

"Aren't you even going to thank me?" she said.

When there was nothing from him, she added, "I should have left you there, for all the thanks I get. Next time, don't call me. I won't be treated this way, you hear me, Cody?"

She wanted something from him, even if it was only gratitude. She wanted it, and it was his to give, and she could go on wanting it because no way would he give her anything after what she'd taken from him. She had bailed him out, and he owed her for that. Then, like she always did, she'd ruined it, hungry for his gratitude and appreciation. A simple thank you would have done it, and yet he'd refused to play his part.

"Get in, Cody, please. Something bad happened."

Letting go of the whole power struggle with her like an outgrown children's game, he asked, "What happened?"

"It's bad, Cody."

"Tell me. Did something happen to Grandma?"

"No, not Grandma. It's Dan and Heather. Somebody shot Dan and Heather."

He heard the words and looked at his mother's face, her tears. He couldn't look at her, had to get away from her.

"Why are you looking at me like that? Last night. At home. Someone broke in and shot them," she said.

He doubled over and threw up everything that was left in his stomach from his partying the night before.

"Oh, my God. Just get in, Cody."

He opened the door and collapsed on the seat, his head spinning, sweat pouring off his face. If only she wouldn't say anything else, he might be OK.

"Where's your truck, anyway?"

"Saddle Lite."

"What happened last night?"

He held his hand up to stop her from saying anything else. His head throbbed, a constant beat of torture. When he opened his eyes, daylight scorched them. He pressed them closed with his fingers. "Drive," he said.

"What did you get arrested for?"

"Stupid bar fight. Leave me alone."

Her face cold as a stone, close to him, no love or compassion now. He'd hurt her again, so easy for him to do it; aware of his power with her.

She drove him to the Saddle Lite. His hand on the door handle, something new in her eyes, a cold distance, as if seeing a stranger. And something else, fear. His mother was afraid of him. It should have bothered him, but instead it gave him finally a sense of separation from her smothering love.

"Cody, I need you to tell me the truth. Did you have anything to do with Dan and Heather?"

He slammed the truck door and she peeled out of the parking lot like an angry teenager. He watched her drive off, a sad, sick feeling in the pit of his stomach that had nothing to do with being hungover. His own mother had asked him if he was a killer. How twisted was that?

■ ■ ■

He had ten dollars in his pocket, enough for coffee and breakfast at the Flying J. That's about as far into the future as he could think. He ate the breakfast burritos in his truck. His body came awake with the simple fuel, the hot caffeine burning through his veins. He was himself again, invincible, alive. And then he remembered—his Uncle Dan and Aunt Heather.

He called Graham, but his phone was turned off or dead. Graham couldn't seem to keep it charged.

He had to do something but didn't know what to do or where he wanted to be. Not home, didn't want to see his mother, couldn't stand to look at her face. He wanted to avoid another shouting match. She had bailed him out, and he owed her for that. Then, like she always did, she'd ruined it.

CHAPTER 6

The frigid air hit him like a welcome slap back into reality. Free! Graham pushed open the heavy glass door of the Justice Complex. He gulped the air like water and filled his chest, filled every cell in his body with fresh air and freedom.

His work boots gripped the hard-packed snow as he jogged to the truck. In a boxer's stance he punched the air, knocked the tightness out of his limbs, light on his feet, a moving target for an invisible opponent. His muscles ached from an hour of unmoving concentration with his mind fixed on his personal survival code: Watch what you do, give them nothing, don't let them put it on you.

The whole time inside, the detective fired his questions, all of them suggesting he'd killed Paige's parents. Too many questions, too many chances to get the answers wrong.

He lit a cigarette, and smoke caught in his throat. He coughed, and a sob came out and took him by surprise. What the fuck! Paige! She must be going crazy looking for him.

His throat hurt and his eyes watered, just the cold, that's all. He held his breath, pushed the feelings down. No time to freak out. He plugged his phone into the truck charger. A few minutes later it started beeping, all notifications of missed calls from Paige.

He listened to the first few calls, and then he couldn't listen to anymore. He could hardly make out the words she was saying through her tears and hysteria.

He didn't want to call her, afraid of what he'd hear. Paige lost it over small things; what the fuck would she do with this? No more running home to Mommy and Daddy when things got tough between them.

Just text her.

Where are u?

Immediately, his phone rang. He should have known she wouldn't let it be that easy.

"Baby, I'm sorry."

"Oh, my God, Graham, where are you? I need you! Why didn't you answer?"

"They pulled me in. I know what happened."

"They're dead, my parents are dead. Oh, Graham, come get me now!"

"I know, baby. Where are you?"

"I'm at the hospital, I need you now, can you come now please, please, Graham."

"I'm in the truck now. Give me five minute, ten minutes."

"Don't hang up. Stay on the phone. Don't you dare hang up, Graham."

"I won't. I got you."

He drove slowly through the quiet Sunday streets, spooked by the recent encounter with the law and not eager to get to Paige. He wanted to show up for her. He wanted to be the man she could count on. He dreaded being with her in all the dark feelings, feared being swallowed by her grief.

He reminded himself she wasn't like his mother. Paige's face lit up whenever she looked at him; he made her happy. Unlike his mother, who lived in a chronic state of depression and who turned her face away from him.

He slowed and entered the circular drive in front of the hospital. Paige pushed through the glass doors, ran to him, and pulled the truck door open. He hit the brakes to keep from dragging her.

She threw herself at him, arms around his neck, hot tears on his cheek. She trembled in his arms, and he held her tight to keep her from shaking into bits. Worse than he expected, this throbbing mess of sorrow, a weight that would drown him if he let it.

After a few minutes, he lifted her hands away and said, "Come on, let's go home. You need to sleep."

She nodded and wiped her eyes. They drove in silence, her head resting lightly on his shoulder. It made it a little hard to drive, but he managed and could breathe again.

By the time they got to his trailer, she was asleep. He carried her inside and laid her on the bed, removed her shoes and the silly flowered backpack she always wore. When he pulled the quilt up to cover her, he was gripped by a sensation of pure love. He didn't need anything from her. It was enough just to love her. The feeling brought tears to his eyes.

In the kitchen, he poured himself a beer and then sat alone in the small living room. He turned on the television, the volume low so as not to wake her, just enough for the comfort of the voices, like when he was a kid with the grown-ups in another room, the safety of that feeling, knowing he was not alone.

He needed the time, though, just him and his thoughts. It bothered him the way the detective's questions had implied he wasn't good enough for Paige.

He wasn't the mismatch for Paige her parents said he was. There were things they didn't know about their daughter that would shock them. The knowledge of Paige's edgy activities was his secret ace in the hole. And it was especially useful because it didn't have anything to do with him. Her parents couldn't blame Graham for ruining their precious daughter. No, Paige had gotten into nude modeling and dancing long before he came on the scene.

She tried to keep it from him, but he'd found the pictures online. At first, she lied when he confronted her. He did a good job of acting. He wanted her to think he judged her for it. Maybe even that it would be a deal breaker. She was a good girl, but he'd found out the truth. In fact, he didn't care at all. So what if she got off on showing her titties and ass to old guys? It turned him on to think of her doing that. He figured out that Paige's parents would oppose her being with Graham. He made a plan of attack when they started putting pressure on her to ditch him. And that had happened right on schedule. Right after the first time he met them, he found Paige looking all sad, and when he asked her what was wrong, she said at first it was nothing.

She was into him; he could tell by how she responded in bed. It was fast and furious between them. He didn't want to lose her just for that reason alone. How often did a guy find a gold mine like that? It started out hot, and it showed no signs of cooling off.

That was when he'd played his trump card. It was tricky. He didn't want her to know he was in fact blackmailing her to stay in the relationship with him. He wanted her to think he knew her better than her parents knew her. That, in ways they didn't understand, she was more suited to Graham than either of her parents would ever know.

Obviously, they could never know about the nude modeling and dancing. Did she know how easy it was these days with the internet for her parents to find out about that? He would help her cover her tracks. It would be their little secret. She could depend on him the way she couldn't depend on anyone else, not even her parents. He loved her, even if she wasn't perfect. Could her parents say the same?

What did she want most? To continue to be a child in constant search of her parents' approval? Or a woman who was secure in the fact that her man loved her even when she wasn't perfect? It was a great speech, a successful speech. From that day forward, Graham didn't need to worry about her loyalty.

He opened the last beer and then lay down beside her in the bed. When he moved her bag to the floor a bottle of pills fell out. A month's supply of Xanax from the hospital pharmacy. No wonder she was dead to the world.

He unscrewed the top and shook four of the small ovals into his hand. A long time since he'd done Xanax; remembering the swooping lightness of it, he washed the pills down with beer. He closed his eyes and waited for the float away feeling to come over him like a breeze on a summer day, just enough to make things a little better.

An hour earlier, he'd been trapped in a room, spooked by the questions, the detective's black eyes on him. The overhead light bright enough for surgery made him feel naked and exposed. So long since he'd been this close to the law. Graham was always on the lookout for extra money. It didn't matter how, only the cash mattered. No one else was there to help him. He got this early on. His old man had gone before he was born. His mother was there, but most of the time he wished she'd left too. Nothing was ever handed to him. If he wanted something, he worked for it or he stole it. Some jobs paid more than others. It made sense to do what paid the most. He wasn't stupid. He didn't judge it. If it put money in his pocket, he did it. Sure, he worked, but big plans meant making money whatever way he could. Just try and let someone tell him he shouldn't.

It bugged him when Paige tried to get him to go to college. She wanted her parents to approve of him, and thought that Graham getting an education would make a difference. She was naïve. Nothing would make a difference. Well, everything was going to be all right now. She'd need him more than ever.

In their eyes, he was doomed from the start because of his old man's screw-ups, the fact he couldn't stay out of a bar fight, and the last one that had ended with another man dead.

Paige was a beauty, and she came with a lot of money. The way she stalked him, though, it did make him crazy. He guessed that was just her way of loving. She was the first person who ever cared where he was and what he was doing.

Only then did he think about how close he'd come to getting busted the night before. Stupid Cody busting his balls for no reason. He was lucky he'd left the Saddle Lite before the cops arrived, the lights flashing in his rearview mirror as he drove off.

He checked his texts. He wouldn't feel bad if Cody got pulled in; he had started it. When he got wasted, he went too far, talked shit, and pushed his buttons.

His mind and body relaxed, everything felt smooth and liquid, and he wanted to go with it, drift off, forget.

He shook himself awake—the money was still in the truck.

She stirred when he sat up. He held himself still, not breathing, and waited until he was certain she was asleep before retrieving the satchel stuffed with bills and placing it in the far corner of his closet.

CHAPTER 7

Snow came down hard and fast on the drive from Laramie to Farson, a barren, isolated route. The erratic movement of snow, like driving through shifting lace curtains, required constant focus. His eyes ached from the pressure of concentrating.

For long stretches of time, he saw no other vehicles, and then a group of two or three semis off the road, the trailers sideways on the ground, casualties of the high winds. Driving this portion of the interstate through the Red Desert gave him a small thrill, the feel of the planet beneath him. He drove slowly and carefully over the treacherous road. There was no point in hurrying.

Nicole's text had come in at a good time. The presentation on changes to the tax law for living trust had been going on for an hour. He'd stepped out of the conference, glad for the interruption, and called her immediately. She sounded panicky, on the edge of freaking out, and spilled the news of the shootings in a rush.

"Oh, thank God, Mark, you need to come home. Dan and Heather, it's awful, I can't believe it, they're dead, someone killed them last night at the ranch."

"Slow down, tell me what happened."

"I don't know. Paige found them this morning when she came home. I don't know why Heather was there. I'm at the

Sweetwater ER with Paige and Bella; they're both being treated for shock. I could use something myself."

"Have you talked to anyone from the Sheriff's Department?"

"No. I haven't seen anyone. I'm here all by myself. I need you, Mark, you know how I get. This is too much for me to handle alone. I'm afraid to sleep in my own house."

He explained about the conference, how if he signed out before the last session, he'd lose the credits he needed to renew his law license. She didn't get it, but she didn't have to, those were the facts.

How would Bella handle the death of another son? This latest tragedy might stress her memory and judgment further. He represented other seniors in his elder law practice and was aware how quickly mental capacity could change.

At some point he lost cell service, and when it picked up again, his phone chirped notification messages. In Riverton, he stopped at the Good To Go gas station for a coffee and found five texts from Nicole. Her neediness under stress wore him down. She knew the trip from Casper took over five hours, and with the added weather he'd be lucky to make it in seven.

He turned off the phone and got back on the road. Nothing he said would make any difference. Only his presence calmed her. The sooner he got there, the better for both of them. Cody being home for the long weekend might be a help or maybe not. The parent-child relationship Nicole had created appeared to be a one-way deal in the kid's favor.

She babied him and tried to blame it on his father's death, and these roles had been honed over time. She never got what she needed from her husband and turned to Cody instead. He recognized the pattern because he had lived the pattern.

How would the kid take losing an aunt and uncle a year after his father's death? Nicole worried about her son's mental health maybe more than she needed to. From what he could see, the kid smoked enough weed to keep himself chill. Nothing he could do about that, Cody didn't like the idea of him from the start and had never warmed up. He'd warned Nicole if she brought him in too soon, they risked Cody's rejection.

As he approached Farson, fatigue hit hard; he wanted his three b's—beer, bath, bed. He didn't want to talk, or listen; he hoped his presence would be enough for her. He'd gone cold when she told him to leave the conference and put her needs first. He knew how to make her happy, and he enjoyed doing it, but it only worked if she didn't ask for it. It needed to come from him; he didn't know why.

He offered to spend the night at her place, and she settled down and didn't give him any trouble. In every relationship one partner is more invested than the other. He always made sure the balance tipped in his favor.

Things were good with Nicole, and he didn't want to lose her. Five miles out of Farson, he texted her.

Be there soon

The daughter, Paige, with no parents, how would she live? The cops would look at her boyfriend first. He'd heard from Bella that neither Dan nor Heather liked him for Paige. A kid named Graham, fancy for a trailer court kid, likely supplementing his income with minor drug deals to college kids. He agreed, the punk didn't deserve the likes of Paige. Picturing him holding her while she cried for her parents, Mark was gripped with a surge of desire. What's the story with this girl?

He called the hospital and asked about Bella, learned her status, stable and able to have visitors. He could visit. It was what he wanted to hear. They had important business to do together. He needed her to be coherent so there could be no challenges to her plans for the ranch. Bella loved the ranch and wanted to keep it a working ranch. The taxes were killing her, eating up the estate, leaving less and less for investment.

CHAPTER 8

Six o'clock on a dark winter morning, an hour before I set the alarm to go off. My cell phone flashed and vibrated and played the first notes of *Rhapsody in Blue*. The caller ID read *Detective Beau Antelope*.

Most likely he'd been up for hours and made himself wait until the half-meridian passed. Somehow, he managed to function without a regular sleep schedule in a high-intensity job as a homicide detective.

"Can you work on this case?"

"Yes, what do you need me to do?"

"Do you know the daughter?"

"Paige? No, I never met her. I didn't think to ask last night, was she there? Is she all right?"

"She was the one who found them."

"The poor girl. How is she?"

"By the time I got to the scene, she and Dan's mother had been taken to Sweetwater Hospital; they were both in bad shape, according to the responding officer. The mother was admitted for observation, and the daughter was discharged last night. Can you meet with her this morning?"

I told him I'd be available to meet with Paige Petrangelo once the workday officially started, after coffee and a shower. He told me I'd find her at her boyfriend's place and gave me Graham Douglas's address in the Elk Street Mobile Home Park.

We agreed I'd call him when I finished so we could ride up to Farson to interview the sister-in-law, Nicole Petrangelo, who would be able to provide the most coherent report of Dan and Heather's life in the weeks leading up to their deaths.

Antelope was a man of few words. That was all right by me. I'd spent years listening to Zeke's charming stories and ended up not knowing how much of what he told me was true and how much was him crafting an image he wanted to be true.

An hour later I walked out into early morning air that cut like glass. When the snow stopped sometime in the night, the temperature plummeted. The snow crunched and sparkled underfoot as I walked to the Jeep.

It was a short drive over to the Elk Street Mobile Home Park. Graham Douglas's trailer was an older style single wide at the end of the last lane with a view of the back parking lot of a convenience store.

The place looked deserted, the blinds closed, no vehicle in front. Was Paige still here? I knocked and waited. I didn't hear any signs of movement in the trailer. I knocked again and when no one came to the door, I got back in the Jeep and called Antelope.

"I'm here, but it doesn't seem like anyone else is. Are you sure she's still here?"

"Hold on, I'll call her."

A minute later the door opened. There was no mistaking the face of grief. Paige Petrangelo was stricken. Tall but bent over, a long black sweater wrapped around her slender body, black jeans, red converse sneakers, blond hair hanging loose around her face, no attempt at grooming.

"Are you the doctor? The detective said someone was coming to talk to me."

"Hello, Paige, I'm Dr. Hunt. May I come in?"

"Sure."

She moved away from the door and into the front room of the trailer. I closed the door, and the room lost its light. Paige sat on a black leather futon and stared at the floor.

I opened the blinds at the front window. Paige looked up and squinted. There were traces of black mascara under her eyes.

I sat at the edge of an oversized recliner, the only other piece of furniture in the small room except for a sixty-inch television on the interior wall.

"I'm so sorry about your parents. I knew them from when we all lived in Cambridge. They were good people, and I'm so sorry you lost them like this."

"You knew my parents? How?"

"Your dad played poker every week with my husband. The two of them were good friends. Once in a while, the guys would get together and invite their wives. I met your mom a few times."

She stared blankly at me. Was she taking anything in? Paige needed context to help ground her in reality.

"I'm sorry, I'm out of it. They gave me some pills at the hospital to calm me down. Graham woke me up before he went to work, and it all came back, so he gave me two more. I just want to sleep. It hurts too much to be awake."

"What did they give you?"

She reached into a black shoulder bag embroidered with roses and pulled out a plastic bottle and handed it to me. Xanax five milligrams, sixty pills. It was hard to tell, but it looked like she had taken more than was prescribed.

Antianxiety medication can give needed comfort and reprieve from intense pain in traumatic situations, but it can also interfere with the brain's natural ability to process painful memories if the medication is used to block out emotional pain. It was a fine balance that, if not managed precisely, could result in a person having more psychological pain later on.

When I handed the bottle back to her, she said, "Don't worry, I'm not going to kill myself."

"I wasn't thinking that."

"Why are you here?"

"Detective Antelope said it might be easier for you to answer questions with a psychologist."

"He's afraid I'm going to do what my dad did, but I would never do that. I can't believe he did that. Do we have to talk about this?"

"Let's talk about the day before. I understand you found them when you went home on Sunday morning. Where were you coming from?"

"I was here. I'm always here now, not officially living, here but I have a lot of my stuff. Before you ask, things weren't good at home, that's why."

"What was happening at home, Paige?"

"Does it matter?"

"Maybe. We're trying to piece together how this could have happened. If your parents were struggling in some way?"

"Everything went to hell when we moved here. My mom hated it. She couldn't stand being on the ranch, the isolation of it. She started going out every chance she got, and it freaked my dad out. He got all controlling. He never used to be like that. I couldn't take it when they'd fight. I should have stayed. They'd still be alive. It's my fault."

She broke down and cried, reaching for the bag and the pills.

"Wait," I said, and she looked at me, her fingers working off the cap.

"If you take more of that, you'll feel a little better right now, but it could also make it harder later on."

"I don't care about later on. I don't care about anything," she said, but she dropped the bottle into the bag without taking another pill.

"I know it's hard to imagine right now, but there will be a time when it won't hurt so much."

"You're right, I can't imagine that."

"It will, though, you'll see. You just have to get through the days right now."

"I don't want to, though, just get through the days. I want my parents alive. I'd do anything to have them back. I feel so guilty saying this, I don't even know if it's true. I'd even give up Graham if I could have my parents alive again. Is that wrong?"

"There's nothing wrong about your feelings."

"I loved Graham, I mean I do love him, but still, they're my parents. I should have been a better daughter."

"What do you mean?"

"They didn't like Graham. My dad especially. He said Graham was trouble and would bring me heartache. Like I was going to listen to my dad right then, the way he made my mom so crazy. That's the other reason I didn't stay at the ranch. I didn't want to hear him talking about Graham. I couldn't stand listening to him anymore. If he wasn't fighting with me, he was fighting with my mom. Now I feel bad. He was hurting and nobody cared. We both left him."

"Your parents' fights, did they ever get physical?"

"You mean did he hit her? Never. She would never have gone back if he did."

"Gone back?"

"She moved out a month ago. Things got that bad. She was at the Days Inn. She called me on Saturday and said she was going up to the ranch that night and would probably stay over. She said I should come by for breakfast. She sounded excited, happy for the first time in a long time."

Hearing her own words, aware of how recently her mother had been alive and happy, brought on her tears again.

"Why did this happen? I don't understand!"

I sat with her for a long time while she gave in to the tears. When she'd finished, she took a deep breath and, for the first time, sat back, arms at her sides, spent.

"I have to go to sleep now," she said in a quiet voice, a statement with no apology.

"That's a good idea. Sleep as much as you can," I said.

"Did anyone tell my Aunt Amber?"

"The Sheriff's Department will be notifying all the family members."

"My dad's the only one in the family who talks to her."

"Oh? Do you know how to reach her?"

"Her number's in my dad's phone. Amber Delman. She lives over in Riverton."

I knew too well what the early days after a traumatic death were like for those left behind. The specific searing pain that comes in the wake of violent death did indeed lessen over time, a long time, years of time. But innocence was forever lost to me.

CHAPTER 9

The Eden Valley is forty miles north of Rock Springs in the middle of the Red Desert. The sister communities of Eden and Farson have a combined population of 594 people, mostly farmers and ranchers. The majority of settlers had come to the valley in 1907 when the Carey Act allowed each settler 160 acres at fifty cents an acre and thirty dollars per acre for water rights from the nearby Big and Little Sandy Rivers.

We drove past acres of straw-colored winter pasture covered with patches of drifted snow from Sunday's storm. In the morning sun the air glistened with tiny sparks of light—ice crystals caught and carried on a current. A mean wind blasted across the open land from both sides of the two-lane highway. Antelope held tight to the steering wheel as the sturdy Chevy Tahoe bucked and rocked under the battering force.

Farson lies at the intersection of US Highway 191 and US Highway 28. We came to the four corners and turned right at the Farson Mercantile Building, famous for its large ice cream cones, then turned right again.

"Nicole's place is just up the road. We're a little early. Do you want to see where the shootings happened? We'll pass the Sanderson Ranch first. We have time for a quick stop. You can get a sense of the crime scene."

"The Sanderson Ranch?"

"What's wrong? You look a little spooked."

"I'm connecting some dots. Who owns the ranch?"

"Bella Sanderson."

"Bella Sanderson is Dan's mother?"

"Yes."

"I didn't put it together. I should have asked."

"What do you mean?"

"I met Bella Sanderson in a professional capacity. I didn't realize at the time she was Dan's mother."

"Would that have made it a conflict of interest?"

"No, Dan never talked to me about his mother, so I went in with no prior impression of her. At the start of the evaluation, Bella said something about her son supporting it. I could have asked her son's name, but I didn't."

I thought back to the day Bella Sanderson had come to my office for evaluation. She'd inherited a ranch her family had owned for over two hundred years. She wanted to leave it to the Nature Conservancy. She worried that this would cause some repercussions within her family.

"It might make it easier for her to talk to you, having met you before."

"Paige said Dan has a sister who's estranged from the family. Her name's Amber Delman, and her phone number is in Dan's contacts."

"His belongings are in the evidence room. I'll check it out. See what Nicole has to say about her, too."

Like most ranches in the area, the Sanderson Ranch raised alfalfa. We turned into the driveway and bumped along the dirt road under ancient cottonwoods.

What it would be like to make a living off this land—the deep connection, the comfort of burrowing, the world held at bay, safe in a cave of earthy mystery?

The main buildings of the ranch were made of dark cedar logs and had been constructed in the mid-1800s. They were hunkered low into the ground as if they were growing out of it and were part of the land. There was a timeless stillness in the clearing they created. The working ranch was still today in the wake of the tragedies.

There were three dwellings on the property: the main ranch house, a much larger, modern log home with skylights and picture windows facing the southwest toward the Wind River Mountains, and a smaller log cabin.

"That's where they died," Antelope said,

The incongruence of the scene was startling. It was a magnificent house, all angles and chimneys, like something out of a fairy tale.

"It's hard to imagine a murder-suicide happening in there. Ever since I started making money, I've dreamed of living in a place like that. Another dream dies," Antelope said.

CHAPTER 10

A mile down the county road, we found Nicole Petrangelo's new residence. The single-story white frame house needed a paint job and a new roof. A late model Ford Expedition with Sweetwater County license plates that read COW-GIRL-4 took up most of the short, gravel driveway. A small yard of patchy grass and frozen tumbleweeds fronted the main road.

"Quite a difference from life on the family ranch. She apologized in advance for what she referred to as her diminished circumstances. When Dan and Heather moved back here, she was asked to vacate the property. Apparently, all the buildings on the ranch are owned by Bella Sanderson. A cold move on her part. Does that fit with the lady you met?"

"I'm a little surprised to hear that. That's a lot of loss for Nicole—first her husband, then the home she shared with him. There's probably more to the story."

Nicole Petrangelo must have heard us pull up in the county issue Chevy wagon. She opened the door as we walked up the driveway.

A petite woman with elfin features, black hair in a pixie cut, bright red lipstick. Nicole wore a black leather skirt, black silk blouse, black suede boots, heavy silver jewelry everywhere.

"I'm Detective Antelope and this is Dr. Hunt. She's a psychological consultant for the department."

"Yes, it's a horrible thing, that's for sure. But come in, come in. It's cold out there this morning." She held the door wide and gave it a hard slam before locking it.

"That's not something I usually do. We never lock up here, it's not the Wyoming way, my husband always used to say. But look where it got poor Dan and Heather. That murderer walked right in, no questions asked. I'm afraid here all by myself. With Bella still in the hospital and Paige, the poor thing, she's gone off to stay at Graham's.

"I wouldn't be here if it wasn't for Cody being home from UW on Thanksgiving break. It's a comfort having a man around. He'll sleep with his gun, too. I don't want anyone taking us by surprise. That's all I need to lose my boy, too, on top of everything else. There's been too much death in this family. I don't know how I'm dealing with it."

"We'll want to speak with him. Is he here now?" Antelope said.

"No, he isn't. I expect him home later. I'm about to go to work. Should I have him call you?"

"Do you know where he is?"

"He's a twenty-one-year-old male, I'm sure you remember what that's like, Detective. I stopped trying to keep track of Cody a long time ago."

"My husband, Jack, died a year ago, a suicide. I'll never get over it. Isn't that crazy? The two of them, gone in a year. Bella thought he might have been murdered. That was the first sign of her losing it. I thought it was crazy at the time, part of her general mental decline. She hasn't been the same since Jack passed."

"What do you mean about your mother-in-law 'losing it'?"

"I wasn't alone in thinking that. Dan agreed. She talked about changing her will and donating the ranch to some nature thing. Can you believe it? That ranch has been family run for years, and Dan came back to help her run it. Jack devoted his life to keeping it going, my life too. Both of her boys sacrificed for her to keep her ranch, and in the end, she wanted to give it away?

"Dan got tough with her, told her to get checked out, get her memory tested. My boyfriend is her lawyer, and he agreed that would be the best thing, if she wanted to change her will, make sure she's competent to do it, or else the whole thing would be a mess later on, anyone could challenge it.

"I don't know what happened with that. Nobody bothered to talk to the family, of course, the ones who know her best, who see how she's failing a little bit more every day, forgetting things, and wandering off all by herself for hours at a time in the cold.

"I wouldn't be surprised if this is the end for her. She was there on the ranch. How is she ever going to stay there again? Thank God, I don't live there still. Was it a random killing? Should I be afraid for my life and my son's life? Is that what you're saying?"

"The medical examiner hasn't ruled on the official cause of death. They were both killed by a single gunshot wound. At this time, it's uncertain if the shots were fired by a third party or if Dan shot Heather and then took his own life."

"Oh, my God, that's horrible. I don't know which is worse."

"Do you have any idea who might have wanted Dan and Heather dead?" Antelope said.

"Dan and Heather—the golden couple. I don't know anyone would want them dead, and in that horrible way," Nicole said.

"Are you aware they'd separated?"

"Heather stopped by the day she left Dan. It took me by surprise. She was a cold fish; either that or she didn't like me. She looked scared out of her mind that day, shaking. She wanted a restraining order and didn't know where to start. My boyfriend's an attorney, and I told her to call him if she wanted help with the process."

"Do you know why Heather left?"

"Only what my son Cody told me. He's close with Paige. Dan got suspicious that Heather was cheating on him. She denied it. Things got ugly between them."

"Did she say why she wanted a restraining order?"

"No, and I didn't ask. I didn't want to know. I just gave her Mark's phone number."

"Could you give me his number? I'll need to talk with him," Antelope said

Nicole reached into a pocket on her cell-phone case and pulled out a shiny black business card with an imprint of the scales of justice embossed in gold.

"Here you go. I give these out whenever there's a need," she said.

"You said you weren't friends with Heather, but she made it a point to tell you she was leaving her husband."

"She was a wreck that day. I've never seen her even a little bit upset, ever. I'm the only person she knows out here besides Bella. I doubt she would have stopped to tell Bella. She would have taken Dan's side, no question. That's the way it is in that family. Blood is everything.

"We weren't close, me and Heather. Because of our husbands and how things were with them. Jack and Dan were close growing up. But that changed when Dan moved away. He went East for college and never came home again.

"In the early years when the kids were young, they'd sometimes come out here for holidays and vacations. I know Jack resented Dan because he chose his freedom instead of the family and helping out with the ranch. You could feel the coldness growing between them.

"After Jack died, and they moved out here, I tried to be friends with Heather. She didn't seem interested. After a while I stopped trying, why wouldn't I? A person can only take so much rejection.

"I know she didn't like living on the ranch. We had that in common. I'm a Wyoming girl, but that doesn't mean I'm content to spend my whole life doing nothing but ranching. I thought maybe we could bond over that.

"Right away she started volunteering at the Community Fine Arts Center down in Rock Springs. She spent a lot of time there. She was an artist herself. She started going there way back when the three of them—Dan, Heather, and Paige—were staying with Bella, and I still lived in my house on the ranch that they later moved into."

"Do you know if Heather joined any other organizations here or in Rock Springs?" I asked.

"I didn't see her much after I moved off the ranch."

"It must have been difficult, leaving your home." I said.

"It's been hard. His life insurance didn't pay out because of a suicide clause. I'm here in this rental for the time being, working at the Mercantile full time now, just getting by, if you want the truth. I would have liked a little time to get myself together. Cody's still in college, so that's a lot to pay. Bella needed her place to herself. Heather was the only one who ever said anything to me about it being hard.

"I'm OK now and happy to be away from the ranch. They want you to think they're a wonderful close family, but let me tell you, it's not like that living inside it. Nobody ever made me feel welcome. Poor Jack never got credit. He loved the ranch, and he gave his life to it, not that Bella appreciated it. She always loved and respected Dan more, if you ask me, because he left and made a name for himself. She was always into that, you know?"

"What do you mean?" I asked.

"She left the ranch herself, got herself a degree—who did that back then? She's more like a man than a woman, if you ask me. Jack didn't like to hear me say it. He loved his mother and wouldn't tolerate anything bad being said about her. Still it was true. She was a snob, an intellectual snob, and she and Dan shared that, and poor Jack was left out in the pasture with the cattle. I don't know how he stood it, but he did. He was loyal to the bone. It was his weakness," Nicole said.

"You called it a weakness?" I asked.

"I'm not saying it's a bad quality, being loyal. But being loyal to people who see you as a second-class citizen, never being able to stand up for yourself, that's weakness, and yes it did cause some arguments between us at first. I stopped fighting it, came to be like Jack, accepting he would never change in regard to his family, like he accepted his place among them, sad as that was. I miss him, I do. My life hasn't been the same here since he died," Nicole said.

"Do you know if they had any problems with anyone in the community?" Antelope asked.

"They didn't talk to me. Bella never talked to me. We weren't confidantes. There could have well been a whole mess of stuff going on in this family, and I would never have known about it. Made that decision a long time ago, mind my business; they would do what they would do anyway," Nicole said.

"Sounds like you tried in the past and it didn't work out."

"Way, way back, in the beginning when it looked like a normal family. I gave my opinion about things, sure. Never made a bit of difference, Bella got even colder to me, and Jack wasn't happy that I made his dear mother unhappy. I caught on quick," Nicole said.

"We need to know the whereabouts of all family members; it's a routine part of the investigation. Was your son here with you on the night Dan and Heather died?" Antelope asked.

"He came home here from Laramie on Friday afternoon. On Saturday night, he went out with Graham, that's Paige's boyfriend. They had a little problem at the Saddle Lite, and

Cody spent the night in jail. I bailed him out myself on Sunday morning. I hope it doesn't cause him too much trouble, taking anger management classes or anything. He needs all his focus for school. It was just a little bar fight, nothing serious. He and Graham got into it about something. He didn't tell me. That's probably the best alibi anyone can have."

"The exact time of death hasn't been determined yet," Antelope said.

"My son didn't kill his uncle. You need to stop suggesting that he could have. Why would he do that? Cody is a good boy," Nicole said.

"As far as I know, Bella was the only other person on the ranch that night. Paige has been down with Graham for some time now. I worry about her. She's had her own problems. She looks like an angel, but she isn't as innocent as she looks. And now she's hooked up with Graham. Who knows what trouble the two of them will get into? He's Cody's friend, but that doesn't mean I approve."

"You said Paige Petrangelo isn't as innocent as she looks? What do you mean?" I asked.

"Maybe you should ask Cody about that. The little I know comes from him. He came home every night sick and tired of hearing all of them talking about how great she was and how she could get a much better boyfriend than Graham Douglas and, if you can believe it, trying to put the blame on Cody. It's true Cody introduced her to Graham, but how can they blame him for the two of them hooking up? He knew the guy, it's not like they're best buddies. It's not like he played matchmaker. He and Paige were out having a few beers at the Eden Bar one night, and Graham came over to say hello to Cody and met Paige and that was that, instant chemistry," Nicole said.

"So that was when Cody told you something about Paige not being so innocent?" I asked.

"I think he regretted it as soon as he said it. As I said, they're true buddies, from the playpen on up. Don't tell him I told you. He might be mad at me for talking about her," Nicole said.

"That's not how we work. You won't be named as the source of our information to anyone else we talk to," I said.

"Well, OK. Paige has done some not-so-ladylike things, nude modeling, even some acting, if you can call it that. Though why she did that, I don't have a clue. It's not for the money, that's for sure. Dan and Heather spoil that girl no end," Nicole said.

"Does anyone else in the family know about this?" I asked.

"We were alone when he said it. But Bella was in the house. And he didn't say it quietly, he was mad, that's for sure. He didn't mean for her to hear it, but she could have," Nicole said.

"And is it likely she would have told Dan about it?" I asked.

"If she knew, it's definite she would have told Dan," Nicole said.

"Do you have any contact information for Amber Delman?"

"I haven't heard that name spoken around here in years. Who told you about Amber?"

"Paige said Dan kept in touch with her. We can find it in his phone contacts. If you have it, it would save us some time."

"Me? I didn't have anything to do with Amber. Jack wouldn't let that happen."

"Sounds like there's a story there. What can you tell us?"

"Lots of problems there. The trouble started way back in high school, and she just kept going with it. The usual teenage things, drugs and all the problems that come with that. I heard she did some time in prison."

"At some point she married; do you know anything about him?"

"He's the whole reason she went bad. Craig Delman, he taught history at the high school when I was there. All the girls loved him. He was one of those teachers that acted like one of us. I guess Amber loved him more than the others. They started seeing each other when she was still a student, way underage. He lost everything, job, his family. I heard he got five years in Riverton, but with probation he was out in no time. Amber waited for him. They got married right away. That's when the family disowned her. That's the story as I heard it from Jack. He told me before we got married and said that was the last he was going to speak of it."

"Do you know if Dan and Heather were having financial problems?"

"He spent a lot of time up at the casino. Other than that, I wouldn't know. Money isn't talked about in this family. It's a given ranching is a hard life; you're lucky if you turn enough profit to keep on doing it. Nobody's getting rich doing it these days. Not with property taxes as high as they are."

"We appreciate your time, Nicole. It's very helpful getting an understanding of the family."

CHAPTER 11

Antelope claimed to be an expert on cheeseburgers. He maintained a five-star rating system of every burger joint in the county. When I told him I'd never had a cheeseburger at Mitch's Café in Farson, he insisted we stop there for a late lunch.

We parked in front of the hitching post in the parking lot of the locals' favorite spot. The small cedar-and-rock building sits right on the edge of the highway. Inside, the café has a cozy, old West feel. From our table by the front window, we watched cattle graze on the ranch across the road.

"You know Nicole was flirting with you?"

"That happens to me all the time," Antelope said.

"It must make your job harder, all that feminine distraction."

"It makes it easier because people let their guard down about things related to the case when they're focusing on something else."

"You're not kidding, are you? Women flirt with you all the time? Under these circumstances when they're being questioned about a crime?"

"I'm not kidding, or bragging, and I make sure not to encourage it or respond to it. It's something I noticed a long time ago, so I use it. I used to think it was the uniform, but I don't wear a uniform anymore."

"When Nicole talked about Bella's mental status, she looked smug and satisfied." I said.

"Not much empathy there."

In the evaluation, Bella had told me about the animosity between them that they each kept veiled from the man who brought them together, Jack Petrangelo. With his death, there was no longer any need for the illusion of family unity, and the gloves had come off. The hostility Nicole harbored for Bella was real. I tried to imagine having her as a mother-in-law. What feelings must Nicole harbor after all those years of playing second fiddle in her husband's life, and what dark actions might those feelings have led her to?

"Complicated family dynamics. A tragic case," I said.

"Three family members died violently within a year."

"Paige said when Heather left Dan, she moved to the Days Inn."

"After I drop you off, I'll stop there and see what I can learn about Heather's time there," Antelope said. He pulled the card from his pocket and handed it to me. "Do you want to talk with the boyfriend?"

"Mark Kastle?."

"You know him?"

"He referred Bella to me."

"Sounds like a man we need to talk to. What's your take on Attorney Kastle?"

"I'm not sure how observant he is. I got the impression he's not the emotionally intelligent type. We spoke a few times. The first time was when he called me to refer Bella for testing to determine if her mental processes were intact or compromised. He needed a professional opinion on her mental competence. The conversation was brief, straightforward, and professional."

"Something tells me the other time wasn't straightforward and professional."

"Oh, it was straightforward."

"What happened?"

"I met my lawyer, Aubrey Hiller, in Green River at a little place near the district court. He sends me cases from family court, custody evaluations mostly, and we were catching up on some of those. It was clear we were in the middle of a meeting. We had file folders stacked on the table between us, and he was typing notes into his iPad.

"Mark came in and went to the counter to pay for a takeout order. On his way out, he stopped at our table, pulled a chair over, and joined us without being invited. I was surprised to see Aubrey act so chilly toward him. It was obvious to me he didn't want Mark there. Mark didn't pick up on it, stayed where he was. We'd finished eating and could have spent more time talking about the cases, but Aubrey paid the check, and we left.

"Out on the street, I asked Aubrey what that was all about. He said it was a long story he didn't have time to tell me then. He told me to give him a call if I was ever interested. But then he gave me the short version, which was something like, in Aubrey's vernacular, 'The guy's a dick. Do yourself a favor, say no when he asks you out.'

"I asked him what made him think he's going to ask me out. And Aubrey said, 'Trust me, he'll ask you out.'

"I parked a few blocks away on a side street. I was unlocking my car when I heard someone walking behind me. I turned around, and Mark was there. I told him he'd startled me. He put his hand on the door of the Jeep and smiled at me like he was clueless about scaring me.

"Standing there, he was too close to me, so I got into the Jeep to put some space between us. It was surreal. I felt afraid even though nothing happened.

"And just like that he switched and got all charming and solicitous, apologized for scaring me. He asked me out without any finesse or flirtation. It was strange, and I was glad Aubrey had warned me."

"Some people see Aubrey like that—successful attorney, big money. Some guys overachieve in all areas. Is it confidence or arrogance?" Antelope said.

"Arrogance, I think. It turned me off. I didn't want to ruin a professional referral source, so I played nice and politely declined the invitation."

"Was that the end of it?"

"That wasn't the end of it. The problem with being polite about these things is it doesn't get through to people with low social intelligence. They don't read the signs. They don't get it. So they keep asking until you finally have to say no in a way that isn't so nice.

"He called me a few weeks later. I said no again, this time no excuses. I think he got the message. He hasn't called me since. Usually, with men like Kastle, if you don't fall for their charm, they just move onto someone else. And when they decide they're done, that's it. It's like you cease to exist. This is not the guy who wants to be friends with you if you won't date him."

"Sounds like he made an impression."

"With the little experience I have of him, I'm willing to say he's a narcissist. I know it's just a small behavior sample, but I'm pretty sure, based on the way he handled being rejected by me. And it's such a minor rejection, the thing that happens all the time in life. Most people learn to roll with it. The Rolling Stones did a song about it, 'You Can't Always Get What You Want.' Narcissists take everything to heart because everything is always about them. It must be a very painful way to live. The way they handle it is with disdain and contempt for the one who hurt or disappointed them."

"I wonder how he got with Nicole?" Antelope said. "What would a woman see in a guy like that?"

"You can be sure he didn't show that side at the beginning.

And Nicole is a widow who was lonely and lost when her husband died. They were married for twenty years. She's not used to being alone. In other words, she was vulnerable, which is a quality that attracts a narcissist."

"Is it safe to say Kastle, being a narcissist, sees something in his situation with Nicole that's of value to him?"

"You mean beyond having a woman who sees him as a knight in shining armor?"

"You and Nicole are different types of women. From what you said, a competent professional woman wouldn't be a draw for him. What do you think he was after?"

"A conquest. If he got me to go out with him, accept him as a sexual partner, I'd lose status in his eyes. He wouldn't see me as a professional anymore, someone of equal stature. I'm a woman, and he would do what comes naturally for narcissists with women. He'd attempt to control me. It would be subtle at first, verbal slights becoming more contemptuous with time."

"Why do you think he referred Bella to you?"

"There aren't many psychologists in the county who do forensic work. I chose to take it at face value and was pleased when he kept the conversation brief and professional. I never heard from him after I sent him the completed evaluation."

"When was this?"

"In the summer, late August, I remember it was right before I went on vacation."

"Do you know if she wrote a new will?"

"My involvement ended when I gave Mark Kastle the report. I have no idea what happened after that."

"Let's find out if she changed the will. Can you follow up with Kastle?" Antelope said.

"I'll call him."

Antelope went quiet and looked out the window. I noticed he'd finished his cheeseburger and fries, and I hadn't yet tasted mine. I'm not good at multitasking, as in talking and eating at the same time.

"You're right about these, best I've ever tasted," I said.

He pointed at the idyllic scene of the cattle grazing across the road.

"Locally grown," he said.

I put the cheeseburger on the plate.

"Thanks, I'm not going to be able to eat this now."

He smiled and gave me a quizzical look.

"Remind me not to take you hunting," he said and went back to staring out the window.

"What are you thinking about?"

"Two brothers commit suicide within two years. What's the likelihood of that?"

"I could research it for you. Suicide runs in families, that's a well-known fact. And their father also killed himself. Familial suicide raises the odds for other depressed family members."

"You were surprised when I told you Dan killed himself. He didn't seem depressed to you?"

"I was shocked. I never would have thought him capable of taking his own life and even more shocked that he'd kill Heather. As far as him being depressed, I never got that sense. But then, we only talked on the phone, and not for long or about anything substantive. I'm pretty experienced at picking up nuances and variations in mood, but I didn't get that from him. I feel terrible that I missed it."

"Suppose you're right and he wasn't depressed?"

"Depression can look different in men. It can look like anger. It can look like obsessive jealousy. Dan didn't talk to me about that. Anger and jealousy—that's a common motivation in domestic homicides."

"Something about the crime scene doesn't fit." Antelope said.

"Tell me."

"I'd rather show you the pictures, and then you tell me what you think. See if you see the same thing I do. Do you think you can handle it?"

"I guess we'll see."

"You don't have to. It's not part of your training, learning to deal with graphic violence, plus you know the guy. Forget I asked."

"Don't do that. Don't try to protect me," I said, surprised by the sudden flash of anger I felt.

He picked up on the shift in my mood, and he changed in response. We were all business now, the playful undertone that had been present in our relationship since the first time we worked together was gone. And that was familiar too. Our conversations often danced on the edge of intimacy, until one of us, usually me, pulled back.

"Next time we meet, I'll have the official copies to show you," he said and signaled for the waitress to bring the check.

"Do you want me to interview Bella?"

"I'll call the hospital, see if she's good to have visitors. Let's get on the road first."

I asked the waitress to wrap the cheeseburger to go.

"I thought I ruined your lunch," he said

"I'm sure I'll get over it," I said and smiled, trying to lighten the mood and recapture the ease between us. But it was too late.

CHAPTER 12

For a long time, I wondered if Jimmy Quinn would ever try to find me, and how I'd feel if he did. As time passed, I imagined that scene less and less.

On the day he finally showed up, he was the last thing on my mind.

All the way down Hilltop Drive I drove half blind, my right hand shading my eyes against the blinding brightness of the setting sun. If I'd seen him before he saw me, I might have turned around and left him there to wait like I waited for him.

I didn't recognize him at first. All the nerve endings in my body switched on, my personal predator alert coming to life. I reached for my bag and touched the curve of the Beretta Nano under the soft leather.

Then he lifted his chin, a move I recognized instantly, and my muscles relaxed a little as the unknown threat resolved, though part of me stayed on high alert, because now I knew the exact nature of the threat.

He looked right at home as he leaned against the porch railing, arms folded over his chest, feet crossed at the ankles, cool Detective Quinn.

His face was hidden in the shadows of the porch, but I recognized him immediately, the shape of his body, the way he held himself, the faux casual attitude—all encoded in my brain for instant recognition.

He must have been freezing in his city detective clothes—leather jacket, wool slacks, polished loafers. He took off his trademark aviator sunglasses and stared at me as I walked toward him. I'd once teased him that his green Irish eyes were his secret weapon and that's why he kept them hidden.

He didn't make a move to meet me—classic Quinn. The world came to him. He expected nothing less.

"What are you doing here?"

"Freezing my butt off waiting for you. Is it always this cold?"

"You know I don't like surprises. You scared me."

"Aren't you happy to see me? It's been a while."

"It's been two years."

The sunglasses were back on, hands in his pockets. You didn't need to be a psychologist to know his defenses were up. I learned early on in our time together it didn't take much to make him retreat. Quinn was a tough guy who went through life with a bulletproof vest over his heart.

"You know about Dan?" he said.

"How did you find out?"

"Paige called me yesterday. I haven't slept since I heard."

"I'm sorry, I know you guys were close. You got out here fast."

"Yeah, it doesn't feel real. I told her I would come out, do what I could to help. She's not happy with how they called it. And you're working on the case?"

"I do some consulting for the Sheriff's Department. No one here needs your help, Quinn, there's an active investigation. It's early days; you know how these things go."

"What resources does this one-horse town have compared to the Cambridge PD?"

"They hired me, what else do you need to know?"

"Make sure they don't screw it up."

The light was dying around us. The sun dropped behind White Mountain, and the temperature followed. I was standing in the cold with a man I never expected to see again, surprised by the coldness in my heart.

"It's good you came for the funeral."

"I came to find out who killed him."

"The coroner's office hasn't ruled on the official cause of death yet, but the crime scene looked like a classic murder-suicide. Dan shot Heather and used the same gun on himself."

"Dan would never do that. I trusted the guy with my life every day for twenty years. I knew him better than anyone. He wasn't capable of that."

His fingers were turning white, and he blew on them to warm them.

"It's hard to believe, I know. You might be too close to make that call."

"Christ, it's cold. Can we take this conversation inside?"

I answered that question with silence and a stare.

"I get it. I know I left it too long, but we need to talk."

"I don't need anything. But apparently you do. So say what you came to say."

He took the sunglasses off, folded them, and slipped them into his pocket.

"Look at me, Pepper."

We stood there in the low light, our eyes on each other. The moments went by, and I waited to feel something.

He turned his head in the direction of the house and something about that, the subtle yet strategic suggestiveness, brought it all back. Every private thing we'd shared in our year together had staked a claim in my body. There was no way I could let him into my home, no way I'd ever allow myself to be behind a closed door with him. And that was a surprise. I'd thought I was over him.

He waited a minute, and when I didn't move to open the door, he said, "You're not going to invite me in?"

"No."

"You don't want me in your house?"

"No."

I enjoyed saying no, to deny him what he wanted.

"I'm at the Outlaw Inn. I know some things about Dan nobody else knows. You need to hear them."

So much was going on inside me. All the feelings I'd kept locked down so I could go on with my life broke free. My heart pounded with excitement and fear.

We looked at each other in the dying light, night coming on fast. Behind him, reflected in the front windows, the last light of day dimmed. In a few minutes that would be gone, and Quinn and I would be standing in the cold and dark, and I might have given in and brought him inside and that would have been a mistake.

"Give me an hour. I'll meet you in the bar."

"Good call," he said.

When he walked past me, his arm touched mine, igniting a quick spark between us. I waited there in the night air that held his scent until he drove off before unlocking the door. That was how little I trusted myself around him.

I took a hot shower and changed into black jeans and a black silk shirt I knew would turn him on. The ritual of getting ready for a lover.

I hadn't told anyone in Wyoming about Quinn because my other story played so well. In that story, I'm a grieving widow whose perfect life was destroyed when her husband was murdered by a patient. That I found his body beside his dead mistress only added to my credibility and cast me as the innocent victim.

But I was far from innocent.

A year before, I had met Quinn, a Cambridge detective who'd testified on one of my cases in the Cambridge Court Clinic.

I was in the courtroom reviewing my report when he was called to the stand. It was his voice, the authority and timbre, that made me look at him.

I hoped he would say something dumb or intolerant so I could forget I'd ever seen his face. By the time the cross-examination finished, it was too late for me to testify.

Court recessed for the day, and I gathered my things and entered the stream of people moving through the crowded corridor. He touched my elbow, firm enough to stop me.

"There's a bar around the corner. Come have a drink with me."

We walked out into the cold November afternoon, already dark at four o'clock, and found ourselves in the warmth and cheer of a neighborhood bar that was sleazy enough to deter the court crowd.

I was married, and he lived with a longtime girlfriend. Without saying very much, we went ahead in spite of those entanglements. Our real lives and the real people we went home to every night existed outside of us, and we rarely talked about them.

It was late when we left the bar and walked through the quiet city streets in a cold drizzle of rain. We kissed for a long time in the subway kiosk before my train came.

A few days later we met in a hotel room on Mass Ave. That's how it started and how it went for over a year until the night my husband was murdered.

I called Quinn before I dialed 911. I was in shock, shaking so hard I dropped the phone twice before I managed to call him. I needed to hear his voice.

He said we shouldn't see each other while the case was being investigated. He was afraid his career as a detective would be jeopardized if our affair was discovered in the process of a homicide investigation.

Not in that moment, nor at any time after, did I think Quinn killed my husband. But I understood that being my lover gave him motive; no one has a better motive for murder than the illicit lover. He said we had to cut off communication so there'd be no evidence of anything between us.

It made sense at the time. Later, I realized if anyone looked they'd find a year's worth of evidence. I trusted him, and he was scared, so I went along to protect him. It meant I was left to deal with the crisis, all the grief and trauma alone. Even after a suspect was arrested and charged, Quinn kept his distance from me. I'd been erased, rendered invisible, as if nothing ever happened between us.

I didn't need a lover who left me when I needed him most. I packed up my Jeep with the few things I wanted from my life and found my way to Wyoming.

I remembered how easily I had slipped into things with Quinn, how I'd agreed to go with him for a drink that first night, and how I'd almost done it again.

I called his cell phone. He picked up on the first ring.

"I'm at the bar with two cognacs waiting for you."

"Don't wait. I changed my mind. If you know something you think will help the investigation, I'll set up a meeting with the detective who's running the case."

He took a deep breath. I waited and after a while he said, "OK, if that's how you want to do it. I definitely want to meet this guy. He'll be happy to hear what I have to say. Set it up. I'm available whenever."

CHAPTER 13

He showed his Sweetwater County Detective ID to the clerk at the front desk of the Days Inn, who took a quick look, earbuds in, his head keeping time to music only he could hear. His employee badge identified him as Jonah, Western Wyoming Community College Hospitality Intern. Jonah tipped his head toward a sign for the administrative offices. Antelope followed him down a dimly lit hallway to the office of the manager, Derek Hastings, and pointed to the open door.

Antelope waited and tapped on the door to get Hastings's attention. In the small office, a dark-haired man in a gray suit focused intently on his desktop screen, unaware of Antelope's presence.

"I'm looking for Derek Hastings," he said.

The manager startled, shut down the computer screen, and swiveled his desk chair to face the door. Like a guy caught in the act of watching porn.

"Can I help you?" Hastings said.

He stood up, puffed out his chest, minor corporate player assuming a practiced stance, an attempt to project confidence. The suit didn't fit right, and Derek Hastings didn't look comfortable in it. More to this guy, Antelope thought. Making a statement with hair pulled into a short ponytail, purple shirt, and Picasso-print tie.

"Detective Antelope, Sweetwater County. I have a few questions on a case we're investigating."

"Sure, no problem. Jonah should have told me you wanted to see me. Interns, not sure why corporate wants to use them, not like they add value in my opinion. Let's take a walk. Time for my smoke break. Bad habit, I know, but I can't seem to quit."

He checked his phone, dropped it in a pocket, locked his desk and office door, and led Antelope out through a door that said EMERGENCY EXIT ONLY onto a six-foot slab of concrete and the open desert. Heating and ventilating units on either side provided protection from the worst of the southwest wind.

He checked his phone again and lit up, took a deep drag, held it, and let the smoke out slowly. A ritual smoker in love with the process as much as the nicotine, the cheap and quick escape from stress.

"I'm all yours. What's this about?"

"I have some questions about one of your long-term renters, Heather Petrangelo. Do you know her?"

The reaction passed so quickly, someone else might have missed it, but he had trained himself in the art of studying faces, the way the body stayed loyal to the truth.

"What's this about? Is she in trouble?"

"I guess you haven't seen the news."

"I'm straight off a hunting trip, rolled in an hour ago, showered and changed in one of the guest rooms. I didn't stop home; my gear's still in the truck. No luck for me this time. What about the news?"

This guy is anxious, Antelope thought.

"I'm investigating a homicide. Heather Petrangelo is dead."

It hit hard. Hastings turned his back to the wind, coughed, lit up again. "No! How? What happened?"

"It happened on Saturday night. She was murdered in her home in Farson."

"In Farson?" He coughed again, waving at smoke already blown away, and closed his eyes. "I'm sorry, this isn't the kind of thing you hear every day."

"Did you know her?"

"We spoke a few times."

"You're surprised she was killed in Farson?"

"Just, you know, she's been here a while. You get to know the ones who stay. She was separated."

"She talked to you about personal things?"

"I might have overhead it in the breakfast area, you know, people talking. Did he do it?"

"It's an open case. We're talking to everyone who knew her. Did she tell you he was violent?"

"No, nothing like that. I'd see her once in a while, but I don't know anything about her life."

"Except that she left her husband."

"Right."

"She was an attractive woman. Did she have anyone coming around? You see her with other men?"

"I'm not out front a lot, so I can't help you with that. I'm sorry."

"We've been told she might have been seeing someone."

"That would be her personal business. It's not our place to get involved in that. Why would that matter? She was separated."

"She stayed here for a while. No one in the family mentioned anything about a separation."

Derek shrugged and threw his hands up. "Listen, I should get back. We've been out here a while. I don't want to leave Jonah on his own for too long; it'll be getting busy soon."

"I'll come back if I think of anything else. You'll be here, right? You haven't got any more trips planned?"

"I planned on going down to Salt Lake for the long weekend to spend the holiday with my parents."

"Give me your cell number in case I need to follow up with you."

"Sure, but can I ask why you'd need to follow up?"

"A woman's been murdered. You were probably one of the last people to see her alive. We're just getting started investigating. And I'm going to need access to her room."

"Sure. You want the key now?"

"I'll take a look now and get the forensics technicians in there tomorrow. I'll secure it with crime scene tape. Has the room been serviced since Saturday?"

"The weekly rentals get cleaned every Friday."

"What's the best time to catch staff members who'd be most likely to know Heather?"

"Kitchen and cleaning staff, you want to be here in the morning; they all clock out by noon."

At the front desk Hastings pushed past Jonah, pulled out a key card, magnetized it, and handed it to Antelope.

"It's in the back, best to drive around. When you come out of the arch, take a right. It's the last unit facing the desert."

■ ■ ■

Heavy satin drapes closed out the last of the afternoon light. He turned on the overhead light and scanned the living room and kitchen area of the unit. Perfect order, every surface cleared, no food or dishes left out. In the bedroom, shirts and sweaters tossed on the bed like she tried on a lot of different things before making a choice—what you do when it matters how you look. The bathroom was the same, cosmetics and hair things used and left out when she'd finished with them.

Heather Petrangelo planned to return to this room. Why did she go to the ranch? Her daughter hoped for a reconciliation. Maybe her visit to Dan was to start that conversation. Or maybe she'd planned another conversation, one about ending the marriage.

CHAPTER 14

It was inevitable. With or without me, he was going to stick his nose into the murder case. Sooner or later, Quinn would come face-to-face with Beau Antelope who was the lead investigator.

Things would go better if I introduced them. I knew both men well and knew the professional similarities they shared would make it that much harder to deal with each other. Picture two male mountain goats facing off on a rocky cliff.

In his role as chief detective, Antelope didn't take well to anyone interfering with his investigations. Quinn wouldn't care about that and could very quickly make himself persona non grata.

I wasn't thrilled that Quinn was in town for a lot of reasons, most of them having nothing to do with the murder. I was intrigued by his conviction that Dan Petrangelo hadn't committed suicide. It didn't sit right with me, either. While I didn't know Dan as well as Quinn did, he didn't come across as someone who harbored violent tendencies. I didn't know Heather well. We'd met at holiday functions sponsored by the Cambridge Court.

My impression of Heather was of a reserved but pleasant woman, ill at ease in the hard-drinking crowd. She stayed close to Dan, who was the center of a group of laughing men. Heather stayed in Dan's shadow, happy to be there.

I invited Antelope and Quinn to meet me at the Sidekicks Book and Wine Bar on Broadway. The two of them sat on the curved white leather bench at the center of the store, and I sat across from them.

We met early on Tuesday morning. A bright and freezing cold day, so cold spidery Jack Frost icing filtered the sunlight on the front window.

The two men couldn't be more different in personality, but had surprisingly similar taste in clothing. Antelope wore a cashmere blazer, a white dress shirt open at the neck, dark jeans, and expensive leather boots. He amazed me with his ability to navigate the icy streets of Rock Springs in designer footwear. Quinn wore a tweed jacket with a black shirt and black jeans, and black suede boots, probably bought for the trip west.

It was warm, the café ovens were in use, and the scent of cinnamon filled the air. Quinn took his jacket off and folded it inside out on the space between him and Antelope. My hands remembered the softness of the gold hair on his forearms. He sat back, his hands flat out on the bench, one leg crossed over the other. Casual, no big deal meeting his old lover's new lover for the first time. Quinn was cool. At least that's what he believed and wanted everyone else to know.

The café was busy and noisier than I had expected with the chatter of other patrons amplified by the high ceilings and exposed pipes. The two men sat in silence. It would be up to me to start the conversation. Why had I thought this meeting was a good idea?

I told Antelope the basics. I identified Jimmy Quinn as an old friend of Dan's and left out the part about our affair. Antelope and I weren't at the stage in our relationship where it was safe enough to tell each other our significant romantic histories. Maybe we could avoid that altogether. He knew about Zeke's murder and his affair. I knew about his long-term relationship with Cassandra

McKnight. They'd grown up together on the reservation and made it out by way of the University of Wyoming.

Though he claimed to be done with her, that wasn't entirely true. At another time in my life, that might have mattered. But after the murders, I changed. I didn't know if the change would be permanent. I didn't want any claims on me, and I wouldn't make claims on anyone else. Antelope was free to be with Cassandra or any other woman.

It didn't take Quinn long to figure out there was chemistry between me and Antelope. He's not a detective for nothing, and he knew me too well, in the way only a secret lover can. He knows my dark side and the parts of my soul I keep from others. That's what makes a secret affair so intense. It's the one place that's home to what you hide from everyone else. At least that's the way it was with me and Quinn.

All of a sudden it hit me that Antelope was at a disadvantage here because he didn't know Quinn's place in my life. I felt a sudden stab of guilt at putting him in this position. And maybe that was a sign that Quinn still held my loyalty. I'd have to think about that later. Right now, murder was on the table.

Time to get this show started.

I looked at Antelope, who watched me, his face still and serious, waiting.

"Detective Quinn is a friend and former colleague of Dan Petrangelo's. He has some information he wants to share from his communication with Dan a week before the deaths that he believes will help the investigation. We all worked together in the court system, and I can vouch for his credibility and professionalism."

I had rehearsed this mouthful last night and this morning. The intention was to get the facts out cleanly without raising any suspicion regarding the nature of my relationship with Quinn. I didn't feel like I owed Antelope any explanations, and I didn't want to further complicate what I knew would be an already complicated conversation. I knew Antelope well enough to know he wouldn't be happy with this challenge to his department's conclusion that the deaths were a murder-suicide. To suggest otherwise was to imply that he and his team had not been thorough in their investigation.

Antelope turned toward Quinn and waited for the other man to speak.

Quinn twirled his thumbs, waited for Antelope to give a sign he wanted to hear him out, tip the power balance in his favor. He was the odd man out, a potentially unwelcome guest in Antelope's territory. Antelope wouldn't give that leverage. Quinn was tough, also impulsive and at times overly confident.

"I knew Dan better than anyone else you'll meet. So what I'm about to say, you should take seriously," Quinn said. He paused and glanced at me, still wanting Antelope, who sat unmoving, to give some sign of interest. When that didn't happen, he went on.

"Ever since he moved back here, Dan and I would catch up on the phone once a month. The last time we talked was a week before he died. What he said sounded like it came right out of a TV crime show and I blew it off. I thought he was being a drama king. You know how he could get sometimes," Quinn said.

"I'm sure you'll tell us eventually."

Quinn enjoyed holding back, building tension—not only with stories. But I didn't need to be thinking about that right now. In fact, I didn't need to think about Quinn's talents in the bedroom ever again.

"We were on the phone catching up on a few things. All of a sudden, he says, 'If anything happens to me, it wasn't an accident.'"

"He said that?"

"He made me promise to look into it."

"We've been told there were marital problems."

"Everyone's got problems," Quinn said.

"This is a hard place to live. Heather was a city girl. I'm not surprised she got depressed."

"Nobody's arguing that," Quinn said.

"She left. He didn't want her to leave. It's an old story—if he can't have her, nobody can."

"Not Dan's story," Quinn said.

"What makes you so sure?"

"I trusted his instincts. I trusted him with my life. Dan didn't kill his wife, and he didn't take his own life."

"If there's one thing I've learned from my work, ten years of listening to people's secrets, it's that we never know the whole story," I said.

"I can't get those words out of my head. 'If something happens to me, it wasn't an accident. If I die, promise me you'll find out who did it.'"

"He was afraid someone was out to get him. Sounds like the thoughts of a paranoid man," Antelope said and looked at me, wanting confirmation for this opinion.

I nodded in agreement. In the interviews with family members, the theme of Dan's jealousy and obsessive fear of Heather having an affair had come up from several sources. It was one of the main reasons she'd moved out of their house on the ranch. According to Dan's daughter, Paige, and sister-in-law, Nicole, Heather could no longer tolerate Dan's constant questioning and tracking her every move and conversation.

"Dan wasn't paranoid," Quinn said.

"Maybe you didn't know him as well as you think you did. Time changes people. Circumstances change people. This place changes people. It's been a year since he moved out here. A lot can change in that time. A lot did change for your friend," Antelope said.

"I know Dan. He didn't kill his wife, and he didn't kill himself. That's not the guy I trusted my life to for years. He wouldn't do that," Quinn said.

Antelope had his own questions about the crime, but clearly he wasn't going to share them with Quinn, an interloper in his territory.

"Dan didn't do this," Quinn said.

"This is a hearsay conversation. You haven't seen the victim in a year."

"I'll be asking questions," Quinn said.

"You're a visitor on this one, Detective. You know the lines. Don't cross any. This is my case."

"I'm not here to make trouble." Quinn stood, grabbed his jacket, looked at me, and said, "I'll call you."

His face was red, and his eyes told me he was about to lose it. I'd witnessed his loss of control a few times and hoped he could get outside and away from us before that happened. Somewhere there would be a kicked-in fender or a busted window. That's what it would take to release the explosive anger; force and pain reverberating back into his body.

It had caused him a few problems on the job, earned him a few stints in anger management therapy. I worried in the end it would cost him his career. Lucky for him, it hadn't.

"I'll get the coffee," Antelope said and went off to the order at the counter. The interaction between the two men had lasted about five minutes. I don't know what I'd expected exactly, but I was surprised at Antelope's curt dismissal of Quinn's information.

Antelope came back with two large mugs of steaming coffee.

"Thanks, what I needed."

"Your friend's not happy," Antelope said.

"Don't worry about Quinn."

"What trouble will he make here?"

"Hard to say. He's got a short fuse sometimes."

"How well do you know him?"

"I referred him for treatment when his temper got him in trouble on the job."

"What do you think about his story that Petrangelo feared for his life?"

"Seems straightforward. Why would anyone make something like that up? Take time to come all the way out here?"

"Petrangelo was convinced his wife was cheating on him. The guy was losing his mind, getting paranoid," Antelope said.

"We heard a lot about him being jealous, possessive, and obsessed with Heather betraying him. That's different from paranoia. When people are paranoid, they believe they are personally targeted for danger."

"Maybe he was afraid someone wanted him out of the way," Antelope said.

"We never found any evidence that Heather was cheating. And Dan didn't tell Quinn the reason he was afraid for his life. He never said anything about Heather being unfaithful."

"There are lots of motives for murder," Antelope said.

"What are you thinking?"

"Start with the obvious and the question we never asked. Did Petrangelo have any enemies?" Antelope said.

"It would be hard to find someone who didn't like Dan," I said.

"How well did you know him?"

"He was Zeke's friend, and Zeke didn't have a lot of friends. Zeke was very image-conscious; he didn't keep anyone around who'd make him look bad."

"Another side came out after he died. Maybe it's the same for Petrangelo?"

"I suppose you're right. We never know people. Especially if they don't want us to know them and work hard at keeping a distance."

"We need to know more about Petrangelo. That's the place to start," Antelope said.

"What about Heather?"

"We'll need to talk to everyone in the family again. Let's wait until they bury their dead."

"The funeral service is Monday. When do you want to get on this?"

"We have one murder on the books, maybe two. No time to waste. You planned to see Bella at the hospital today; how about you take Cody and Mark Kastle?"

"What do you want to do about Amber?"

"I'll take her. It will even out the numbers, and first contact should be someone from the Sheriff's Department," Antelope said. "Does Quinn know about her?"

"I haven't talked to Quinn about the case, if that's what you mean. You should know I wouldn't do that. That's why I set up this meeting. It's your case, and you call the shots. I'm a consultant. Which means I'm here to help. I don't have decision-making power."

"You taught me over-explaining is a sign of defensiveness," Antelope said.

"I'm not happy he's here."

"What's the story there?" Antelope said.

"I don't like being reminded of the past. And Quinn's a hothead, impulsive."

"You trust his instinct on this?"

"He knew Dan, and he's a decent detective."

"He thinks we missed something. Let's find out if he's right," Antelope said.

We left the café and walked up Broadway to where my Jeep was parked at the intersection of C Street. Storm clouds heavy with snow sat low in the sky, a sense of foreboding in the still, crisp air. Christmas decorations were up in many of the shops that lined Main Street, but I couldn't find a hint of a joyful note inside me.

"I'm heading to Ethete tomorrow to see my family. If this thing blows open, it could be a while before I have time again. Let's hope the weather doesn't shut Thanksgiving down," Antelope said.

"Everyone could use a break," I said.

"Keep Quinn in check," Antelope said.

"No one controls him, certainly not me."

"There's a story there. I can deal with it if you ever decide to tell me," Antelope said and walked away in the direction of the Sheriff's Department.

CHAPTER 15

Paige ran to him and almost knocked him over with the strength of her hug. Quinn was her father's best friend, and she'd greeted him like this for as long as she could remember. He had always accepted her love like a happy kid himself. He didn't have any children of his own, and that made her feel like he was a second father to her.

And now here he was, and she was so happy to see him. And not only that, he was the one person who didn't believe, couldn't accept that her father had shot her mother and turned his gun on himself. Finally, someone she could talk to about her fears.

After hugging and crying together, Paige led the man she called Uncle Jimmy into her grandmother's home. The home she had shared with her parents would require professional cleaning after the Sheriff's Department finished collecting the forensic evidence from the crime scene.

Before Uncle Jimmy arrived, she had gone into the house alone, even though her grandmother offered to accompany her. She wanted to face it alone. It was time she grew up and stopped depending on other people emotionally. She'd never wanted this, never wanted to be more emotionally mature. Her parents had kept her sheltered and dependent until she'd rebelled when they moved her here to Farson She had freaked out then because her life was so different, but the rebellion was another way of being immature. She'd settled down when she met Graham, and now she could see that she had transferred her dependency from her parents to her boyfriend.

He pointed out to her how she was being too dependent and needed to grow up. At times he sounded harsh, and it hurt her to be reminded that she was alone in the world now. Graham was right. An orphan at eighteen years old, she better get used to the fact that no one would ever love and care for her the way her parents had.

She held onto Uncle Jimmy's hand as she pushed the heavy wooden door. Inside the house was warm, and a fire crackled in the big stone fireplace. A cozy room, so different from her last image of her parents' house.

Quinn looked around, and she watched as he took in the quaint western furnishings and the log walls. Everything about the place was so different from their house in Cambridge. There she'd lived on a tree-lined street in an old New England cottage that her mother had transformed into a showplace with her good taste and ability to find treasures for DIY rehab in thrift stores.

She broke down at the memory of her childhood home, which she loved and missed to this day. Whenever she thought about her mother, it was an effort to hold back the tears. At some point she would let herself have a good cry with Quinn. But first, they'd talk. It wasn't the right time. She didn't want him to think she was a baby who couldn't handle talking about her parents' deaths.

"Different, right? Can you see why I hated it here at first?"

"Nothing like home," Quinn said.

"I made some coffee for us, and my grandmother made blueberry muffins. Make yourself comfortable like you always did at our house, and I'll bring everything from the kitchen."

"Can I take a look around first?" Quinn said.

"It's all closed off. The tape is still up."

"I know my way around crime scenes. I won't disturb anything. You have a key, right?"

He came back with a look on his face that told her the death scene got to him. She set the coffee mugs and the plate of muffins on the coffee table, and he sat on the plaid love seat opposite her.

"Cheers, kiddo," Quinn said and held up the mug in a toast. For a moment, it was old times, the intimacy of the cheerful toast. She had been five years old when the ritual started. She had walked in on Quinn and Dad drinking beer in the kitchen. Quinn raised his glass in a toast and said, "Cheers!" Paige said, "I want to do cheers too." Dad had said, "You're too young to drink," but Quinn got up and poured her a glass of milk and made his first ever, "Cheers, kiddo." It had become their thing.

She held up her mug, smiled, and sipped the hot liquid, the first measure of comfort since learning her parents were gone.

"I'm so glad you came. I feel so alone since it happened."

"I make it a point not to do funerals. But I wanted to come. For your folks, I made an exception," Quinn said.

"I don't know if I can do it."

"I'll be right beside you. We'll do it together. Deal?"

"Deal. Every morning when I wake up, for a few minutes, it's like it didn't happen. I don't want to go to sleep, because it's too hard when it hits me and I remember it all over again."

"You know, I don't think it went down the way they're saying," Quinn said.

"I'll never accept it. I don't care what that backwoods coroner says. My dad didn't kill my mom. He loved her."

"They were having problems, I heard."

"He didn't kill her!"

"Hold on, kiddo, I don't believe that for a minute. I'm going to work out what happened. Can you stand me asking questions?"

"Yes, sorry, ask me anything. I'll keep it together."

"I know it's tough."

"I'm OK. Mom hated it here. She started going out a lot. She was bored and out of place on the ranch. She missed being social. I think it took Dad by surprise, how she wanted to be out of the house and all the new friends she was making. He didn't have time for that with all the work on the ranch."

"He missed his work. That I know," Quinn said.

"It's like we were all thrown in an alternate universe. I know he was unhappy, too. Why did he make us come here? They'd still be alive if we stayed home where we belonged."

"Dan belonged here. This was his home, too."

"He changed. I didn't like what he became. I feel bad about that now."

"What do you mean?"

"He turned into one of those creepers who read their wives' text messages. He even put a tracker on her car! When she found it, that's what did it. She packed some things and went to stay at a residence hotel in Rock Springs. She called to tell me where she was and made me promise not to tell him. Isn't that crazy? You know them. How could this happen to them?"

"I don't know. Sure doesn't sound like the people I knew. Dan said you moved out. Is that why?"

"They fought all the time. Because he was questioning her and accusing her of seeing other men. Once he got started, he couldn't stop. It's like he turned into another person. Once when Graham came to pick me up, he heard Dad on one of his rants. It bothered him so much he asked me to stay with him, and I didn't have to think about it twice.

"Dad would have tried to stop me, so I left without saying anything to either of them. I texted Mom and asked her to please understand it wasn't her I was leaving. I didn't want to see Dad acting that way. I was afraid I'd end up hating him."

"What you said there that he turned into a different person.

That's what people think. That he snapped, and that's why he was able to do the thing."

"She went back to him that night. She knew him better than anybody. If she thought he was OK, he must have been OK."

"The last time I spoke to him, he was spooked. I need your help figuring out who he was afraid of."

"What did he say?"

"He made me promise that if anything happened to him, I'd find his killer."

"He said that? My dad was afraid someone wanted to kill him? Who would want to do that?"

"Now don't get mad at me. I know this is a hard question. Is there any chance your mom was cheating on him? He thought she was seeing someone. Was he wrong about that?"

"It wasn't like that, though. She just needed a friend, that's all. She needed someone to talk to about how bad things were at home."

"So, there was someone. Did you meet him?"

"No, and I don't know his name or anything about him. I only know because she was always on the phone. She'd get a call and be all happy, just like a teenager. I got mad and thought, he's right, she's cheating!

"'Is that your boyfriend?' I said. She got real serious and explained to me how sometimes things happen that you don't intend to happen. She told me there was someone who was very supportive and listened when she needed someone to talk to about how bad things were at home. She said she wouldn't even know this person if Dad didn't get jealous and controlling. He wasn't the cause of it."

"And you have no idea who this guy is?"

"I didn't want to know. I didn't want to judge her, but I did."

"Her phone is in evidence, so we can probably find him."

"That's the other thing, she deleted every text she got from him. It made her look like she had something to hide, and I told her that. She just said she got used to doing that because of Dad being so crazy jealous, and it's nobody's business who she talks to. But now that I'm saying this, maybe Dad was right to be jealous. Maybe she was having an affair. Oh, I hate this conversation! I feel like I didn't even know my parents and now I never will!"

"Welcome to adulthood, not a pretty place to live."

CHAPTER 16

Bella Sanderson had changed since we met in my office in July. She looked smaller and thinner, lying prone in the hospital bed, without the imposing air her height added. She smiled when I walked into her room, but her face held no sign that she recognized me. A slight concern; I gave her a minute, as these were not normal circumstances. An MRI and CT scan would determine if she'd suffered a stroke after learning of Dan and Heather's deaths. Short-term memory loss and even amnesia are soft signs of transient ischemic activity.

The room was dim, the overhead lights off. I reached for the switch, but she stopped me.

"Please don't turn the light on. I have a terrible headache."

I moved closer to the bed so she could see me in the light that filtered in through the vertical blinds.

"I'm Dr. Hunt. We met in the summer when you came to my office."

"I remember you. Do you work here?" she said.

"I'm a consultant to the Sheriff's Department trying to figure out what happened with your son and daughter-in-law."

"It's good to see a familiar face. I feel better knowing that. Dan admired you so much," Bella said.

"I have to confess when you told me your son said you should see me, I didn't know Dan was your son. You mentioned a son, but I never asked his name."

"Probably my fault, the way I'm communicating these days. People tell me I forget things all the time; either that or I'm repeating myself."

"I'm so sorry for your loss, Mrs. Sanderson. I can't imagine what this must be like for you," I said.

"Please, please, call me Bella."

"Bella it is. Are you up to some questions?"

"I'll do my best."

"There are a few things that we need to know right now. I'll keep this visit short; I don't want to stress you. I'll have more questions later," I said.

"Go on, please, I'm all yours. I'll help in any way I can. I owe it to my dear Dan and his sweet Heather. If ever there were two people who didn't deserve to die like that, it was those two. Not a mean bone in either of their bodies. And poor Paige, whatever will she do now that she's lost them?" Bella said, tears flowing freely over her face.

"Is this too much? I can come back," I said.

"Paige came running from their place screaming and so upset she could barely say the words. I knew it before she told me; there's only one thing that can make a person react that way. I knew someone was dead. And when she could finally talk, that's when I learned it was the two of them," Bella said.

"That must have been so awful for you."

"I went dead inside, stone cold, I couldn't feel a thing. Paige was shaking so hard, all I could think of was that phrase, *going to pieces*. I put my arm around her and held on tight. I never knew anyone to cry that hard. After a few minutes, I got her to walk with me to the phone, and I called the sheriff. It seemed like forever before we heard the sirens and saw the lights. I got up to go to the door, and it was like all the feelings I had inside, the weight of them, just pulled at me, and I went down. I never lost consciousness because Paige began screaming again. It must have been that sound that kept me from going under. But I couldn't get myself up. That's how I ended up in here."

The door opened and Bella smiled at the silver-haired doctor who walked in and took both her hands in his.

"I am so sorry, Bella," he said.

She shook her head and bit her lip, made an effort to hold back the tears that brimmed in her eyes.

"How did you find me?" she asked.

"The hospital always notifies me when one of my patients is admitted. They send me the test results, and we can follow up when you're discharged. They'll even set up the appointment for you."

"This is Dr. Hunt. She's a psychologist. She probably knows more about me than you do."

"Tom Hamlin. I've been this lady's doctor for over forty years. I'm glad she's got someone to help her through this," he said.

"That's not why she's here, Tom, she's working with the sheriff, trying to figure out who did this horrible thing."

The doctor looked confused, and I knew what he must be thinking. The news would have reported the shootings as a domestic homicide.

In the dark room, with a headache, in the throes of new grief, Bella still was able to discern the questioning look.

She looked back and forth between us, wary and frightened.

"What do you two know that I don't?"

"The Sheriff's Department is looking at the case as a domestic homicide. It's a preliminary finding that could change, but right now it appears that Dan did this."

"They think my son Dan did this? Dan killed Heather? Dan killed himself? Impossible."

She put her hands over her eyes as if to close out the unwanted, unfathomable reality.

"You both need to leave now. Please, I need to be alone."

Dr. Hamlin and I left the room together and hesitated before parting ways, as if the sorrow we'd just witnessed somehow held us in its grip.

"I know she said you're not here in the capacity of her therapist, but I do hope you can help her deal with everything. This is only going to make it harder to deal with her diagnosis. See if you can get her to change her mind about treatment."

I nodded and didn't tell him that he'd just violated patient confidentiality. I wondered if he assumed I knew about Bella's medical condition because she said I knew more about her than he did, or if he just wanted to make sure that I knew.

■ ■ ■

Bella heard the door close and felt grateful to be alone. She wanted no more intrusions from the world, which had once again given her more than she felt she could handle. The only thing that gave her any solace was the fact that the pain of living would soon come to an end. If Tom's visit did anything, it reminded her of her own mortality. She thought about the last time she saw him. It had already been a month living with and trying to accept the death sentence.

They had sat together in silence, the two of them, as she considered what he'd said—glioblastoma, an aggressive form of brain tumor, less than year to live.

He'd been her doctor for forty years, their relationship a strange mixture of distance and intimacy. The things he knew about her life and her body, her children's bodies, the way her husband died by his own hand. Had he ever suspected the reason John killed himself?

She recalled awkward times in the months after John died when he had looked at her as a woman, not a patient.

The way he acted had repelled and disgusted her. She'd considered changing doctors, but he had taken care of all three children also. When it came time for her next annual visit, she scheduled with him, and by then he had returned to his place as her physician.

Now his empathy enveloped her, intimate and warm, in the small office. They'd known each other forty-five years, Bella and the man who'd been her doctor since he was a resident in internal medicine, and she was a new bride. She'd accepted the referral to the oncologist. A particularly aggressive form of cancer. Treatment might buy her a little more time, but that would be measured against the quality of her days, he said.

The weight of the gun at her waist gave her comfort, like the hand of a lover, as she took in the news. Late afternoon and suddenly the light in the room darkened. He turned on the desk lamp, and she saw it had hurt him to tell her.

Outside, a mass of dark clouds moved across the wide expanse of desert where the wind shook the sagebrush and scattered lacy remnants of snow from the last storm. Like me, she thought. Here for a while, then gone.

She'd walked out into a swirl of lazy snow, started the truck, and waited for the heat to come on, surprised to see her hands shaking when she turned on the windshield wipers. At Hilltop Drive, she took a left in the direction of Dewar Drive instead of heading north to the ranch.

She didn't have a plan. When she turned onto Interstate 80 West, she knew where she wanted to be. Semis and long-haul truckers raced past making the most of the time before the weather closed the road.

The last Green River exit, Flaming Gorge Way, led to Wild Horse Canyon Road. Twenty-four miles on a dirt road to Highway 191 north of Rock Springs, the long way home. Not the smartest thing to do with a blizzard coming on. But she didn't have to be concerned any longer about making the right or the smart choice.

She followed the pavement for a mile until she got to the unpaved portion where she pulled over and shut off the engine. An outcropping of white rock flanked by ponderosa pines marked the spot she needed to see.

She stood at the edge where the gravel road crumbled into the mountainside. Below were the Green River Twin Tunnels and the busy interstate, the sound of the speeding traffic silenced by an angry wind thrashing in the branches of the junipers and pines.

This was place where Jack left the world.

Two years since he'd taken his own life, and she'd never understood why he did it. A strange peace came over her. It no longer mattered what had driven him to that decision. Each person gets to make that call for themselves, and no one else has the right to interfere or even question why. For the first time she accepted his decision to leave the world, leave the people he loved without saying good-bye.

She wanted the same for herself. She wouldn't follow up with the oncologist. She wanted to leave this life on her own terms, in her own time. That was the gift of the prognosis—her time here was limited, and she could stop finally worrying about doing the right thing. She thought about crashing and meeting the end on her terms. She was afraid of the inevitable pain ahead.

So many people died on this road. Wyoming roads were reliable killers, both accidental and intentional deaths. Drive past the turnoff to the ranch and up into the mountains, find the right place on the narrow mountain road, and drive off the edge into oblivion. That would always be an option as long as she was strong enough to get behind the wheel.

She felt the gun at her side. Even better, she thought, a sure thing, a strong way to go out, and a family tradition.

■ ■ ■

The day she learned she had a brain tumor she felt so many things—weak and helpless when she heard the diagnosis and then strong and determined when she realized she could take control of her dying. And now, lying in a hospital bed, attached to tubes and machines, she was devoid of any sense of empowerment.

She couldn't think anymore; her head hurt, and she felt so sleepy. The world as she knew it had changed. This knowledge spun in her mind, an unfocused swirling galaxy of hot pain she wanted to avoid. She closed her eyes, shut off her mind.

The spinning stopped, and as her thoughts landed in the space she dreaded, she remembered, Dan was dead. Do something about it. She couldn't abandon him, though his murder brought her own death closer, her cells revolting, rejecting life. Why?

CHAPTER 17

Something important you should know. Not going do it on text.

The message came through when I left the hospital. After a year with Quinn, I knew he wouldn't give up. I agreed to meet him for a drink at Sidekicks. The drive downtown took me out of my way and farther away from home. The main point was to avoid drinks in the bar at the Outlaw Inn.

He was at a pub table near the bar, his eyes scanning the early evening crowd.

He stood and moved toward me with his arms open for a hug. I turned away, made a big deal, took a long time taking off my hat, scarf, jacket, and gloves.

He rapped on the bar and pointed to his glass. The waiter came over to take my drink order, and Quinn ordered another cognac. Bright eyes and easy smile, the first flair of confidence I'd seen in him since he arrived in Rock Springs.

"Nice spot, I like it better at night," he said.

"I'm glad you approve."

"Your kind of place, it's got a Cambridge vibe to it."

"You got me here. What did you want to tell me that you didn't want to do over text?"

"Score one for me, Doctor Hunt's intrigued."

"I'm way past playing games with you, Quinn. I was on my way home when I got your text. This better be good."

He stretched out his arms, cracked his knuckles, and took a deep breath, getting ready.

"Listen, the Dan situation, that's not the only reason I came out here. Give me a little credit."

"I'm listening."

"Before we go there, though, Paige told me maybe Dan was right, and Heather did have someone on the side."

"If that's true, it supports the murder-suicide hypothesis, provides a time-tested motive."

"Works both ways. Gives the other guy a motive if she went back to him."

"We agreed we'd share information when we were all together, keep it simple."

"My bad, I figured we're here, what's the point in waiting? Did you forget I don't play by the rules?"

"We check in with Antelope tomorrow. Let's hold off. I've been working on this case all day. I could use a few hours break."

"Have it your way. You want something? Appetizers look interesting."

"I don't want anything. Talk to me."

"You're not going to like what you hear."

"I got that."

"You're a smart woman, no secret about that."

"If it was a happy thing, you would have spilled it. You're not good at containing yourself."

"You know me well," he said, and gave me a long poignant stare. "Better than anyone, in fact."

"I'm not interested in walking down memory lane. You got me here with that provocative text. What's the important thing I need to know?"

"Do you ever think about when she gets out?"

"What are you talking about?"

"Kelly Jones. The nutcase who shot your husband."

"She's serving a ten-year sentence."

"Time off for good behavior, time off for time served, aced a psych eval that must have been done by a deaf-and-blind moron."

"When is this set to happen?"

"First of December. Parole board met last month and approved it."

"That's ten days from now."

"Hence my urgency in wanting you to know."

"An email would have been quicker sent the minute you got the word."

"Did I have an email?"

"You didn't have an address either. How did you find me?"

"You left your forwarding address with Victim Services. It was just a PO box but, hey, I'm a detective. It wasn't hard to locate your place."

"I find this pretty hard to believe given all the publicity the case got, the sensationalism."

"You'd think, right? It usually goes that way. But some feminist group got behind this and has been waging a PR campaign casting her as a victim of male oppression. What's a poor girl to do when she falls in love with her shrink, and he doesn't love her back? Blast him with a Glock nine millimeter, apparently."

"You're kidding. How could anyone think that way? It was cold-blooded, premeditated murder, a double murder, and one of the victims was another woman. That's insane."

"And that worked on her behalf as well. Insanity defense. Out of her fucking mind with unrequited love. Driven mad by the man she trusted to heal her. Let's hope some opportunistic journalist doesn't get her to sign a contract and turn this soap opera into a book or maybe even a major motion picture. The world we live in today, that could happen."

"Why didn't you just let Victim Services do the notification? That's the point in my providing them with my address."

"Yeah, I should have done that."

His hands were incongruously elegant on his otherwise tough-guy body. His fingers were splayed on the edge of the table making small indentations in the linen cloth. Under his starched blue Oxford cloth shirt, every muscle was taut. He looked like he was about to spring from the table. This was Quinn hurt. One calibration away from angry. He was graciously giving me time to make things right. The veins in his neck pulsed, and his green eyes were laser-focused.

"I get it. You didn't want me to be alone when I found out. I always admired your chivalry; it set you above the pack. Coming out here was a grand gesture. Don't think I don't know that."

With each word he visibly relaxed, his face softened, and his jaw unclenched.

"If that's your version of thank you, I'll take it."

I nodded at him, and he took his hands off the table and sat back in his chair.

"You're welcome," he said.

I didn't know what else to say. I registered the news of Kelly's release—a disturbing development, something a reasonable person could be rightfully concerned about. It's a preferable state of affairs to have your husband's murderer contained behind lock and key in the Framingham Women's Prison than at large in the world.

I had no fear of Kelly Jones. We had shared the same position in Zeke's emotional landscape. He'd spurned both of us in favor of my drop-dead gorgeous friend Carmen, a bilingual clinical social worker with a black belt in karate. Did she regret the hours spent training so she could defend herself when needed? I'd always been a little jealous of Carmen. Everything came so easily to her, and the things that didn't, she took anyway. That she ended up dead at thirty-two didn't balance out the bitter heartache, the slicing agony of her betrayal.

My best friend having an affair with my husband was a wound that could have gone on bleeding. Though they both deceived me, hers was the greater harm, the assault to the sisterhood, the greater hurt.

Kelly, the double murderer, on the other hand, was a different story. She was every therapist's worst nightmare—a triple threat, diagnosed with borderline personality disorder, bipolar disorder, and polysubstance abuse disorder. Zeke was fascinated by her.

Zeke hand-picked his patients. He was that good, and his reputation earned him referrals from distinguished colleagues. He was a superstar in the inbred world of psychotherapy in the Greater Boston area—a shrink to the stars, but in the academic arena.

He didn't like complicated cases. He liked cases he could turn around and show off as his own accomplishments. Kelly, a mental train wreck with an IQ of 160, however, turned Zeke on. In layman's terms, this combination of clinical issues could range from insecure, unstable, and needy on a good day to paranoid, rageful, and impulsive on a bad day. Depending on which substance she chose to manage her intense emotions, Kelly could be passively stoned or wired for vengeance.

She didn't have a license to carry the gun. It belonged to her father. He had shot himself when she left home to go to the Massachusetts Institute of Technology, where she'd won a scholarship to study biomedical engineering.

She stayed in school and financed what the scholarship didn't cover by selling off part of the ranch she inherited. I learned this from reading the notes in her chart before having all of Zeke's medical records destroyed.

Before I moved out here, I couldn't distinguish one huge Western state from another. It's literally by accident that I live in Wyoming.

Interstate 80 is the major east–west highway across America. In winter, the Wyoming portion is often treacherous and frequently shuts down due to blowing snow and high winds. An hour after my Jeep spun out on I-80 westbound near the first Rock Springs Exit, it closed for two days. My uncharted travel was interrupted long enough for me to know I wanted to stay.

The fact that my husband's killer had grown up on a ranch somewhere in the West was locked away with all the other things I never wanted to think about again.

"What are you thinking?"

"First thing she'll do—get outta Dodge," he said.

"Torrington's a day's drive from here. We won't exactly be neighbors."

"Not a challenge for a determined psychopath."

"I'll deal with that, when and if it happens. All I can focus on is this case right now."

"Here's what I came to tell you. You need to move back to Cambridge."

I couldn't hold it back. I laughed in his face.

"That's what I get for wanting to save your life?"

"It's been twenty-four hours since you showed up, and already I feel just as fucked up as I did the last time you were in my life."

My cell phone vibrated in my purse, my emergency phone and my main connection to patients after-hours. But the name on the screen wasn't a patient. It was Beau Antelope.

"You two have a personal relationship?"

"Not your business," I said.

It was as if Quinn could read my mind. Right from the start, he had shown an eerie ability to zone in on my private inner world. He'd broken all the barriers I kept in place between myself and other people, smashed through the walls. I let him see me.

That's the reason I never forgave him for ditching me after the murder. He knew what I was going through and left me in that mess all by myself.

My phone vibrated again.

Quinn was a quick study, though, and as soon as my eyes met his, the smile vanished.

"What's going on?" he said.

"I have to go."

He assumed a clinical emergency, didn't ask any questions, signaled the waitress for the check.

I put my coat on, keys in my hand.

"Wait up, I'll walk with you."

He pulled out his wallet to drop a hundred-dollar bill on the table.

We walked to my car, the only people on the empty street on a still, bitter cold night. A few stray snowflakes swirled, lazy and innocent, the first sign of a blizzard.

"You need winter gear," I said.

"I'm a Cambridge detective. We're a tough breed."

"This isn't Cambridge. You'll freeze to death walking around like that," I said.

"I guess you still like me."

I stopped walking. When he noticed, he turned around.

"What? Why'd you stop?"

"Here's something important *you* need to hear. You left me at the worst time of my life. You blew it. There's no coming back from that. Not a chance. I will never forgive you for that."

He moved back as if shoved by an invisible enemy. He got it, perhaps for the first time, he understood the extent of the damage he'd done—the absolute destruction of my love.

The problem with having someone know you to your core is never being able to keep something secret from them. Quinn knew me like that.

I left Quinn standing on Broadway with his plan to spend the rest of the night pub-crawling through Rock Springs.

I turned on the heater and the fan full blast. The sound was impressive, but cold air would still be circulating by the time I got up the hill to my place.

I had big plans for being in bed five minutes after I walked in the door.

As I turned onto Hilltop Road, my cell phone rang and flashed Antelope's number.

"I learned something interesting today about Bella Sanderson," I said.

I realized was doing what Antelope always does on the phone, bypassing greetings and going straight to the main reason for the call.

"What's that?"

"Her primary care doctor came by and inadvertently let me know she recently received a diagnosis and needs treatment that she seems to be avoiding. He didn't say what it was, but the way he said it made it sound ominous."

"She might open up about it, being in a vulnerable place."

"Listen to you! She might, or she might go the other way, shut down even further. That would be my guess. Also, she was pretty emphatic that Dan would never kill himself."

"Is that right? What did she say?"

"That's it. She shut down and basically threw me and the doctor out at that point. I'll revisit it when she's stronger and out of the hospital. Anyway, you called me?"

"Yeah, there's something else I want to say, if you have a minute."

"Sure."

"I want to clear the air—in case you had any questions about the way things went with us after we closed the Stacey Hart case. I never called."

"I figured you got busy. Not a big deal."

"This is awkward. I should have just left it."

"You gave the impression you wanted to spend some time together, talk about something other than murder. And then that never happened. Is that what you mean?"

"It must have seemed weird to you."

"That you disappeared?"

"I didn't intend for that to happen."

"It's fine. You don't owe me an explanation."

"I've been thinking about you, thinking about calling you. I was going to call you and then this case came down."

"You called me and here we are."

"But the thing is, you need to know, I was going to call to talk about something other than murder."

"OK."

"A few days after I wrote the final case report, something strange happened. I don't want to go into the details right now. Some things that happened in that case, some things got to me, triggered some stuff for me. I needed some time to get right with myself. You know how that can go. What do they call it, processing? That takes time. It got most of me for the last five months."

"I understand, that happens."

"OK, then, so we're good?"

"Sure. We're good."

He was silent, and I realized my response sounded cold and flippant. Here he was offering me something sincere and private, and I was still holding the line to make sure he didn't get too close. Now it was my turn to take a risk.

"Thank you for telling me. I did wonder what happened."

"It's good to have you on the case. It's going to be a tough one."

"I know, but that's how we like them, right?"

After we hung up, I sat in the driveway while the Jeep got toasty warm, enjoying the small thrill of what just happened. I meant it when I told him he didn't owe me an explanation for the brief moment when he opened a door and then closed it. But it felt good to know there was a reason behind his behavior. It gave me a warm feeling to know he'd been thinking about me and getting ready to open that door again.

CHAPTER 18

A homicide investigation isn't always a methodical, orderly progression of obtaining information. In my work with the Sheriff's Department, I've learned to be flexible, to move in and out of interviews and places, not knowing if what I'm hearing will make any difference in solving the case. In the end, it all comes together, but you can never tell in the middle which piece of information will be crucial, which conversation will be a waste of time.

When I signed a consulting contract with the Sheriff's Department, it meant cutting back on the number of hours I could devote to my psychotherapy practice. To cut down on business expenses, I set up my professional office in the sunroom of my home. It had a separate entrance so my living space remained private.

The sunroom was on the southwest corner of the house. Even on a winter morning, it was toasty warm. I watered the plants and poured my second cup of coffee.

In preparation for my meeting with Mark Kastle later that afternoon, I called Aubrey Hiller. I left him a message that I wanted to follow up on the comment he made about Kastle the day we had gone to lunch. I hadn't been interested before, but now that he was involved in a homicide investigation, I was curious to hear "the long story."

My attorney was a bit high maintenance. He never answered the phone; he had to be prepared before entering a conversation. He was not a morning person; by his standards, any time before noon was too early to do business.

On the day before a major holiday, he might not even be in the state. He owned a small private plane and took off for a weekend or a day, sometimes a few hours, to fly to Las Vegas, Santa Fe, or Tucson. Aubrey loved the sun and the desert. He once said he didn't see the point of flying into the rain.

I didn't expect a call back right away. I had an open block of time and planned to finish writing a custody evaluation due in court next week.

The phone rang and changed those plans.

"Can you talk to Cody Petrangelo? I've been trying to track him down for three days. He just showed up here, and I need to be in court in five minutes."

"Sure, send him over."

"Hold on a minute. I'm pulling up a report. See if you can get him to talk about it. OK, here it is. On July fourth, deputies responded to a nine-one-one domestic violence call at Sanderson Ranch from Bella Sanderson. Cody and Nicole were there visiting, an argument started, Cody put his fist through a wall, shoved Nicole out of the way when she tried to stop him from leaving. He was gone before the officers arrived. That's it. I'd like to know what they were fighting about. He's on his way, all yours."

Ten minutes later, Cody Petrangelo knocked on my sunroom door. Black jeans and a hooded sweatshirt, no gloves in a Wyoming winter, his hands looked painful, red and chapped.

Short and slender, a male version of his mother. There was little life in the sleepy green eyes, and his skin was winter white and dull. He bit his fingernails to the quick. As he talked to me, he was working on his thumbnail.

Unlike his mother, he didn't seem to care about impressions. He wore all the right clothes without any awareness of how things would go together. He reminded me of some homeless people who got expensive second-hand clothes from donation centers.

His voice revealed a gentleness that his appearance belied. If you met him on a dark street, you might think of him as a small-time drug dealer and do your best to keep your distance. Cody Petrangelo was shy; in addition to his depressed mood, I could also detect the signs of social anxiety. The initial impression came off as menacing, low-grade danger, but a second look revealed a soul afraid of being seen and judged.

"Is this where I'm supposed to be?" His bloodshot eyes scanned the room. He looked exhausted and wired at the same time.

"Come in, Cody, I'm Dr. Hunt. You're in the right place. I work with the Sheriff's Department. I told Detective Antelope it would be easier for me to meet with you here."

"He's been blowing up my phone, but now he doesn't have time to talk to me."

"We work together. We've been meeting with the family, trying to understand what happened at the ranch Saturday night."

"My uncle shot my aunt. How fucked up is that? Sorry about the language."

"You're OK. These things don't happen without a reason. Do you have any idea why he might have done that?"

"I live at college. I'm hardly ever back here. It's not like I have a home since my mom moved off the ranch. Just one more of her moves to screw up my life and mess with my head."

"I understand she moved so your uncle and his family could have the house."

"You talked to her? Is that what she said? She's always got a way of explaining things that makes her look good."

"Why do you think she moved?"

"I don't think, I *know* why. She wanted to have her boyfriend around without anybody making a big deal about it."

"And who would make a big deal?"

"My grandmother. I heard them fighting about it. She thinks it's too soon for my mom to have another guy. She's pretty sharp, my grandmother. I agree with her. I didn't want to see some other guy in my dad's house. It wasn't even a year, and she's got someone else there."

"You're talking about Mark Kastle?"

"That's the dude."

"And he's also your grandmother's lawyer?"

"I guess. I don't pay too much attention to stuff like that. Like I said, I'm not here much. But, yeah, my grandmother said something about my mom making a fool of herself flirting with him the first time he came to the house."

"How about you, do you ever argue with your mom?"

"Are you kidding? That's all we do."

"Detective Antelope told me about an incident last summer. You and your mom got into it at your grandmother's place, and you put your fist through a wall. Sound familiar?"

Cody made a fist with his right hand, opened it and wiggled his fingers. "I did some damage. Twelve weeks of physical therapy. Good as new."

"Were you aware your grandmother called nine-one-one that day?"

"That's why I took off. People overreact. That stuff happens with my mom and me. She has a tendency to piss me off."

"What does she do?"

"Like I said before, I can't stand the guy. She won't let it rest. Keeps pushing it. I push back."

"Tell me about your relationship with your Uncle Dan."

"I pretty much didn't have one. Honestly, I didn't want anything to do with him. He took my dad's place. I didn't want to think about that, the reason he was there. Me and Paige are close. Two lost souls, you could say."

"What do you mean?"

"Both of our lives are fucked up. My dad was dead, her dad dragged her out here. She was lonely, miserable as fuck. The last time they came out here to visit, she was just a little kid. She grew up. She's cool. We hit it off."

"You introduced her to Graham."

"Best thing ever happened for both of them. That's what they tell me. Is she ever gonna be normal again? She's fucked for life, right? Her dad killed her mom. That's fucked up. Even more fucked up than my situation."

"It's possible it didn't happen that way. It's possible both of them were murdered."

"Really? This is weird, but that would be better right? It would mean I'm not related to a psycho. It's bad enough my dad killed himself. It ups the odds that I'll do the same someday. Yeah, I looked it up. Don't laugh, I'm thinking of changing my major to psychology. I don't know, they might not let me in. I'm too fucked up already."

"Let's talk about something that happened recently. You and Graham had a fight at the Saddle Lite. What happened there?"

"The bartender overreacted. It wasn't even a fight. Nobody threw a punch. We argued, I shoved him, he shoved me back, and I landed on a table. I guess some drinks got spilled, and girls started screaming the way they do. Graham took off like he always does. You won't catch him near any trouble.

"One of the girls helped me get my ass off the floor. I was enjoying some female attention when the law showed up."

"What were you arguing about?"

"Nothing. Bullshit. We both had a buzz going. I was busting his balls. I said he owed me for fixing him up with Paige. How else would a mutt like him get a girl like her? I was joking, but we both know it's true."

"Any idea why he got so mad that night?"

"It was my fault. I was in a weird space being back here. I set him off. I touched a nerve. Graham doesn't come from the best family. But that doesn't matter, he's not like his dad."

"What about Graham's dad?"

"You're not from around here, are you?"

"I moved out here two years ago. What's the story there?"

"He's locked up for killing a guy in a bar fight. That's weird, that's what we're talking about here. Graham doesn't even remember the guy, it was that long ago. He's got the same name, but he's not that guy. Everybody just needs to give him a break with that."

"But that night you didn't give him a break."

"We went back and forth. I could see it was getting to him. I kept going. I told him in the end she's a good girl. She'll do what her parents want her to do. Then he said he'd worked out a plan, he wouldn't let anything get in his way."

"What do you think he meant by that?"

"Graham can talk his way into anything. He figured he'd win Paige's parents over eventually. I pushed him too far that night. But it's fixed, we're cool now. He thought it was funny I was the one who got arrested."

CHAPTER 19

I finished my interview with Cody and headed to Green River. The trip took twice as long as usual, I-80 was packed, travelers headed east and west for the Thanksgiving holiday. An unusual experience on the open roads of the West.

Mark Kastle cleared his schedule to meet with me after the morning session of the Green River District Court. He invited me to meet in his home office, which turned out to be an expansive adobe residence with a view of the Green River.

He opened the door dressed in spandex workout clothes, with a towel around his neck. He bowed at the waist, spread out his arms, and welcomed me into his home.

"Come in, Dr. Hunt, great to see you again. Hey, I appreciate you making the trip down this way. Gave me a chance to fit in my Peloton workout before our meeting."

A handsome man who knew it, he played up his youthful looks, wore his white-blond hair buzzed short and spiked on top. Refined in speech, elegant, and arrogant in the way he moved.

"I'm happy to get out of my office."

"You can see why I prefer doing business here."

By Sweetwater County standards, the house was a showplace with glazed tile floor, stucco walls bordered with mosaic tiles, burnished copper accents—clearly a decorator's work.

"It's a lovely space."

"Come back this way; my office has the best view in the house."

With glass walls on three sides, the office ran the length of the building and looked out across the river to Expedition Island and the nature and walking trails.

"There's ice water, coffee, tea, whatever you like there on the bar. Help yourself. There's even some green smoothie in the blender. I started a cleanse, gearing up for the big day tomorrow."

"I'm not sure how much work I'd get done in this room. Great views."

"I set it up to have that spa feeling, modeled after a resort I stayed at down in Mexico and didn't want to leave."

"Makes me want to plan a vacation."

We sat across from each other on white upholstered sofas, surprisingly stiff and uncomfortable. Mark crossed his legs at the knee and projected a sense of sexual confidence that teetered on the edge of predatory. I thought of the way he'd startled me the first day we met and had second thoughts about meeting alone with him.

"Wouldn't we all like to escape right now? Nasty business up in Farson. And our co-client, Bella Sanderson, brings us together once again. I suppose we should get down to business. You work for the Sheriff's Department?"

"On a consultant basis when a case overlaps with the mental health domain."

"As this one undoubtedly does. What do we know so far?"

"I'm sure you understand, I can't discuss an open investigation."

"Of course, my bad. I will withdraw the question. You can't blame me for being curious, though. Nothing like a seedy family drama. How can I help?"

"We need some basic information on the family. I'd like to get your impressions of Bella Sanderson."

"So, Bella. She hired me to draw up a new will for her and, as I mentioned at the time, I sent her your way. I picked up on something in the way she communicated that I couldn't nail down. Frankly, your findings surprised me. I hoped testing might pick up what I experienced. But apparently, the issues are too subtle at this point."

"Can you say more about what you observed? We met for a few hours in a structured test setting. Sometimes we miss things. You know, same as when your car's making a noise but when you bring it in for service, the noise disappears, and the auto techs can't find anything."

"Good analogy. So you want me to describe the noise, so to speak. Here goes. She'd be talking and, every once in a while, she'd lose track of what she was saying. The words would trail off to the point where she'd stop talking altogether, and then she'd start up again, not always in the same place she left off, but close enough that the conversation went on in the same subject. At the same time, she'd get to the end of whatever idea she tried to explain. But she hadn't said anything new at all, just the same thing in a slightly different way. While she gave the impression she'd clarified everything."

His voice was hypnotic, I found myself having the very experience he described.

"I have some questions about the will."

"I understand the law requires that I cooperate with an investigation of a crime, even if it violates a client's confidentiality. But I'm having trouble seeing the relevancy of my client's will to Dan Petrangelo murdering his wife?"

"It's possible we're dealing with a double homicide."

"I understood from the family that it was a suicide, same as the brother, tragic."

"We're waiting for the coroner to make that determination."

"Can I ask what makes them suspect homicide?"

"I can't talk about the details of an open investigation."

"I honestly don't see what difference it makes now. In her original will, she directed all her assets be equally divided between her sons. Are you aware there's a daughter who has been estranged for many years? There's a clause in the will that specifically states she is not to inherit from the estate. I don't know the story there. Bella wanted to change the will to bequeath the ranch, the house, and all the land to the Nature Conservancy, with the idea they would continue running it as a working ranch and an educational and historical entity.

"That would change the financial status of her family for generations. You can see why I wanted to be sure about her judgment."

"Do you know why she wanted the change?"

"She didn't get into it in depth, and this is where I'd question if she could fully explain her thoughts. She said at one point she wanted to set Dan free. She didn't believe he'd come home because he wanted to be a rancher, but because of the obligation. She described it as a way to bring an end to what she called 'the hostage situation.'"

"Did Dan know about this?"

"As you can imagine, he didn't like it at all. He threw away a high-paying career to come back here and run the place after his brother killed himself. To him, the change in the will was a slap in the face after everything he'd sacrificed.

"I understood that. You wouldn't believe all that I've seen in my work. We say family is the strongest bond and blood is thicker than water. That's not been my experience in estate planning for elders. For a lot of folks, rather than being a safe haven, family is a danger zone.

"Dan came to me in confidence. He thought she was losing her mind. For as long as he could remember, Bella had talked about holding onto the ranch, preserving her family legacy. It was my idea to get a mental health evaluation. It would protect everyone. She was opposed to the idea at first, but that's not unusual; most people get defensive when their mental capacity is questioned. Dan pushed her. He had the most to lose if she went through with the change. I don't think she would have done it, if the idea had come solely from me. Hearing it from two people she trusted convinced her to schedule with you."

"Where does that stand? Has she executed a new will?"

"I gave her your report and told her to look it over and let me know when she wanted me to draw up the changes to the will. She hasn't yet directed me to create a new document for her signature. It's like she's forgotten about it. I haven't heard a thing about it since. That's not unusual either; these things can feel urgent and then get stalled. No one likes to think about death, and making a will makes death real. It's denial, but I'm not telling you anything you don't know."

"Thanks, that's helpful background information. I imagine you have more than a professional perspective. I understand you have a personal relationship with Nicole Petrangelo."

"Nicole's a lovely woman, a good friend. I like to think I provide some emotional support. She's had a lot to deal with, her husband's suicide and her son's emotional problems."

"How did the two of you meet?"

He hesitated for just a second, then patted his stomach.

"You have to promise not to tell anyone. You can't tell by looking at me because I work out, but I have a weakness for ice cream. Nicole works at the Farson Mercantile. I'm a big fan of their super cones so I'm there a lot in the summer. You know how it is practicing in a small town. It's almost impossible to avoid dual relationships. You're probably not used to that working in a major city. I bet you have a different experience here."

"I know what you mean. It's hard to avoid. Clients aren't bound by the same rules of confidentiality. They come up to me when I'm in line at the movies, getting a tire changed at Big O, waiting for my number to be called at the deli meat counter. It can happen anywhere. I return the greeting and try to end the contact as quickly as possible."

"The way I look at it, meeting interesting people in the course of my work is a bonus."

"Nicole said she referred Heather Petrangelo to you. Did she become a client?"

"Not officially. She came in for a consultation about a restraining order. I told her she didn't need an attorney for that, she could go to the district court and complete the paperwork herself. There's a fee to have the papers served. Couldn't be easier. Of course, people are often upset, and things can feel overwhelming. That was certainly the case with Heather."

"Nicole said Heather was afraid Dan might hurt himself after she left, and that's why she took his gun out of the house."

"Smart woman. Prophetic as it turns out. I advised her about the court's policy on firearms in domestic situations. Once she filed a restraining order, Dan would receive notice to turn in any weapons in his possession."

"Are you aware that she never filed a restraining order?"

"I'm not surprised. It happens a lot. A woman might pick up the paperwork and then never file it, or if she does, she could change her mind a few days out and void it by not showing up for the court date. For those who do show up, the restraining order is put in place for six months. Sometimes the woman will violate the order and contact the guy, and sometimes he contacts her, and she doesn't report it. Human factors undermine a system that could work. Again, another area where you probably know more than I do about why that happens."

"I've taken up enough of your time. I understand we'll both be at the Sanderson Ranch tomorrow for Thanksgiving dinner."

"I spent the weekend at a conference in Laramie cooped up in a hotel ballroom with two hundred attorneys, and I've been in court until an hour before you got here. I've had my fill of people for a while. If it was up to me, I'd spend the day alone with the best takeout available. But Nicole insisted, the show must go on, so I won't disappoint.

"I never liked holidays. Is that pathological? People from happy families have that luxury. Does everyone do this with you, open up about their problems and their past? That's all you get from me today, Doctor."

CHAPTER 20

Antelope typed Amber Delman's name into the state law enforcement database and learned about her recent release from the state penitentiary at Riverton after serving a sentence for possession of methamphetamine. Because she had opted for the state's new drug court program, she'd ended up with a reduced sentence and would satisfy the remainder of her sentence on probation with the Sweetwater County Probation and Parole Department under the supervision of Cassandra McKnight.

He might end up paying a high price for the information he wanted; rarely were things simple when it came to Cass. It was two o'clock in the afternoon, on the day before a holiday, but he didn't doubt she'd be in her office. Her rigorous work schedule qualified under his definition of workaholic. A hedonist off the job, he pictured her pumped for the long weekend, ready to party, which put the odds in his favor. Factor in a pure heart and no secret agenda, and it might not be a total shitstorm.

It had been over a year since he'd last seen her. A year of strength and focus and his life in balance—the most stable year of his adult life. The silent phone in his hand held the power of a land mine, if he gave it that power. As half of the equation, he intended to keep his half from going off in a flurry of hot destruction.

He stood, put the phone on the desk, and pressed speaker. He didn't want her voice so close to his ear. He pulled the number from his contacts and called her.

The phone rang for a while, and he imagined her seeing his name on the screen and deciding to let it ring on. That worked: leave a message, ask for the information, a professional call and nothing more.

Her voice filled the room—her sultry, soul-singer voice, her smooth-as-satin, smoky voice. So many times, that's all it took, the sound of her voice, to drop whatever and whoever from in his life and send him running back to her.

And it always went bad. Each time in the bruised aftermath he told himself to remember what they were like together: sick, toxic, dysfunctional, codependent—every label he could throw at it. But logic always lost in the battle with his caveman brain.

That's how it went until the last time he'd walked out of Cass's house and knew he wouldn't be going back. It didn't feel like he was walking away from her, but rather, toward something else. He didn't have a new woman in his life, just a sense that he could find one. For the first time, he might find a connection that wouldn't leave him and the other person in shreds.

He could thank Pepper Hunt for that, but he never would. It was because of knowing her, seeing the ordinary person behind the title, that freed him to get professional help to figure himself out. His intense fear of opening up to a therapist and being judged decreased.

Therapy had always been a foreign concept. Not the thing you did in his world, though his world had changed, became more nuanced, more isolated, than when he first left the reservation. He scheduled with a psychologist in Casper, a three-hour drive away, to keep the whole deal private.

Though he still had more work to do on the case, he felt suddenly lonely and restless, and he began to shut down the open files on the computer. Thanksgiving never meant anything to him, but he needed a break. He wanted to be home like everyone else instead of alone in the empty, quiet building.

He pulled into the passing lane on I-80 and headed to the liquor store, avoiding the traffic jams and fender-benders on local roads on the day before the holiday. When his phone rang, he took it from his pocket and kept his eyes focused on the speeding vehicles switching lanes at high speed.

"What a surprise, Beau, so nice to hear from you."

"Thanks for getting back to me."

"You sound so serious. You called me?"

"I'm driving. Let me call you back. Five minutes."

"I'm about to head out. We can catch up later."

"Stay there. I need information from your files. Hang on, I won't be long."

"Whatever, Beau. It's the start of a freaking holiday weekend, and I'm sitting here alone. You have five minutes."

And there it was—the essence of Cassandra McKnight, caught in a two-minute segment of conversation, a creature of constantly shifting moods and impulses. He took a deep breath, grateful for the reprieve, time to get back in the mindset he needed to be in before he talked with her.

The phone rang a long time before she picked up, every action a power play in Cass's world. She answered in a flirtatious mood. He'd have to play along or risk offending her.

"I just listened to your voicemail. What do you want to know about Amber?"

"I need to reach her for an official notification of a death in the family. I've got a cell that's turned off and no voicemail set up."

"I don't know about any family, just her loser husband, who she tells me is also now getting his shit together in recovery. A kid in foster care scheduled to go back to her care soon. Tell me it's not her kid who died?"

"It's not her kid. She has family up in Farson, and there's an eighteen-year-old niece who wants her to know. If she follows the news, she knows already. You heard about the shooting up there? Two people dead. Her brother and his wife."

"The murder-suicide? I hate those domestic violence cases, love turned to hate, everybody dies. Maybe I can relate, who knows. Amber's been doing good. I hope this doesn't set her back."

"She's one of the few who'll make it? You still have that optimistic streak."

"I have to think that way. It'd be too demoralizing if I didn't have some hope. You know the story. Some bad things happened to her that weren't her fault, but she thought they were, and that's what she lived out. She made the right choice with drug court, though, got some decent treatment, early release. She's in a supervised work release program we've got going with the Little Wind River Casino. Are you ready for the home address? I've got a landline, too."

He typed the address and phone number into his phone contacts.

"A little advice for dealing with Amber. You should watch yourself."

"Why is that?"

"There's something about her that gets men crazy. Some of them even go to jail. She's an addict in every way—booze, drugs, and sex. She's clean and sober. I know that because she pees for me every week. We haven't yet figured out how to test how many guys she's doing. She's an untreated sex addict."

"That's a real thing, sex addiction?"

"And she's your type."

"What type is that?"

"Crazy beautiful. Emphasis on crazy."

"I'm warned. Enjoy the time off."

A done deal. One thing left to do—say good-bye.

"When will you be in Riverton?"

"Tomorrow."

"I'm staying at the Wind River Casino. Bunch of friends getting together trying to avoid the family drama. Come by. We'll catch up."

"I'll give you a call. Don't wait for me, though; we'll see how the day plays out. I don't want you to pass up any fun."

"Did you forget who I am? Don't worry about me, I'm living life, same as always. You're the one turned all serious. Call me, Beau."

Happy to be off the call with Cass, he headed home with the hope of a quiet evening and just one more thing to do before he could forget the case for the night.

■ ■ ■

Once home, Antelope opened his laptop and googled Craig Delman. As the sites started loading, he brewed a strong pot of coffee, filled a heavy pottery mug, and added a shot of Jameson whiskey.

When he got back to the computer there were pages of hits. Craig Delman, age forty-six, Riverton, Wyoming. The man had a clean record, with one significant exception.

A third-degree sexual assault felony charge which had been prosecuted fifteen years prior and for which he had served three years in the Wyoming State Penitentiary in Riverton, later completing ten years supervised parole out of the Green River Probation and Parole Office. He had paid his debt to society on the legal side.

It had been a sensational trial for Wyoming, a high school teacher as sexual predator with a student. The *Casper Star Tribune*, the state's largest newspaper, covered the trial. Craig Delman testified that Amber Petrangelo was the only female student at Farson-Eden River High School he approached for a sexual relationship. For her part, Amber testified that all the sexual encounters between herself and Craig Delman had been consensual, and that she initiated at least half of said sexual encounters, which began in her junior year and continued for over six months.

It was obvious that the defense attorney had groomed Amber to testify in support of Delman. The strategy didn't work, and he received the maximum penalty for statutory rape in the state of Wyoming. And now they were married. It was a crazy world. Sometimes other peoples' lives made him feel normal.

CHAPTER 21

On Thanksgiving morning, Bella sat at her kitchen table with the first cup of coffee of the day and looked out the ranch lands and the Wind River Mountains. It was early, and at the horizon the sky shimmered in a delicate icy blue, so fine and temporary. She didn't take her eyes off it, knowing it would be gone within minutes. She was surprised by the deep sense of contentment that filled her even in this moment of darkest grief. She could sit here all day looking out at the land and not be bothered by people. In a few hours, her house would be filled with guests for Thanksgiving dinner. She would have canceled, but there were others to consider. She was not the only one grieving.

When she married Jack, Nicole had taken over the production of Thanksgiving dinner, and she offered to continue the tradition. Bella should have been grateful Nicole was willing to take on the project, but she dreaded the effort it would take to pull herself together and talk to people as if she cared about anything. Because right now she cared about nothing and no one; however harsh that sounded, it was the truth.

Every year, Nicole hosted Thanksgiving dinner in her house. That was impossible this year. The house remained closed off with crime scene tape, a shock every time she saw it.

And it hadn't been Nicole's house for a while now, one of the many changes that had rocked her family this year.

Last month, when she got the cancer diagnosis, Bella thought that her illness and death would be the next big thing.

It felt foreign and impossible to take it in, and she didn't want to take it in. She'd never told anyone, and she was glad about that. Because now they had the deaths to deal with.

How would they all manage without Dan and Heather? Holidays always brought memories of the missing ones. She hoped the day of being together brought more comfort than pain for everyone involved.

She thought about Amber, missing for so long—not missing, banished. Strange now to think there could have been something powerful enough to make her disown her daughter. The idea of intentionally distancing herself from her daughter rose to a level of absurdity now that two of her three children were dead.

And the reason that she had sent Amber away in anger took on a new meaning. Maybe there was a message, something she should learn, from the terrible loss of her two sons.

She thought back to the day Amber had appeared at the ranch, wearing an air of confidence Bella hadn't seen in her since she was a teenager, the year before she ran into Craig Delman like a car crashing into a brick wall. There was something else, too, excitement she could barely contain. Bella noticed the restlessness, the inability to settle in one place, as she moved through the rooms of the house she had grown up in, like a stranger seeing them for the first time.

It was a Sunday, the day Amber came to visit, and Nicole and Jack and Cody had come for lunch. Usually when Amber made the trip to the ranch, there was tension among the family members. Bella had never gotten over the fact that Amber had chosen Craig Delman over her family. She'd made a decision never to speak his name, which meant it was impossible to have a conversation with Amber about anything of substance in her life.

That day, the conversation was lively with Amber leading the way, and Nicole, always so hungry for friendship, quickly joined in. Jack seemed pleased to see Nicole enjoying herself, and after a while he relaxed, and the mood shifted and became lighter, each person at the table seeming to relax and open up. It was a feeling that had been absent from the family for a long time. She wanted to grab hold of the moment and freeze it, keep them all together in the sweetness. She'd had the same impulse at other times in her life, and knew that it wasn't possible; nothing, especially happiness, lasted forever. Only the bittersweet longing went on and on.

Jack and Nicole stayed longer than usual while Amber played a card game with Cody. This is how it could have been, Bella thought, how it would have been, if Craig Delman had left her daughter alone, chosen someone else's teenage daughter to be the object of his perverted passion.

It was early evening when the others left and she was finally alone with Amber. It was a warm night in late summer. They sat on the porch and watched the sky grow bright in the long hours before sunset. She could almost feel the earth's movement, the inevitable surrender to night. Amber stirred and she knew something was coming, the reason for the visit, and she couldn't stop it.

When Amber finally started talking, it was worse than Bella feared. Amber explained how she often felt lonely and cut off from the family, different from the others, not as good as her brothers or her parents. In one of her lowest moments, she'd gotten interested in genealogy and started researching the family history. She knew there must be other people in the family she had something in common with, others who had done worse things than she had. When DNA kits became affordable, she expanded her research.

And then she stopped talking, and the two of them looked at each other. Amber must have been waiting for her ask the question, but Bella was still clueless at that point.

"Do you know what I found, Mother?" Amber asked.

Something in the way Amber looked at her suggested it was a trick question, with an answer that would elude her and then stun her with its obvious simplicity and rightness. It seemed that the answer took form in her mind at the same time she asked the question.

"What is it, Amber, what did you find?"

"Did you ever wonder where he is?"

And Amber waited and watched her and saw in Bella's face that she was right.

"What are you talking about?"

"You know, I can see it in your face. The baby you had when you were twenty-one and unmarried and gave up for adoption."

"No, it's a mistake. Get your money back on that thing."

"It's science, mother, ninety-nine point nine percent accuracy."

"It's wrong, Not a hundred percent. I don't believe it."

"You don't believe it? You lived it! I'm the one who had a hard time believing it, believing that someone as self-righteous and judgmental as you are ever made a mistake!"

"You're wrong, Amber, and I refuse to talk to you about this any further. You need to forget about this. I forbid you to talk to your brothers about this. It's nonsense, and you would only upset them the way you've upset me."

"You forbid me? You tried doing that in the past, and look what happened! I'm still with him even though it drives you crazy."

"Leave. Now, and don't come back here with your lies."

"How do you like it? Being shamed for choices you made."

"Go, now."

That had been four years ago, and she had not seen or spoken to her daughter since. Did Amber know about the deaths? It had been five days since it happened, and she imagined all the news stations had covered the story. She didn't want to see it and avoided turning on the television or reading the paper.

She'd call her after the others left. It was the right thing to do. Her address book contained the landline number for the house in Riverton, assuming she still had that phone, assuming she still lived in Riverton.

CHAPTER 22

Jimmy Quinn managed to get himself invited to Thanksgiving dinner at the Sanderson Ranch and asked me to go with him.

The next thing he asked was what he should wear.

"I brought one suit for the funeral. I can't wear it twice," he said.

With his fashion consciousness, he stood out among the detectives, an overcompensation for a childhood in the Cambridge city projects.

I told him jeans and a flannel shirt would be fine for a holiday dinner on a ranch in Farson, Wyoming. He shopped anyway. His wardrobe back home on off-duty hours, which he spent wining and dining his status-conscious, social-climbing girlfriend at trendy, upscale restaurants and bistros, didn't include casual clothes.

Back when Quinn and I were a thing, I'd been bothered by unwanted feelings of jealousy about Jessica. Maybe I still was. It made no sense. I didn't want him now. Maybe I envied her ability to inspire him to try so hard to please her.

"What do you think? Cowboy enough?" he asked when he got in the Jeep.

"You bought out the Boot Barn," I said.

"That place isn't cheap. I dropped some cash there."

"I like your style," I said.

It was important to him, and it didn't cost me anything to give the compliment. It was my contribution to what later happened between us, which I guess was inevitable, though I hadn't seen it coming. That's how closed off I was to him, or at least that's what I told myself.

Quinn turned his attention to me. Of the two of us, he was the clothes horse.

"Even girls don't dress up on holidays out here?"

"Watch those non-PC comments," I said.

"What'd I say?" Quinn asked. He looked genuinely confused.

"Girls?" I said.

"You are a girl," Quinn said.

"I'm thirty-six. I left my girlhood behind years ago," I said.

"I like you in dresses," Quinn said.

"Sorry to disappoint." I said.

"I'm teasing. You look hot in those jeans and boots. A whole new look I can incorporate into my fantasies."

I pulled off the road, a dramatic move I hoped would help make my point. I didn't want to deal with another day of his arrogance.

"Knock it off, Quinn. Did you forget what I said the other night? I'm using the little bit of goodwill I have left for you to deal with this situation.

"Two people are dead. Otherwise, we wouldn't be talking. You can put the two of us in a cold case file.

"I'm under contract for this case. I don't need your help. Control yourself and quit trying to play me, or I'm taking you back to your motel, and you can get yourself up to Farson."

He slumped in the seat, his head resting against the window. He watched the road and vehicles speeding past. Nonverbal feedback in the form of eyebrows raised and lowered.

I rated his emotional development in the ten- to twelve-year-old range.

Great, I was stuck with a middle-school jerk. Why did I ever want to be with this guy?

"You wouldn't know about Dan feeling threatened if it wasn't for me," Quinn said.

Defensive, fragile ego, allergic to criticism, committed to salvaging his self-concept.

I didn't want to fight with him.

"We appreciate the information. It didn't come up in the preliminary interviews with the family. Let's leave our stuff out of this and do this together as professionals, OK?"

"We? You and Antelope, you mean? Do you have something going with him? I thought I picked something up when I saw the two of you together," Quinn said.

"I'm not talking about my personal life with you."

"Gotcha! You just answered my question! He's your personal life."

"You're incorrigible. And you're wrong."

"Trying to be a friend here."

"I have standards for friendship you don't meet."

"Never mind, not my business," Quinn said, and went back to slumping and watching the road.

During the affair we didn't argue, and now looking back, that was probably because we didn't really talk much. Hard to believe I considered leaving my marriage for a man I'd never had a substantive conversation with. If we'd had real conversations, I probably would have picked up on the stubbornness, the arrogance, the self-centeredness.

As a trained psychologist I have knowledge, I have experience, sometimes I have awareness. So, why did I waste my time with the kind of men I wasted my time with?

I know any time spent looking at the faults of the other person in a romantic relationship is just more wasted time. So much better, not easier, but time well spent to look at myself. I was there in all the places with all the people who wasted my time and broke my heart.

Halfway to Farson a storm came through—zero visibility, black ice, blowing snow, fun times. After five minutes of white-knuckle driving, it moved on.

"That was freaky. Good driving, Doc," he said.

"Storms out here are different. Everything's different. That's why I like it."

"Different how?"

"Out here everything is harsher, sharper, bolder—the wilderness and the weather are always right in your face. There's a total lack of refinement that I find refreshing. It's not a place to let your guard down. The wind blows all the time, stirring things up. It keeps you sharp."

"You gotta admit, this place could pass for a low-budget witness protection program locale. The kind of place no one would choose if they had a choice."

"I feel at home here."

"I hear a couple of those boutiques on Newbury Street closed this year. There was a major drop-off in profits in retail clothing when you left the greater Cambridge area."

My right hand struck his arm and landed a punch with power. We glared at each other; caught in a time warp. His eyes widened with a mixture of shock and pleasure. We used to do this; he'd provoke me, and I'd protest with a quick punch. A time-travel moment: the instinctive reaction and the familiar intimacy it revealed. How it could still be there despite my mental resolve to never go near this man again, never let him get close enough for a second strike.

"Harsher, simpler, bolder. That goes for the men out here, too?"

"You have no right to ask about my personal life, Quinn."

"I used to be your personal life."

"Past tense. Leave it there."

The wind picked up and the snow started up again. All the way up Highway 28 we were the only vehicle. Hard work keeping the Jeep on the road, straining my eyes in the dizzying flurry of whirling snow, like a snow globe shaken by an invisible hand. Quinn sulked beside me. He rubbed his right hand over his chin, a gesture that meant he was considering whether to speak the words in his mind or hold back. Often when he made the choice to speak, the words came out fast and stung like a back-handed slap.

"How's the beautiful Jessica? Still the most eligible bachelorette in Jamaica Plain?"

"Funny. You have a way with words."

"Just making conversation."

"You really want to know? Or are you busting my balls?"

"Both. You don't have to answer if it's a sore subject."

"I might be getting married."

"That's been your campaign statement for as long as I've known you and a good while before that. It's not news."

"There's something else."

"Sounds like you want to tell me something."

"She's pregnant."

"When's the big day?"

"We haven't set a date yet."

"What are you waiting for?"

"The results of the DNA test."

"You've got to be kidding me. You made her do that?"

"What? I'm supposed to take her word for it?"

"For Christ's sake, Quinn, she's been waiting around for you to marry her for years. Now she's pregnant, and you're questioning whether it's yours? She ought to get smart and leave your ass."

"We broke up for a while. She was with another guy. It's a fair question."

"You don't think she knows who the father is? She doesn't know if it's you or the other guy who knocked her up?"

"She's sure it's mine. Women know these things, apparently. Something to do with the timing, the day of the month, whatever."

"And you don't believe her? Is that what you're saying?"

"I have the right to know. Are you saying I don't?"

"Do what you have to do."

"Thanks for the support."

We rode the rest of the way without talking. Quinn slouched away from me and stared out the window at the scenery, pouting. I enjoyed the silence.

We turned onto the ranch road in time to see Cody running from the house. He took off across the fields. Nicole stood on the porch watching him. When she saw us, she came over.

"Is everything all right?" I said.

"It's Cody. He just can't handle the thought of me and Mark together. It's just going to be the four of us for dinner."

"What happened to the others?" I said. The idea of spending an afternoon with Nicole and Mark Kastle didn't sound very appealing.

"We're all a hot mess here. It's just me and Mark at this point. Bella said she's not up to it; she has one of her headaches. Paige said Graham got a chance to work overtime and she can't think about eating. And there's my son running through the fields like a crazy man."

"He's getting way out of line." Kastle had come out and was standing beside Nicole, a protective arm around her shoulders.

Nicole looked up at Kastle and said, "I should have told him you'd be here."

"He needs to grow up and accept that you have someone in your life."

"We're all having a hard time right now. I feel like I want to give up. I just spent six hours cooking and nobody wants to eat."

"What do you say, folks? You want to join in our holiday festivities?" Mark Kastle said.

I looked at Quinn. He gave me a dead-eye stare that translated roughly to "Are you fucking kidding me? Let's get out of here." I told Nicole not to worry about us, the Outlaw Inn was serving a Thanksgiving buffet.

CHAPTER 23

At the last minute, Cody had decided to surprise his mother and drive out to the ranch because she'd begged him to come, because it was Thanksgiving, because she'd guilt-tripped him about his grandmother feeling sad if he didn't show for dinner.

Nicole didn't get along great with his grandmother, but she used her to manipulate Cody when she needed to. The two of them didn't outright fight, but he felt the tension between them. He loved them both, and it used to make him sad when he was a little kid. It was one of those things he couldn't do anything about, and so he ignored it.

He'd learned this from his father: If it's bigger than you and it won't budge, find a way to get around. It was good advice. It worked for boulders and bears and also for the relationship between his mother and grandmother.

He should have known Mark Kastle would be there. It was going to be hard enough to see his mother. She should have told him.

They were in the kitchen when he came in. His mother at the stove, her back to him, fussing over the steaming pots, laughing, Kastle right there behind her, pushing himself against her.

He left the door open and cold air filled the room. They both turned around.

"Cody, you're here." She looked surprised, her face flushed, caught in a moment.

"Come in and join the party."

Maybe if he hadn't said that, Cody could have dealt with the slimy smile and challenging look.

"Fuck the two of you and Thanksgiving too."

．　．　．

He'd walked the fields to try to calm down. Why did it matter so much about his mother and Mark Kastle? He didn't trust the guy. He had left the ranch and driven the mile down the road to the house his mother rented. He found his father's old laptop stashed with his clothes in one of the unpacked boxes from the ranch. Why hadn't he done this earlier? He had driven himself crazy with all the stories he made up in his head when he could have always known the truth.

He almost opened it right there, he was that eager to know. He didn't want to take a chance of her showing up with Mark. He took the laptop and charger and left.

He stopped at the Get and Go for a six pack and some snacks to take the place of the Thanksgiving dinner he never had and told Graham he was headed to his place. With Graham working and Paige staying at the ranch, he'd have Graham's place to himself for the night, all the time and privacy he needed to do his research.

His father was a simple man and used the most predictable associations for passwords. Using his initials and birthdate, he was able to learn that she started having an affair with Mark Kastle in May. His father died in October. Bingo. What a bitch.

He wanted to hurt her.

There was only one email that showed any promise. The phone number and address of Mark Kastle's law practice was there at the bottom.

CHAPTER 24

On Thanksgiving morning, Antelope took his time getting on the road. It was a holiday after all, and the rest of the population was getting a slow start, warming up for a big meal and an afternoon in front of the television watching football.

He'd have more luck making the trip in person than trying to get anyone in the casinos to take action on a request for information on a holiday. It would mean more hours clocked for him, but at least he stood a chance of getting answers.

His intention was to visit all three casinos first and head to his mother's place whenever he finished up. And if it took all day to ferret out the answers, he'd grab some food from the last casino restaurant and head back to Rock Springs. She might find out later he'd been in the area, but by that time he'd be gone. It was always better if she was upset with him from a distance.

He planned to make a loop tour beginning with the Shoshone Rose Casino in Lander, move on to the Wind River Casino in Riverton, and head back south stopping at the Little Wind River Casino in Ethete, where his mother lived.

It was a clear day, and he made good time on the way over. The weather channel predicted snow later in the day, which could complicate things, slow him down, or keep him longer in places he didn't want to be.

He arrived at the Shoshone Rose before noon and was surprised to see the parking lot full on this family holiday.

He removed his sunglasses as he left the bright day to enter the artificial light and glitz of the hotel lobby. Slot machines lined every wall.

He disliked gambling and found it hard to see it as anything other than throwing away money. There is no winning strategy for playing slot machines where the odds are one in 49,836,032. Dan had played poker where the odds varied dramatically and were determined by skill. Luck plays a role in the random cards dealt, but the way you play them determines whether you win.

He chose the Shoshone Rose as his first stop for another reason. Cassandra's brother worked here and would likely be able to put in a word for him. Clay, a workaholic and a single gay male on the low, didn't have a family to give him an easy excuse for asking for the day off. Clay volunteered for the double-time holiday shifts. Difficult any day, but especially on holidays when society gave permission to drink, Cassandra's family could get out of control.

Despite the number of cars in the lot, the main casino had a sad, empty feel to it. The bright, gilded, cavernous space easily absorbed the patrons. The slots made their noises, like wild birds calling out for mates in a deserted forest. A few loyal patrons stood in the mostly empty aisles between the machines.

The tables held the real action—blackjack and craps, where the odds of taking home some cash on a holiday were better. He walked through the casino, a large room with high ceilings and plush carpets. The muted sounds of gambling—fluttering roulette wheel, brushing croupier's rake, cards shuffled and slipping, dice bouncing on felt—broke the silence of the carpeted room. The sound of the human voice—a distraction, a curse, bad luck—unwelcome where the stakes ran high.

A strong smell of booze in the closed rooms. He wouldn't mind a drink; it would help his mood as he made his way through this day, and yet, impossible on the job. And he wouldn't have wanted to stop at one, not here in this place that indulged human vice.

Some corporate decorator had conjured Satan's salon—red velvet draperies, red satin wallpaper, red-and-gold stripes in the plush carpet. There were women here, too, but they didn't hold top billing. Here money ruled, money and the desire for money.

Clay McKnight stood at the far end of the room dressed in a black tuxedo with a silk shirt in a deep cabernet color that didn't coordinate with the decor. Casino clothing no doubt ordered by someone in another branch of the business who didn't understand that not all reds worked together. His eyes roved the room and swept past Antelope but quickly turned back when recognition hit. The slightest movement of his head before he started across the room.

By the time he reached Antelope, his face had begun to shift out of his professional blankness into some version of his private self where eagerness and friendship still existed. He held out his hand and pulled Antelope in close with his other arm.

"Beau, long time, good to see you, man," Clay said.

"Likewise. So this is your spot. Looking good."

Clay straightened his cuffs. "Fancy casino clothes. Have you seen Cass?"

"We're meeting up later."

Clay raised his eyebrows, surprised. "OK, yeah, you two go way back."

Clay was nervous. What had he stumbled into? "Something wrong?"

"All good."

"I'm here on business."

Clay stepped back, an involuntary distancing from anything related to police business.

"I need to find out if a guy I know owes any money here."

"Half the guys we know on the rez are running a tab."

"This would be a white guy out of Farson running a big tab."

"Not too many guys of that description come in here or come back here if they lose. You're gonna find someone like that up at the Wind River."

"Who would I talk to here?"

Clay tilted his head and pointed a thumb at his chest.

"Right here."

"You're the man?"

"Cass didn't tell you?" Clay said.

"What?"

"I'm an assistant security manager. I know the ones who are into us big. None of them are white. Nobody lives in Farson."

"Are there records I could see?" With big money, there had to be computerized records of significant debtors to Shoshone Rose.

"We got everything the big ones have. But that's not how it works. The men who need to know, know."

"Can you get it for me?"

"Official inquiry?" Clay asked.

He looked away and scanned the room, clearly getting uncomfortable, afraid that he had overstated the importance of his position.

"I'm investigating a homicide. It doesn't get more official than that."

"We have procedures. It's a holiday. The office crew is off."

"But you're in charge today?"

"Give me a name. I'll let you know."

"The victim's name is Dan Petrangelo. I appreciate it. You still have my cell number?"

Clay took his phone out of an inside pocket of his jacket, scanned contacts, and nodded. "Spell that name for me."

"Thanks. I owe you."

"You should go now."

"I'm headed to Wind River. You know anyone there might help me out?"

"Ask for Alonzo Smith. Use my name. Might help. Not everyone will be cool talking to you. If you know what I mean."

"I hear you."

"Give my sister a kiss for me."

. . .

As he drove up to Riverton he considered his options. He could head straight to Amber Delman's place or default on his usual work-before-play mode and call Cass. Something in Clay's manner when he talked about his sister, made him wonder what was going on with Cass. He checked the rogue idea, he was here to work; whatever Cass was getting herself up to, that was none of his business now.

He parked in front of a simple ranch house on the last street on the border of the town of Riverton. A chain link fence enclosed a small yard in the back. Bright plastic playground equipment and a top-of-the-line barbecue grill shared the small space—everything covered in winter grime and the dredges of dirty snow.

Behind the house, as far as he could see, stretched an expanse of undeveloped prairie land, wide as a sea. Tall yellow grasses swayed and bowed, a chorus of slow-moving dancers in the wily, circling wind.

Signs of an upgrade in process: a new roof and double-pane storm windows. Through the new mahogany door, he heard the competing sounds of a football game at top volume and a country music track, giving the feeling of a party happening on the other side of the door.

He rang the doorbell, and musical chimes played in the house. A man yelled, "Amber! The door!"

She opened the door with the start of a smile that stopped when she saw him.

Amber Delman was a clone of her mother. Still a beauty, with the signs of hard living in the eyes, a dullness even makeup couldn't brighten. Long pale hair, the lemon color of winter grass, softened everything.

He looked at the girl Craig Delman had wanted so much he had willingly thrown his life away, and in that moment, he understood Cass's caution.

Some people have a life force so powerful and brilliant that, at the slightest disturbance, it detonates and destroys.

"Oh," she said, soft as a whisper, "I thought you were someone else."

A second later, she looked past him to the street and registered the county vehicle.

She gave him a cagey look, her eyes narrowed. "What do you want?" she said, before he could tell her his name.

"I'm sorry to disturb you on a holiday. I'm Detective Antelope, looking for Amber Delman."

She glanced at the ID he held out to her, stepped onto the stoop, and closed the door.

"That's me. I'm Amber. What's this about? Am I in trouble? I didn't break probation. You can ask my parole officer, all my tests came back clean."

"You're not in trouble. I'm here on another matter. It's about your family."

Her eyes widened, and she folded her arms in front of her. Amazing how the body responded, setting up the defenses so fast.

"I never see them. Whatever happened, don't look at me for it. You can ask my husband, he'll tell you, I'm dead to them."

"It's about your brother, Dan Petrangelo. I'm afraid it's bad news."

Piece by piece, that's how you do it, let it sink in. The mind can only handle so much.

"What happened?"

"I'm sorry to tell you, your brother and his wife are dead."

He could see it happening. Everything shut down for Amber Delman.

"Dan's dead? What happened? I talked to him last week."

"He died at home on Saturday. A gunshot wound."

"An accident?"

"No."

He let sink in. The facts were a lot to take in.

"Shot? Murdered you mean?"

"The coroner hasn't ruled on the official cause of death. It's possible what we have is a murder-suicide situation."

She slumped back and opened the door. "Oh, my God, Craig! Get out here!"

The sounds of the football game died. A melancholy country song played in the background.

"What is it, hon?"

"I need you!"

When he reached her, Amber Delman fell into her husband's arms. He held her and looked at Antelope.

"What the hell's going on?"

Craig Delman could pass for an out-of-shape high school football coach. His chest had relaxed into a beer-drinker's paunch. An inch of white skin showed at the bottom of a gray sweatshirt. Still recognizable from the mugshot on file when he went to prison for statutory rape. Twenty pounds heavier, chiseled jaw and cheekbones softened, blond hair cut short and streaked with gray.

"Dan and Heather Petrangelo were fatally shot. We're waiting on the coroner to determine if we're dealing with a double homicide or a murder-suicide."

Craig pulled his wife close and cradled her in his arms. Neither one of them spoke.

"There's a funeral service Monday morning at the Eden Valley Church, eleven o'clock."

"She won't be going to that. They all treated her like trash. Come on, let's go inside, honey."

He turned to leave and met a woman coming up the walk.

"Is there a problem? I'm Amber's sponsor."

Craig came to the door, "Come on in, she really needs you now."

CHAPTER 25

A half hour later in the parking lot of the Wind River Casino, he called Cass's cell from the car. He didn't want to waste time walking around looking for her or surprise her with another guy. It'd been years since they were together as a couple, but he tried to avoid seeing her with someone else. The few times it happened, history had staked a claim and left him racked with toxic jealousy.

She answered on the first ring, her voice a soft purr he associated with alcohol or waking from sleep.

"You here?"

"Parking now."

"I'm in the room. Come up. Three thirty-one."

Before he could say no, she ended the call. Time to get business out of the way first. He knew her sleep habits, and from the way she sounded, he figured she'd already be asleep again.

The Wind River Casino had more business than the Shoshone Rose. He made his way through the lobby and followed the signs to the administrative offices, down a long narrow corridor away from the noise and crowds. He found the reception area for casino security at the end of the hallway secured behind a reinforced glass wall.

A woman with waist-length hair sat at a glass desk smoking while a big man bent over her and nuzzled her neck. When the security buzzer announced his arrival, they both froze. She crushed the cigarette and fanned the air. Alonzo Smith disappeared behind the door with a brass nameplate that identified him as Director of Security Operations.

When Antelope reached the security window, the woman gave him a flirtatious smile leftover from the scene he witnessed. A jolt of interest, a sexual thrill being near her.

"What can I do for you?"

Her magnified voice echoed through the security sound system, surprisingly masculine and robotic.

Up close under the glare of fluorescent lights, gray streaks in pale blond hair, fine lines at her eyes.

He placed his Sheriff's Department ID into the tray, and she took her time examining it and passed it back to him.

He asked for Alonzo Smith.

She pressed a button on the white desk phone.

"Sweetwater County detective out here, sir."

"All right, send him my way, Yvette."

Alonzo Smith had the smooth baritone voice of a radio announcer.

Her use of the word *sir*, his brusque manner had Antelope picturing the two of them in a dominant-submissive sex scene.

Alonzo Smith, a tall black man with a gray goatee that matched his three-piece suit, stood behind a bigger glass desk flanked by two white leather chairs.

"Must be something big going on to get Sweetwater County here on a holiday," Alonzo Smith said.

Antelope sat and gave him a brief description of the case and the reason for his presence in the casino.

"Here in the Wind River Casino, we're always happy to cooperate with law enforcement. Of course, there are policies in place, and we must proceed through the proper channels. I'll have Yvette prepare the paperwork. Fill it out and she'll do the rest."

A different league altogether, mentioning Clay's name would gain him nothing. He filled out the paperwork provided. By Monday at the latest, the information he wanted would be faxed to the sheriff's office.

One o'clock. With any luck he could finish up at the Little Wind River Casino and be at his mother's place in time for Thanksgiving Dinner at three. He made up his mind to do that. Cass would have to deal with it. He shouldn't have called her.

He passed the busy casino and the Red Willow Restaurant where patrons were lined up for the Thanksgiving buffet. He walked through the tiled lobby and opened the glass doors to the parking lot and the vast prairie beyond.

Outside in the still and windless afternoon, silent snow came down fast and straight, like arrows dispatched to turn the harsh and barren landscape soft again.

In his mind, the trip to Ethete doubled in length. The air turned colder. The peaceful snow could turn too, without warning, into a raging blizzard, no way of knowing. With the sudden chill, a melancholy feeling came over him. The casino behind him was the last place of warmth and light for miles.

Inside, a sleeping woman waited for him in her bed. The notion of work and a schedule to keep made no sense at all. He turned around and made his way to the elevators that would take him to Cass.

He knocked a few times, but she didn't open the door. It took him calling her on the phone to rouse her from sleep. She came to the door with a bedsheet pulled around her bare shoulders, and the remnant scent of alcohol, a look he couldn't read in her half-open, bloodshot eyes. The look contained elements of seduction and condescension and summed up his decades of entanglement with the now-naked Cassandra McKnight.

He could turn around and leave, and it would make no difference between them. He was too close and caught up in her web.

"Late night, too much party," she said, turning back into the dark room.

He found his way in the sliver of muted light at the edges of the drawn curtains. As always, Cass had turned the heat to full blast. He told himself he wanted to rest a while before getting back on the road, took off his jacket and boots, and stretched out beside her on top of the bed.

Cass stirred in the bed beside him and threw the heavy brocade quilt over his head, enclosing the two of them in the tent-like cover. He stroked her face, a blind man wanting to know her in the darkness. She kissed him with a gentleness, long forgotten, softly, for a long time. He let himself receive the unexpected tenderness. She rested on him, so light and so still as he drifted off to sleep.

Then he startled awake, his body jerked with a sudden frightening sense of suffocation. She bolted up, fear in her eyes, as if she'd forgotten he was there. She smiled, bent down, and kissed him, bruising hard and full of the old need, pinned his hands at his sides as if to keep him from escaping. The heat of her body burned through his clothes as she worked to get them off him with her busy, fevered hands.

He didn't want to do this with her, but if he stopped, he'd have a scene he didn't want.

She was all over him, hands and mouth, busy and eager to get on with business. The action stopped; Cass was gone and he was alone; he lay half-dressed in the bed. In the bathroom, the familiar sounds of Cass being sick from drinking. She'd want to sleep, have no interest in him or sex.

She got into bed and turned her back to him.

"Sorry," she said, and instantly fell asleep.

Her long body stretched the length of him, soft and warm. His palm rested on her skull, a sea-shell curve under the fine silk of her hair.

For all the trouble she'd always been, for all the reasons she was nothing but wrong for him, his body held the other truth about her. As fragile and tentative as it was, he felt a familiar sense of safety, or something close to safety, and he slept.

■ ■ ■

What felt like a long time later, a bright band of sunlight at the window woke him. In her sleep, Cass turned toward him, her eyelids fluttered and followed the action of her dream. He kept his movements slow and quiet, found his scattered clothing in the shadowed room, and dressed.

When he opened the door, light from the hallway swept across her still, sleeping form. He closed the door behind him and walked back into the world he once thought he couldn't live in without her.

As he stepped off the elevator, weariness descended. He resisted a strong urge to turn around and climb back in bed with Cass. He found the Cee Nokuu Café and ordered a large black coffee and an Indian Taco to go. He made his way carefully over the glazed surface of the parking lot. A cold wind whipped around him, slapped him awake. Back in the car and ready to work.

He didn't pass another car on the drive to Ethete. He enjoyed the solitude in these drives through wild lands never seeing another person. Instead of music, he listened to the wind as it howled and moaned across the high desert like spirits pulling him into a lost and forgotten world.

As soon as he walked into the Little Wind River Casino, he knew that Dan Petrangelo wouldn't have spent enough time here to lose a lot of money. The place catered to locals, not one non-Native to be seen, and off the beaten track. He figured Dan Petrangelo would be drawn to the familiar feel of the Wind River Casino and even the smaller Shoshone Rose. The Little Wind River Casino looked too shabby to be appealing.

The more he thought about it, Dan Petrangelo would choose the Shoshone Rose, the shortest drive out of Farson by at least a half hour. He hoped Clay could access the information he needed. After completing the paperwork at the Wind River Casino, he wished he'd done the same at the Shoshone Rose. He'd fallen into the trap of relying on connections within the Native community instead of following the accepted procedures of law enforcement.

He looked for someone in authority in the Security Department working the holiday at the Little Wind River Casino, but all the administrative offices were closed and locked up. It didn't matter, he found his mood slipping in the dreary surroundings.

When he got back to the car, he found three voicemails, two from Cass and one from Clay. Cass, mad as hell he had left without saying good-bye. He didn't listen to the second one. Minutes later she called again.

"I'm sorry for my last message. I bet you thought I was drunk sick. I'm pregnant, Beau. Lucky you, no chance it's yours. I'm doing it different this time; I'm having this baby. You may not be the baby-daddy, but you're my soulmate. I'm not going anywhere, so don't forget that, Beau."

For a driven career woman who claimed she never wanted to be a mother, Cass had a casual approach to birth control and the same with abortion. The times they went through this process together, she comforted him.

Each abrupt, tidy ending rocked him. He grieved without her, and each time his heart closed off to her a little more.

He could always count on Cass to remind him why he wasn't with her. Since she was a little girl her moods had changed as quickly as the Wyoming weather. Her spitfire personality matched her passion in bed, and she fought like she loved—too hard and too often. He didn't want to fight, while the smallest thing set her off. She was too much for him. It saved him from longing for something he couldn't have.

It took a minute to settle himself before he could listen to Clay's message.

Clay sounded excited and pleased with himself. "I got what you wanted. Your man was here. This was his spot. He owed big but he paid it all off. He's clear with the Rose."

When he called Clay back, he learned that Dan Petrangelo incurred a $10,000 debt at the casino that he'd paid off a week before his death. Because he'd cleared his tab at the Rose didn't mean he wasn't into one of the other casinos. Antelope would have to wait until Monday for that information.

There was nothing else for him to do in Fremont County. Seeing Cass again and having to fight both her and his mother when it was time to get away home to Rock Springs would have been too much.

He arrived back in Rock Springs before the buffet closed at the Outlaw Inn. When he turned into the parking lot, Pepper Hunt's Jeep was parked in front of the office. He remembered she had told him Jimmy Quinn had a room there. He drove past the stone canopy and the main entrance to the restaurant and back onto Elk Street and headed home.

The trip to the reservation had stirred up the usual mix of feelings it always did, longing and regret, knowing he didn't belong anywhere, not even in the place that should be home. And the trip down memory lane with Cass had left him weary to the core and irritated by his own weakness and hers.

He had nothing left in him to deal with people. And he didn't want to see Pepper Hunt with Jimmy Quinn.

It was easy to pass up Thanksgiving dinner. It never made sense to him anyway, Natives celebrating this day.

At home he reheated the leftover chili he had made for Sunday's football game, got out the chips and salsa, and chose a new craft beer from his monthly club collection.

Then he realized it was in these moments when he was alone and enjoying simple creature comforts that he experienced the truest sense of home. Home wasn't a place; it was more a state of mind that he controlled.

CHAPTER 26

On Friday morning Antelope walked the two blocks from his office to the Community Fine Arts Center. The small art museum had an impressive collection and was known throughout the mountain West as an oasis of culture in the desert. The times that he'd visited he experienced it as a break from the ugliness of the world.

The historical, nonprofit, multi-arts center maintained a permanent collection and also showcased the work of local artists. On his first visit, he was surprised to find paintings by Norman Rockwell and Grandma Moses among many other esteemed artists.

He couldn't remember the last time he visited this indoor space that gave him the same sense of serenity he'd only known on the open prairie.

Margaret Brannon, the director, sat behind the visitors' desk and smiled when she saw him. Early sixties, a halo of gray curls, bright-eyed, one of the most positive people he ever met. A break he intended to be brief often expanded into a long conversation with Margaret about their shared impressions of an artist.

"So good to see you, Detective. It's been a while since you've been in. But here you are! We have some new things. You'll be happy you stopped in."

"I'm always happy in this place. But today it's a case that got me here. Can we talk in a private place?"

"Yes, of course, let's go to my office. You won't mind if I eat my lunch while we talk?"

The window in her small office looked out on an alley and the fenced-off houses of the next street. At this time of year, the birdbath was frozen and the plantings protected by tarps. The walls were covered in student artwork, plants filled every inch of the window sill, climbers and trailing vines spread to the ceiling and the floor. A Tiffany lamp he recognized as authentic gave the room a gentle amber glow. He longed to stay in the quiet and beauty of the cozy room.

She poured two cups of tea and brought them to the desk.

"The way you like. This is the first time you've come here on business. I assume you're here about Heather. I couldn't believe it when I heard it. Such a lovely person."

"That's what I'm told. When did she begin as a volunteer here?"

"At least a year ago; yes, right at the start of the holiday season last year. I can check my records for that exact date if you need it."

"That's close enough. How well did you know Heather?"

"You know me, I like people, and I like talking about art. So did Heather. She was a painter herself. We showed some of her work here in the spring. But like most of the people I meet here through my work, it stayed at that level. We didn't develop a personal friendship, if that's what you're curious about."

"What were her duties as a volunteer?"

"Anything we needed done. She was very enthusiastic. She enjoyed setting up shows and giving tours of the gallery. She taught a few student classes, too."

"How many volunteers do you have? How many people would she have met in her work here?"

"There are people in and out of here all the time. The Arts Center is a popular place in the community. Or do you mean the volunteers?"

"Volunteers, staff, anyone she might have met here."

"Let's see, there's myself and two part-time assistants, five volunteers . . . well, four now. We have an advisory board with five current members, and we need one more in case you might be interested. Oh, and the members, of course, the local artists affiliated with us, there are easily fifty of them. Why do you want to know? May I ask that?"

"We're trying to develop an understanding of the victim, a standard part of the investigation process."

"The *Rocket Miner* reported it as a case of a domestic homicide. Did something change?"

"That was a premature call. The coroner hasn't filed an official report."

"Are you saying it might be a case of a double murder?"

"That's a possibility. It's too soon to know."

"You think it could be someone she met here?"

"There's nothing that indicates that."

She finished her lunch and put the flowered lunch bag back in the drawer. "Is there anything else, Detective? I should get back to my post."

"Thanks for your time. I'll take a walk through the gallery while I'm here."

"I think you'll enjoy this week's artist. He's got quite an impressive display, very dramatic work. We can talk about your impressions the next time you come in."

Natural light from a skylight provided a quiet backdrop to the brilliance of the colors on the large canvases that lined the walls. The artist painted landscapes and still-life scenes and a few human figures, all women, in silhouette or from behind. Something about the position of the figure in the last painting caught his attention.

The woman had her back turned away, as if in her own world, out of reach of the viewer. The artist had perfectly conveyed a feeling of longing. He couldn't read the scrawled signature at the bottom. The sign on the wall, printed in purple calligraphy was clear, identifying the local artist on display as Derek Hastings.

He took pictures of each of the paintings on exhibit and walked out into the bright cold morning. When he took out his phone to call Pepper Hunt, he saw that he'd missed a call from the coroner. He played the voicemail that confirmed they were dealing with a double homicide. The coroner had definitively ruled out suicide as cause of death for Dan Petrangelo.

He felt his heart beating and adrenalin coursed through him, things were starting to move. Pepper answered on the first ring.

"I've got two updates that kicked things into high gear. The coroner fast-tracked the autopsy and ruled out suicide. We are now officially investigating a double homicide.

"Hastings lied about not having a personal relationship with Heather. I'm at the Arts Center. There's an exhibit of his paintings. And the woman in the paintings, she looks like Heather."

"I'm headed to the Days Inn now. Why don't you meet me there?"

CHAPTER 27

She managed to sleep through the first holiday without her parents with the help of Xanax. When she finally woke up it was Friday morning. The house was too quiet, no sounds of her grandmother moving about. She wondered if she was alone and felt instantly afraid. The fear was enough to keep her in bed. She pulled the heavy quilt up over her head to block out the light. She wondered if she would ever again feel happy to get up in the morning. With her parents gone, her own life seemed pointless.

She hated waking up. There was always that tiny space of time when she didn't know. Then the great punch of grief that knocked her back into the new and horrible reality that would forever be her life.

A few times she woke to use the bathroom. Sometimes those minutes awake gave her enough momentum to put the kettle on and boil water for tea. Then it was easy to make instant oatmeal, her new favorite food, the only thing she could keep down.

A darkness trailed along behind the grief and added a layer of poison. She was beginning to feel afraid of Graham. The first time it came to her, she felt rocked to her core. Her stomach ached with spasms, she got sick. That wasn't true, she wasn't afraid of Graham. She was just so tired.

She slept again, and when she woke up, both the grief and the fear were still with her.

Graham was her world. Even though her parents hadn't liked him, she had stood by him. They were the ones who had taught her to love unconditionally. They hadn't liked his background, he wasn't from the same class, a history with the law, nothing serious. Her father had shown her his record. It made her so angry with her father that he would have done this, gone behind her back, behind Graham's back, and found out all this undesirable stuff about him. Things he was working hard to change and to forget. It made her feel even more protective and loyal to Graham.

She knew she wasn't as perfect as her parents believed. Graham knew about her little issues and loved her in spite of them. Her parents wouldn't even want to go there.

Graham had asked her to lie to the detective who'd treated him like a suspect in the murders. Unbelievable, incredible. How could anyone think Graham would do that to her? He loved her. He was her boyfriend. He would never do that.

The night her parents died he came home late. She woke up from a bad dream, surprised when he wasn't there. She checked her phone. It was after midnight. He got off work at ten. Then she remembered, he planned to meet up with Cody at the bar. She worried when he was with Cody who seemed to be getting worse not better a year after his father died. She didn't understand then what Cody was going through. Only now that her own parents were dead did she get it. It would never be over. She hadn't made a big deal about it. Graham hated it when she questioned him. He said it made him feel like he was on a leash.

It surprised her when he asked her to lie about it.

"I came straight home. I was with you all night. Just say you remember, OK?"

"But you were out with Cody."

"Just do it, Paige, don't make my life harder. I don't need this hassle," he'd said.

Since Graham came into her life, things had changed. People had died. First her Uncle Jack, then her parents. Graham had been her lifeline throughout all the loss. Was he the cause of it?

CHAPTER 28

I met Antelope in the parking lot of the Days Inn. A biting wind came off the desert, and the flags above the marquee snapped and waved like furious birds caught in a strong current.

I held my coat closed at my neck and felt the sting of desert sand that swirled and eddied around us. It was hard walking against the force of it, and Antelope took me by the elbow and led me into the quiet of the lobby where the front desk was unattended.

He made a fist and tapped the bell to summon a clerk.

"This guy flat out lied to me, and I'm not happy. He'd better be here and not on another hunting trip. He probably lied about that, too." he said.

"This must happen a lot in your work."

"You'd think I'd be used to it, but it gets me every time," he said and tapped the bell again with more force.

Derek Hastings rounded the corner, wearing a customer-service smile that disappeared as soon as he saw Antelope's face. His anger pulsed and filled the space like an alarm.

Hastings stopped in his tracks, and for a split second it looked like he might turn and run, but he didn't. He stayed where he was and rocked on his heels, patted his shirt pocket, and pulled out a lighter and a pack of Marlboros.

"Detective. Sorry you had to wait. We're running short-staffed today. Was there something you wanted? I don't have anyone in who knew Heather, I'm sorry, I know you wanted to talk to some people."

"It's you I want to talk to," Antelope said.

"Well, you got me, I'm here. Come on back, here's Jonah now, back from break."

"This is Dr. Hunt. She's a psychologist consulting on the case."

Behind us a door opened, and a blast of cold air circled the lobby, screeching like an invisible banshee. The ginger-haired adolescent found his place behind the reception desk and adjusted his earbuds. He nodded at Antelope. When Hastings said, "Take over, Jonah," he gave him a nod too.

"Come on back, I was just headed out for a smoke break."

Antelope stepped in front of him and blocked his way outside.

"We're going to do this in your office or mine."

"What's this about? Did something happen?"

Jonah paid no attention to the scene playing out. He was in his own world, moving to the beat of music only he could hear.

"Not here. In your office," Antelope said.

We followed him down the hallway and into a small office. He closed the door behind us. The window behind him shook in its frame while the wind raged on, and balls of sagebrush rolled across the desert floor.

Hastings sat behind a desk so big it dominated the room. Antelope and I sat on folding chairs squeezed into the remaining space.

"I'll start by saying you could be facing obstruction of justice charges for interfering in a homicide investigation."

"Should I have a lawyer here now?"

"If that's what you want to do, you can have your attorney meet you at the Sheriff's Department."

"Or we could stay here?"

"We could stay here, and you can tell us the truth about your relationship with Heather Petrangelo."

"I already told you about that."

"I visited the Community Fine Arts Center today. It seems like you left some things out."

He put his head in his hands, his chest moved with deep breaths. "Give me a minute." We waited. He looked at us and tears fell from his bloodshot eyes. "I need a cigarette."

"Tell us about you and Heather."

"We met at the Community Arts Center. She needed a friend, that's how it started. She called it an emotional affair. That's all it was. Nothing physical, well, not what you think. It didn't get that far."

"Why did you lie about it?"

"I didn't want it to look bad for her. I mean she's dead. No one has to know. What's the point?"

"I'm going to need the names of your hunting pals, and the exact date and time you left Rock Springs, the area where you camp. Everything that can substantiate your story that you weren't in the area at the time she was murdered."

"I can get that for you, no problem."

"When was the last time you saw her?"

"Friday, at lunch. It was my treat because she put a lot of work into getting my show up. I guess you saw that."

"Did she say she was worried about things with her husband?"

"I'm glad you're asking about this. I didn't think I'd ever see that money again. She needed money to pay off a gambling debt for her husband. I gave her two thousand dollars to help her out. Did she have that money when she died?"

CHAPTER 29

A Chinese restaurant on the Friday after Thanksgiving turned out to be a popular place. Antelope secured a private booth in the back near the kitchen. There was enough lively conversation going on around us that there was no need to worry about anyone overhearing us. It was hard enough to hear each other. We took turns at the buffet, afraid to leave our table unattended.

"What do you think of Hastings's story about giving Heather money?" I said.

"It fits. It's not the first we've heard about Dan and gambling debts. Where is it, though? Not at the crime scene."

"It explains why she was at the ranch that night."

"If she came with money, we need to find out who has it."

"Only a few possibilities: Bella, Paige, or the killer. Neither one of them said anything about finding two grand," I said.

"I'm inclined to wait until after the funeral to ask them about it."

"What did you learn on your casino run?"

"Turns out Dan was a regular at the Shoshone Rose."

"So, Nicole was right."

"Two weeks before his death, he lost $10,000 in a high stakes poker game."

"Could that be the reason he told Quinn he feared for his life?

Kitchen sounds from the pass-through window—orders called out ready for pickup, clanging of pots and their covers, scraping of silverware and plates. We had to lean forward to hear each other, and our voices sounded like whispers in the loud room.

"Anyone he owed money to would rather have him alive. Still valuable input from

Quinn, though."

"I suppose. His perspective on Dan, that he wouldn't kill himself, it fits with my own."

"You don't like that he's here, though, am I right?"

"It messes with my plan when people from the past show up in the present."

"What plan is that?"

"Keep moving forward. The past is gone."

"I thought psychologists were always digging into the past?"

"Just long enough to figure out where we went wrong so we can do something different. Because what's happening right now, right here in this moment, we created it; every step we took brought us here."

"I don't know yet where gambling fits in to what happened to Dan. That debt was paid off, but Dan didn't pay it. The check came through an account for the Sanderson Ranch Trust, signed by Bella Sanderson; she's the one who controls the trust."

"Sounds like an addiction. How'd I miss it?"

"Why should you have known?"

"I pride myself on being insightful. It's a psychologist thing."

"If a person isn't a friend or a patient, how are you supposed to know their deep, dark secrets? That's the stuff we all work hard to hide, the things we don't want anybody to know."

"Here's one of my secrets. The point of therapy is to make the unconscious conscious. We want to seduce the shadow side of the personality, where the dark secrets live, to come out and play. In the daylight, these forces lose their power and the shame they carry. It's hard work. It's also a lot of fun. What does that say about me?"

"Don't feel bad. Some of us catch a high working homicide. I'll keep your secret if you keep mine."

"So she bailed him out. I wonder if it was the first time and if it has anything to do with her decision to leave the ranch to the Nature Conservancy rather than in the hands of someone who showed himself to be financially irresponsible."

"Dan's gambling problem didn't come up in evaluation?"

"No."

"How do you explain that?"

"Shame, or maybe she didn't know about it at the time. That was four months ago. It's also possible, if she did know about it, that she didn't consider it relevant to what she came in for—an evaluation of her own mental status. She didn't discuss any of the specifics of why she wanted to change her will."

"You didn't find any evidence of memory problems. How does she seem to you now?"

"I saw her two days after the deaths, and I didn't do a formal assessment, so it isn't a fair comparison. She seemed frailer, quieter; she didn't recognize me at first, but none of that is surprising considering the circumstances."

"You'll need to see her again to follow up on this. There's that saying—follow the money. What did you learn from Mark Kastle?"

"Bella hasn't changed her will yet. She wanted to leave the ranch to the Nature Conservancy. Dan thought she was losing her mind and pushed for the evaluation. Hearing that she paid his debt and knew about his problem, it looks like she started to see Dan as financially irresponsible."

"If Dan was bleeding her dry, Bella might have done more than change her will."

"Bella as the killer? Are you serious?"

"Drumming up hypotheses. With murder, everyone's a suspect, especially the close ones. It goes against what we want to believe about family, but it's true, most murders are committed by someone close to the victim. And you're the one who told me, when women murder it's usually for financial and security reasons. Kind of fits here, doesn't it?"

"You know, I had the same feeling the other day in Bella's hospital room that I had when she came to my office. She's a strong person, fortified almost, powerful and resolute. Think of a dam containing and managing the force of a river. That's the sense I get from Bella Sanderson. And what she's holding back is an unending sadness. There's so much grief there, you could drown in it."

"Not every killer is a sociopath. Imagine what killing does to the soul of a normal person."

"I don't want to."

"Just because someone's suffering, it doesn't mean they're innocent."

"This adds another layer to the relationship between mother and son. And it makes me wonder what part that played in any problems Dan and Heather were having. The more we learn about this family, the more they look nothing like what they show to the world."

"Speaking of hidden things. I pulled up this report. It's old. Fifteen years ago, Bella Sanderson made a nine-one-one call on a domestic violence situation between Jack and Nicole Petrangelo. The case was dropped because Nicole refused to press charges. This family has more than their share of secrets. Can you talk to Nicole again and see what you can shake loose?"

CHAPTER 30

Nicole turned on the small lamp on the kitchen table, and the low wattage gave off a comforting glow. She hated the overhead fluorescent one that reminded her of her shifts at the Mercantile. The rest of the house was dark around her, a cave in a hillside.

She'd lived in this house a year now, and it still didn't feel like home. It was her own fault. She had resisted it, didn't want to be here in these small rooms. Heather had called it *cozy*, but she was just trying to be nice to offset the guilt about living in the house that had been Nicole's for so long.

Was the night always this quiet? Or did each death, first Jack, then Dan and Heather, leave it stiller and stiller? She was afraid to move, afraid to stir anything up.

It wasn't yet five o'clock, and it was full dark. She thought about Bella sitting alone in her house on the ranch, the darkness closing in, isolated in her own private grief. Her mother-in-law was a cold fish who showed no interest in her. When she first married and came to live on the ranch, she had tried to get close to the woman. She'd done it for Jack, but it didn't seem to matter to him, and after a while she'd stopped trying.

She missed Cody. She no longer felt close to him. He'd been so distant since Jack died, as if he blamed her somehow. He had gone off with Paige and Graham and would probably stay in town. Young people needed each other at times like this when sudden death disrupted their naïve view that life was good and easy and made for them.

She remembered when she'd felt that way—it had been so brief, her time of innocence. Her youthful happiness had ended when she married Jack. No wonder she had done what she did. When she reacted to her own despair, it had been a long time in the making. She had to forgive herself, she had to.

A spark of anxiety flared in her gut. She had to get a grip, or this feeling would grow into a panic attack and leave her curled in a ball, sobbing on the floor, until it was done with her.

She looked at her phone—five o'clock—permission to start the evening. She pulled the curtains closed over the west windows. She wanted no witnesses to her routine. The sweeping black night outside gave her the creeps. Enclosed within her own home, the world shut out and far away, she was safe. With no one to notice, she filled a tall glass with ice cubes and poured the vodka to the top.

With the first drink, her brain cells sent out little points of light, turned her thoughts brighter, made it possible to sit alone in her own house for a few hours without freaking out until Mark arrived. And then everything would be all right.

Mark always helped her feel better. She had known when she first met him that things were going to be different in her life. And she'd been right. The first day she met him, her life started on a different trajectory. Some of the things she did because of Mark were not always the right things. But she refused to feel guilty. She had put up with a lot in her years with Jack.

Sometimes she was angry about being displaced from her home, and she hated Bella for her selfishness and control. The truth was that house was a prison, and now she was free to live the life she wanted.

If only Cody liked him, everything would be perfect. It bothered her a lot that her son hated the man she loved so much. Of course, it was hard for him, losing his father.

Why couldn't Cody see how happy Mark made her? Didn't he want his own mother to be happy? Didn't she deserve this happiness?

CHAPTER 31

Sunday morning, I woke early to find a missed call and voice-mail message from Nicole asking me to call her, ASAP. I took my time with a shower and made coffee and scrambled eggs before returning her call.

"I'm at Mark's place in Green River. I was too scared to stay at my place last night after what happened."

"What happened?"

"Cody had a major meltdown, I mean a full-blown paranoid episode; he even barricaded himself in his room. Nothing I said could calm him down. Mark tried to talk to him, but that just made things worse. I told you how it is with those two.

"Mark called nine-one-one for an ambulance to take Cody to the hospital. But Cody heard the sirens and took off out his bedroom window! Without a coat! In this weather! But the sher-iff picked him up and took him to the hospital. It was terrible, they had to restrain him, he fought hard. I've never seen him like this before.

"Anyway, the reason I'm calling you is you might get a call from the hospital. They asked me if he had a therapist in the community, which he does have over in Laramie, but I don't know her name, and besides, he's here now, so I gave them your name.

I hope it's OK that I did that? He's irrational and talking crazy. He needs help."

"He's in the right place. The staff at Memorial has a lot of experience dealing with adolescents and young adults," I said.

"This isn't your average teenage stuff. He's not himself. The murders got to him. He's gone paranoid. He doesn't even trust me, his own mother! Can you believe that?"

"I understand how upsetting that must be for you. Do you have any idea what brought this on?"

"The murders brought it on! What else could it be? You saw how he was the other day! Running off like that. He took off and didn't come home until last night. And then this happened! And you know what the worst thing is? He said I'm the one who needs help. And then he said something really crazy, he said the two of you, meaning Mark and me, the two of you are in this together. And he made this noise, a terrible noise, like a growl. It was so scary hearing that sound come from my son."

"I can see why you're so upset."

"Cody's had his issues, but never anything like this. What's happening to my family? It feels like everything is falling apart."

It was clear she was having trouble dealing with this latest development with Cody on top of everything else. It seemed like a good time to follow up on the report of the domestic violence call. I suggested she come in to meet with me, and she agreed.

An hour later we sat across from one another in my office.

"Thank you for seeing me on a Sunday, Doctor. I'm such a mess."

"I've been wanting to talk with you about the family. If I'm going to help Cody, I need to know a little more about what happened with your husband's suicide. Are you OK to talk about that? I know that losing a loved one to suicide is one of the hardest losses to bear."

"It's the guilt that gets to you. Like I should have seen it coming and done something to stop it."

"That's what most people feel. There weren't any signs that Jack was in a bad state of mind?"

"Jack wasn't a happy man, but that was nothing new. I didn't notice him being any more miserable than he usually was, to tell you the truth."

"That sounds hard. It wasn't a happy marriage?"

"How many of those have you seen? We were like everyone else. As happy as people can be trying to make a life together in difficult circumstances, if you know what I mean," Nicole said.

"What do you mean?"

"Living on the ranch with his mother watching over everything, never giving anything over to him or letting him run the place his way. She had her own ideas about how to do things and always deferred to Jack if she had any doubt. Jack always stayed a child in her mind. It made me mad on his behalf. But you could never say anything to him about it. He was fiercely loyal to her. I don't know, maybe it bothered him and got to him and that's why he did what he did like his father before him. Anyway, when I was looking for an answer to why, that's what I came up with.

"Jack had a tendency to be possessive. At first, it made you feel special, but after a while it felt like you couldn't breathe. After a while, I put my foot down and told him I'm not living like this. I'm not like your mother, content to live my life for this ranch. I need something else, or I'll lose my mind alone out here all day. That's when I went back to working part-time at the Farson Mercantile."

"How did he take that?"

"He wasn't happy about it. The money I made helped out, and he started to accept it. People don't change though, do they? He always had an eye out, waiting for something to happen. I could feel it. I suppose he wanted me to accept that about him, but I never could. So I understood when Heather left. It's not easy living with someone who doesn't trust you. My husband was a difficult man, an angry man."

"Cody's temper, did he get that from his father?" I asked.

"I guess you could say that, I tried my best to keep him from seeing us fighting." Nicole said.

"Was Jack ever violent with you?" I asked.

"Why would you ask about that? What difference could that possibly make now?" Nicole asked.

"We both want to understand what's going on with Cody. Anything, even if it seems remote and unconnected, could lead us in the direction of what happened on Saturday," I explained.

"It was years ago. And it was minor as those things go. But it happened," Nicole acknowledged.

"Sometimes these things leave long-lasting emotional scars even years after they've stopped," I said.

"That's how it was with me and Jack. I never would have called the police. It wasn't that serious a thing. Any man can be pushed to lose control. I wasn't the one who pushed him. We both knew that. Sometimes things could get to be too much even for him with Bella, and at times he took it out on me. She never understood that, though, never knew how much she contributed to him being unhappy."

"Was that the only time?" I asked.

"It wasn't that bad. I stayed, didn't I?"

"Did Cody see his father being violent?" I asked.

"It wasn't at that level," Nicole said, engaging in a familiar pattern of denial and minimization that had made it possible for her to remain in the situation.

"The police report cites facial injury, and Bella gave a statement saying she heard you scream."

"I was screaming at him, and he couldn't take it anymore. It happened under certain circumstances like when we were arguing about his mother. I learned to manage it by avoiding the situation, and it didn't happen anymore. End of story. And I still don't see what any of Jack's and my private business has to do with what happened to Dan and Heather," Nicole said.

"It looks like there's a pattern of violence in the family."

"You asked if Cody saw it. I've been worried about him. He hasn't been the same since Jack died. I'm worried he could hurt someone, the way he gets so upset."

CHAPTER 32

Cody felt claustrophobic. He had to get out. Locked up in the psych ward, he was a sitting duck. The charge nurse told him that the law allowed them to hold him for seventy-two hours for observation. At the end of the three days, if they determined he was a risk to himself or others, they would ask him to voluntarily admit himself for psychiatric treatment. If he refused to do that, they would have a judge decide whether there was enough medical evidence to commit him for treatment against his will.

If he had any chance of getting out of here, he had to know what evidence they would use to recommend a continued stay in the hospital. He couldn't remember a thing about the night he was taken to the hospital. He had a right to know, and he asked the woman at the desk if he could read the notes in his chart.

He half expected her to tell him it was against the rules, but she didn't say a word. It didn't take any effort at all for her to hand the chart to him. She pushed away from the desk and rolled her chair three feet to the shelf behind her and grabbed the chart with his name on it. When she opened the thin chart, the note was right there. The note written in longhand with the words, "Sweetwater County Sheriff's Department" at the top of the page.

She placed it on the counter before him and tapped it with her index finger. Her long nails were painted a glossy red and had a Christmas tree on the tip.

"You have to read it here. I can't let you take it," she said.

He gave her a nod and put his hands on his hips to show her he had no intention of taking off with the chart.

The note was written in thick block letters as opposed to cursive and was easy to read. He didn't recognize the person being described. It flashed through his mind that someone had misfiled this report and that it belonged in someone else's chart. But, of course, nothing was familiar about the scene he was reading about. He'd hoped that what he read would bring back his own memories of that episode. But that wasn't the case. It was as if these things had happened to someone else; nothing of that time had been recorded in his conscious mind.

He stood there, reading the page over and over as if hoping the repetition would spark some trace of memory he could build on. It was a chilling experience reading about something he had lived through but couldn't recall. He shivered and folded his arms across his chest as goosebumps rose on his flesh.

"Are you doing OK there?" the woman at the desk asked.

He nodded again and kept his eyes on the page. The note was written and signed by Deputy Antelope at 2:10 a.m. on Sunday, December 1.

"I'll put this back if you're finished with it," she said.

For the first time he heard caution in her voice. She was speaking to him like he was a mental patient and maybe she had made a mistake giving him access to this clinical information. Knowing she was seeing him that way added to the cold rage that was rising in him. In that moment, his mind focused on a single sentence in the report:

Officers responded to a call from Attorney Mark Kastle at Sanderson Ranch in Farson, Wyoming, reporting homicidal threats made by Cody Petrangelo, age 21, paranoid psychosis.

He grabbed the chart, tore out pages, threw the metal binder to the floor and stomped on it. He cut his foot on the edge, and that made him angrier. He picked up the chart and heaved it against the wall.

On his back on the floor with three people on either side of him. The secretary watched from her chair at the desk. She looked at him with sad eyes and shook her head from side to side.

He tried to shake free of the hands on his ankles, thighs, and wrists.

"Hold on there, the nurse will be here soon with something to help you calm down."

It would be like that night. He'd get another dose of a drug that would knock out his memory of this moment. *I have to remember. I have to remember so I can get out of here.*

He woke up sweating in a too-hot room. It was dark with an inch of light slanting across the floor from the partially open door. The hallway beyond was quiet, but he could hear the low sound of faraway muffled voices—the other patients eating dinner in the dining room on the far side of the unit.

His head hurt from sleeping too long and the aftereffects of the strong antipsychotic medication. It had been late morning when he'd asked to see the police report and freaked out. He calculated that the injection knocked had him out for at least eight hours. He sat up too fast. His head spun.

Still under the influence of whatever it was they used to sedate him, he remembered it was twelve hours before he came to after the first time.

He was trapped here, and the fact that the staff could do whatever they wanted with him and turn him into an unconscious lump of clay got him angry all over again. But this time he had a different idea. He wouldn't give them another chance to subdue him. He had to keep his mind clear and his emotions under control to figure out how to get out of this place.

Even in his compromised mental status he understood with uncomfortable clarity how a person could end up in a mental hospital for years. All it took was vehemently protesting that you shouldn't be there to convince people that you should be. Act crazy and you are labeled crazy. He got it now. He had to remember and keep himself in check.

And his mind shut as if he had used up all the energy it had for the moment. He surrendered to dreamless sleep.

CHAPTER 33

The weather mirrored the mood of the day when Dan and
Heather were laid to rest in the Eden Valley Cemetery. Rain was
a rare occurrence in the high desert of southwest Wyoming. It
began in the dark of the early morning hours and woke me from
sleep with a loud, steady insistence, battering the roof tiles trying
to get in.

The lonely sound unsettled me, and I couldn't sleep again.
I got up and turned everything on—lights, gas fireplace, coffee
maker. Humans weren't meant to startle awake in the dark at
the sound of loud noises. My nervous system responded to the
alarm with its reliable regimen of traumatic stress responses—
flood of adrenaline, accelerated heartbeat, muscles wired and
ready to move.

I'd been dreading the funeral. I wasn't thrilled with the
rude and early start the rain created. Except for the recent
snowstorm, the temperatures had been mild, the ground not
yet frozen. Dan and Heather would be buried now instead of
instead of in the spring. The thermometer outside the kitchen
window showed thirty-five degrees Fahrenheit. A few degrees
colder, and the current downpour would have been a major
snowstorm. The Petrangelo family would have the funeral and
burial without delay, and with the support of friends and family

who had traveled to be with them during the immediacy of the loss. There would be a sense of closure that came with the finality of relinquishing the bodies to the earth. That, at least, was something to be grateful for.

The brief funeral service was graveside in the Farson-Eden Cemetery, behind the chapel. The rain had stopped, and the sun was bright and high in a pure blue sky. It was too beautiful a day for a funeral. The Eden Valley looked like a postcard of a community known for peace and tranquility. It was an unlikely setting for murder. Was the killer here at the funeral service? I wondered how many others were thinking the same thing and looking suspiciously at the other mourners, all friends and neighbors of the deceased.

The air was sweet and still and cold, and the sun made the temperature tolerable.

The three women in the family lined up at the head of the graves, Bella in the middle, flanked on one side by Nicole and on the other by Paige. It must be hard for all of them, each for their separate reasons, that Cody was absent, unable to grieve with them, alone in the hospital. I wondered where Mark Kastle was.

As soon as we arrived, Quinn and I split up. I joined Antelope, who stood alone and slightly apart from the group, while Quinn went straight to Paige. They stood together throughout the service, his arm around her shaking shoulders. Graham Douglas stood to the side and let Quinn take over the burden of emotionally supporting Paige in her grief, a job that would be his full time when Quinn went home.

Graham had a big job ahead of him. He was a young man who didn't seem to have much experience dealing with the emotional side of life. Paige had led a loved and sheltered life as the only child of doting parents. In an instant she'd lost them both, after having lost the home and the city that had contributed to her stability for eighteen years.

Graham had only been on the scene for a year. Did he have any idea what would be required of him in the months and years ahead with Paige? Would their young love survive the challenge of Paige's grief? At their age, they should have been experiencing all the excitement and wonder of the expanded world, but instead the loss would weigh their spirits like a heavy anchor. It was an open question whether this tragic event would solidify their relationship or be their undoing.

Just as the service was about to start, Bella held up her hand to signal the minister to wait.

Everyone turned to see a tall woman in a long black coat slowly making her through the rows of headstones. The wind caught her long blond hair, and she caught and twisted it into a braid and secured it with both hands. When she reached the group of mourners, she stood alone at the other end of the caskets. She and Bella made eye contact, and Bella nodded, and the minister began the funeral prayers.

This is Dan's sister, Amber, I thought. I caught Antelope's eye and he gave a brief nod.

It was the simplest and briefest funeral I ever went to, and I found myself feeling grateful that it passed so quickly. The mourners dispersed and got into vehicles parked along both sides of the highway into Farson.

Antelope and I hung back and took a last private moment with the murder victims.

"These things shouldn't happen," he said.

He looked tired and sad, filled with the weariness that came with a job that brought him close to people in their darkest times. It was impossible not to be changed by the pain of others.

"That was tough. How are you doing?" he said.

"It's never easy, is it? You come to pay respects to one life, and all people you lost show up and want your attention. I don't know about you, but I've had too much of people dying. Are you going to the ranch?"

"I'll skip it. It's hard to make small talk when two people are going into their graves. The juxtaposition is too much for me. I get the point—the living need each other. It messes with my appetite, so what's the point of going to the party?"

"It's amazing how much Amber resembles Bella," I said.

"I'm surprised to see her. When I told them about the funeral, her husband made a point of saying she wouldn't come. I guess she changed her mind."

"Death has a way of doing that. We don't always get a second chance. Better to do the thing than regret that you didn't."

"I'll be grateful for anything you pick up on."

"I think I'll take this opportunity to get to know Amber."

"Let's check in tomorrow."

"I have some things scheduled in the morning."

"Give me a call when you're free."

Quinn broke away from Paige and headed in our direction. Antelope saw him coming; he turned and walked away without acknowledging Quinn.

CHAPTER 34

The old log house held a chill in spite of the fire roaring in the big stone fireplace. I regretted giving my coat to the young woman from the Mercantile who served as a hostess and a waitress. I scanned the crowded room looking for Bella, but she was nowhere to be seen.

Nicole must have read my mind because suddenly she was at my side and said, "If you're looking for Bella, she went upstairs to lie down. She has one of her headaches. It was a tough morning. If I didn't have to be here, I wouldn't."

"You're a good hostess. I'm sure Bella appreciates it," I said.

"Well, I try," Nicole said.

"Where's Attorney Kastle today?" Quinn said.

"He'll be here soon. He had court this morning. I'll see you folks later," she added. "I have more things coming out of the oven."

"Why did you do that?" I said.

"What?"

"Ask her about Kastle."

"He's always around, but he's not around at the most important time."

"She gave you a reasonable answer."

"She gave me an excuse, the same excuse he gave her."

"You only met him once, but you seem to have developed strong feelings about him."

"I'm like that. It's the detective in me, I can read people, don't act like you don't know that about me."

"Give me your read on Kastle."

"He's a player."

"That's it? You don't like him because he's a player."

"I know what you're thinking, it takes one to know one. But he's a serious player."

"I don't care for him myself, he's arrogant. But Bella trusts him, Dan did, too."

"I thought arrogance turned you on?"

"It used to, that's how you got your chance."

I shivered and rubbed my arms to get the circulation going. Quinn put his arm around me and gave me a quick hug. Instinctively, I moved away. He feigned a shocked look.

"Don't," I said and looked at him long enough to make sure he understood I meant it.

He narrowed his eyes and shook his head and walked away. A few minutes later, he was talking with Amber at the entrance to the porch. She leaned against the doorframe, and Quinn stood over her, his arm stretched out above her head, holding them together in the small space. I recognized the stance; it was a thing he did to send a message: he was the alpha, he had control. Her pretty face was flushed, and she nodded excitedly as she talked to Quinn, her right hand clutching his arm. Quinn had his cop face on, not moving a muscle or giving any reaction to what he was hearing. I wondered why he had taken that pose with Amber and what she was saying to him.

I made my way over to them to hear for myself firsthand. When I approached them, they abruptly stopped talking. I gave Quinn a look he should have read as *Introduce me*, but he didn't. Amber looked at me and at Quinn.

I said, "I'm Dr. Pepper Hunt. I think you must be Amber. I'm a friend of Dan's from back East, I'm sorry for your loss. He was a good man, a good friend. It must be hard losing a brother," I said.

"I had two brothers and now I have none. They both killed themselves. I understand, I've been on the brink myself."

"Don't say that around her," Quinn said and pointed in my direction. "She's a psychologist, she takes that talk very seriously."

"How did you know my brother?" Amber said.

"He was in a weekly poker game with my husband," I said.

"Dan loved poker. He loved playing cards, all games really. He taught me how to play. He was a good big brother."

Her eyes filled with tears. She caught them in a tissue she kept folded around her index finger. "Excuse me," she said. "This is hard."

She walked off in the direction of the bar, which had been set up on a six-foot folding table in front of a bank of windows that showcased the Wind River Mountains. A low bank of charcoal clouds were moving in fast. Rain and sleet beat against the windows. The peaks of the Wind Rivers looked ominous, shiny and dark, cut by darker shadows along their cracked and rocky ridges.

"What were you two talking about?"

"Dan was her hero, the one person in the family she could trust. If she told him a secret, he'd take it to his grave with him. You know how that goes; people only see the good stuff about dead people. I'll tell you one thing. That woman is trouble."

"What makes you say that?"

"Something about her. I got a bad feeling. She's like a beautiful poison flower. And Dan told me she felt like she wasn't good enough, like she was the black sheep in the family. Not because of who she chose, it goes way back, it's the reason she fell for that loser Craig. You know, like the two of them deserved each other."

Mark Kastle walked through the front room. He was soaking wet and looked annoyed.

Nicole went to him and leaned in for a kiss, but he pulled away and shook the rain off his coat. She made a pouty face, which he ignored. She brought him a towel and took the wet coat away. He checked himself in the mirror, threw his shoulders back, entered the great room, and walked toward the buffet table.

Halfway there he stopped and spun around, headed back to the front entrance where he found Nicole. He put his arms around her and whispered in her ear, and the two of them disappeared.

Quinn saw it too, the quick turnaround. We looked in the direction Kastle had been headed before he changed his mind. Thunder boomed and rolled followed by flashes of lightning that stabbed the ground and took the power out. Amber Delman stood alone in the dark. Rivulets of rain streaked the bank of windows at her back, and her face glowed in the candlelight. She stared, unmoving, at the place where Mark Kastle had been, as if she'd seen a ghost.

"Those two know each other," Quinn said.

A few minutes later, the lights came on, and guests began the process of leaving. The storm passed and the sky lightened up. As we made our way to the door, we heard Nicole introducing Amber to Mark Kastle.

"Looks like you were wrong," I said.

CHAPTER 35

Amber was shaking as she drove as fast as her old car would go. What the hell was going on? She couldn't believe her eyes when she first saw him and then when Nicole introduced them, she had to play it cool. Now she wondered if that had been the right thing to do. Probably not because she never did the right thing. What should she do? Did she have to do anything? Maybe just go home and forget about her family again. She knew how to do that.

She called Craig and told him she was staying overnight in Rock Springs to have lunch with Paige. Craig got nervous about her being away overnight, and she understood that. If any man had a reason to worry, Craig did. She promised she'd be home before dark. She wanted to go home now. Craig made her feel safe.

The first stirrings came as the lights of Rock Springs came into view. A hot tickle and itch, alive and hungry in every screaming cell of her addict brain. The way the idea latched on like a virus and wouldn't let go, leaked toxins into her brain chemistry, hijacked her thoughts. She needed it. Now, right now.

Remember, think about what's at stake, the things you'll lose. Craig. Annabelle. Oh, Annabelle, don't ever think I don't love you. Mommy loves you. I just need to do this one more time. I promise. Once. I'm doing better. But it's hard. So hard.

I gave up everything else. I can give this up, too. I will give this up.

Paige had recommended the Days Inn because her mother liked staying there. And it had the convenience of being the first motel on the road into Rock Springs from the north. She'd get a room and figure it out, set up a temporary home base.

The Saddle Lite Saloon across the street. No way was she going in there. She didn't want to throw away eighteen months of sobriety.

She walked into the lobby, and she knew. All she had to do was want it, invite it with her desire, and it would come to her like a gift. The ease of it thrilled and reassured her, she had permission.

"Jonah," his name tag said. Young and wiry, a taut body, muscles their own right size, not gym perfected. The red hair—a bonus—all gingers were super-sensitive. Jonah, shiny and new.

Jonah smiled when he handed her the room key and told her where to park. He checked her out, too. She smiled back, just the right amount of encouragement. He was too young, too inexperienced to risk doing anything more.

He told her about the twenty-four-hour snack bar and vending machines in case she got hungry later. She told him she'd come back after she got settled in the room.

"I guess I'll see you later, then. I'll be here all night," Jonah said.

"I guess you will, Jonah."

The first thing she did when she got in the room was to find the card the detective had given her. She called the number and asked if he could meet with her in the morning. They made a plan to meet at ten o'clock, and he told her how to find his office on C Street in downtown Rock Springs.

CHAPTER 36

When Jonah walked out of the warm room, icy air sliced his skin like a knife cut. The late-night, frozen stillness, a quiver of wind, the mellow call of an owl at home in the old, gnarled tree behind the property.

He knew as he lived it, this night would stay with him; as an old man, he'd hold the raw husk of it in memory.

She had a name, a name he never used in the time he spent with her—Amber Delman, written in cursive in the guest register. She knew his name. She said his name when she invited him to her room. She called out his name when they were together in an intimate way.

The sound of his name coming from her, like she knew him, had always known him. He regretted not saying her name, a silly regret among all the things he could regret.

When she walked into the lobby, he'd never seen anyone more beautiful. Blond hair fell in soft waves around her face. When she smiled at him, he knew he'd do anything to be with her one time.

He was still trying to get to first base with his girlfriend. So he was more than surprised when the woman in Room 108 paid him a visit to ask a few questions. She hung around the lobby looking gorgeous and making him wonder if she was flirting with him. Then she was gone, and he must have been wrong all along. Of course, she wasn't interested in him. How could a woman like that ever be interested in him?

He pictured the woman he'd left in the bed, how she had smiled and praised his skill, but it was nothing he'd ever practiced, nothing he'd done before. He couldn't believe his luck, how this gorgeous woman just opened the door and let him in. It was in stark contradiction to all the times when he tried hard and failed at the same thing this last year in college.

. . .

Later that night as he sat at the front desk, he heard the wet sound of tires in the slush and snow. A truck rolled by, exited the parking lot, turned right onto Elk Street toward I-80 West. His eyes fixed on the passenger window and the woman with the curtain of gold hair.

The CCTV camera would have captured it, except by that time he had disabled it so there'd be no record of his visit to her room. The camera often malfunctioned; that's how he knew to reset it.

Until that night, nothing of significance had ever happened in his life. Too bad he'd never be able to tell anyone about the most exciting thing that ever happened to him—how a beautiful woman seduced him with mind-blowing sex, and later that night she got murdered.

CHAPTER 37

It didn't help that I let Quinn pour me a second cognac as I shivered in my Jeep in the middle of a storm on Wild Horse Canyon Road. The day had begun with a funeral and burial. I wanted to touch life again, taste it, hold it in my arms.

■ ■ ■

It was his last day in Rock Springs, and Quinn wanted to see the place where Dan's brother had killed himself. When I asked him why, he said there was something about the death that didn't feel right. He hadn't been able to sort out what it was and hoped that viewing the scene in person might help.

We left the Sanderson Ranch and drove south on Highway 191 to Wild Horse Canyon Road, a twenty-four-mile unpaved road over White Mountain and down to Green River. When I told Quinn the road would take us off the grid, there'd be no cell service, and he might see some of the herd of 1500 wild horses, his eyes widened.

"This is the wild West!" he said.

"I'm a cowgirl now."

"You're never going back to Cambridge, are you?"

"There's nothing there for me. This is my home now."

We rode in silence the rest of the way over the mountain. When we got to the place where Jack Petrangelo shot himself, I parked, and we started out for a short hike in the hills two miles out of Green River.

The weather had been crazy all day, and as we walked a biting wind came up, stinging our faces. Angry storm clouds loomed overhead and dropped a mix of stinging sleet, snow, and ice pellets that swirled around us like hornets.

"We have to go back now, or we'll lose our way," I said.

"Why? It's a little snow. I like this. I like intense," Quinn said.

"It's not like snow back East. It's dangerous. We could die out here," I said. I grabbed his arm and tried to turn him around. "Come on," I said, "I'm not kidding."

He walked with me then, his arm around my waist and held me close against him.

"Don't worry, I've got you. Nobody's getting lost on my watch," he said.

It was a good thing we turned around when we did. By the time we got back, snow feathers were swirling. Inside the Jeep I turned on the heat, and we spread our frozen fingers in front of the hot air vent.

"I can't believe you live here. This place is crazy," he said.

"You said you liked intense," I said.

"Let's warm you up."

He took both my hands in his and rubbed them and got the blood flowing. The old ways worked, and I relaxed in his hands.

"I got something better."

He unzipped his backpack and pulled out a bottle of cognac and two small glasses.

"This will help," Quinn said, and poured my favorite drink.

"Same old tricks. Did you steal these from the hotel?" I said, clinking his glass with mine.

"Don't tell your man. I don't want to get locked up in Sweetwater County."

"I don't have a man," I said.

He raised an eyebrow and downed the rest of his drink. "I used to be your man," he said.

"We hooked up in hotel rooms; then I went home to Zeke, and you went home to Jessica."

"That's harsh. Is that how you see it? A side thing?"

"We had this conversation already."

I finished off the cognac and held my glass out for a refill. I didn't like where things were going. Walking beside him, our hips touching, moving together in that easy rhythm our bodies fell into had brought it all back, and I convinced myself I didn't want it back.

"You never said good-bye."

"You blocked my number," I said.

"You could have come by."

"Oh, did I hurt your feelings? Fuck you."

"You know why it had to go like that. I went into survival mode when I heard they were looking at you for the murder. I couldn't be near that. I couldn't afford another screw-up."

"Do you hear yourself? Everything you said was about you."

"You did OK without me."

The rage came up fully formed as if it had been waiting for this perfect moment, I didn't think about it. I slapped him so hard it turned his head and sent the glass of cognac flying from his hand. He grabbed my hand as it came back to slap his other cheek and stopped it.

He pulled me close and kissed me hard. I struggled and tried to get out of his arms. He held on tight, and I kissed him back angry and greedy. I bit him hard on the mouth, and he didn't pull away. He grabbed my breasts. I clawed at his neck. He pulled me on top of him, hard and ready.

That would have been the time to stop. That was the moment I didn't want to stop.

"Jesus, I missed this. I thought I'd never hold you again," he said.

Both of us panting and sweating. So many times, like this.

"I want you so bad," he said.

I covered his mouth.

"Quiet," I said.

We took off enough clothing to do it in the small space and went at it hard and fast, without foreplay or tenderness. We did it like we always did---in a hot frenzy, in stolen moments, with the clock ticking, our real lives on hold.

It felt shameful to want him without loving him, my eyes and heart closed. All the feelings I ever felt for him churned into a wanton meanness. I wanted to hurt him.

He moved in all the ways that used to work for me, tried too hard and came too fast. I wanted to come. I cried instead. When he was done, he rested his head on my chest, and I turned away so the tears wouldn't reach him.

I didn't want questions. It wouldn't have mattered what he did. When it was good between us, and for too long after he broke my heart, just thinking about him made me come. No matter what he did today, orgasm was not an option, a sure sign I was over him.

His body felt too close, too warm, too heavy. I shifted away, got free of him.

"Jesus, look at that!" Quinn said.

I opened my eyes to see snow whipping around the Jeep.

"We need to get out of here," I said.

Outside the wind keened like a banshee. Usually, I'm loud during sex. Today was different. So, there was the closure. He got there at the same time.

"Pretty quiet today, kid," he said.

I got back in the driver's seat and zipped up my jeans.

"Don't be crude," I said. Buying time. I didn't want to have that conversation.

"More than anything, that's what got me off, thinking of the sounds you made when we did it."

"My foot's asleep," I said and stamped my left boot against the door to start the blood flowing.

"I didn't read it wrong, did I? Tell me I wasn't the only one who wanted to do it?"

"You didn't read it wrong."

"Because you know I don't go where I'm not wanted."

"I'm OK. Please stop talking. I need to concentrate on driving if I'm going to get us out of here alive."

Twenty minutes later, the Hampton Inn loomed out of the blizzard, the first welcome sign of civilization.

"Look at that, a Hampton Inn. That was our place back in the day. You should have told me we were this close. Would have been a hell of a lot more comfortable."

"Is that a complaint, Quinn? I hope that's not a complaint."

"No complaints. I could use a drink, though. You spilled the last of mine."

"Sounds like a complaint."

He snapped his fingers.

"I got it! I think I figured out why Dan's brother shot himself up there."

"Are you going to tell me?"

"The hotel! Nobody thought about that?"

"About what?"

"What we were talking about. You said it."

"Said what? What did I say?"

"We hooked up in hotel rooms and went home to other people. What if he found his wife in that hotel with someone else and he drove up the road and blew his brains out?"

CHAPTER 38

They kissed for a long time at his truck, and Paige held onto him until he broke away, his strong hands on her shoulders, putting some distance between them. She began to cry; she needed him so much. She wanted his arms around her, holding her together. The fear that threatened to take over since the morning she found her parents was rising higher. Without Graham she knew she would fall apart.

"You can't leave."

"Hey, it's OK," Graham said.

"I don't want you to go."

"I'll see you tomorrow."

"Tomorrow? Why can't you stay here tonight? You're not going out, are you?"

"Is that what you're worried about? I can't believe that's where your head goes even now. I'm working tonight. I have to make up the hours I've been taking off to be with you. Go inside; she needs you, that's what you said," Graham said, taking her arms from his shoulders and lightly pushing her away.

"Call me later? She goes to bed early," Paige said.

"If it's not busy. The boss doesn't like me on the phone. I told you that."

"Thank you for doing that. I don't know how I could have gotten through it without you."

"You need to take some lessons from your grandmother. She's a rock."

"I know. I love you so much. I get scared I'll lose you."

"I love you too. Now go be with your grandmother. I'll see you tomorrow."

Paige watched him drive away, down the long gravel drive to the state road where he stopped to wait for the road to clear. The brake lights on the Dodge came on, and he signaled a left turn and headed in the direction of Farson.

She wondered why she felt so anxious every time Graham left her. If they were really in love and meant to be together, shouldn't she feel secure even when they weren't physically together? Her parents hadn't felt Graham was the one for her. Could they have been right?

Even Quinn had asked her about Graham, how she met him, and if she trusted him. At first, she thought he was being the protective uncle she'd always known him to be. But something had changed, and he looked at her so intently, and for the first time he talked to her like a detective. He told her that her father didn't trust Graham. His words kept coming into her mind. When everything settled, she faced the implications of what Quinn told her.

"This will be hard to hear, but I think you have the right to know. Dan didn't want Graham in your life. He wanted to offer him money to go away. If he did that, what do you think Graham would do?"

"Graham would never leave me," she said. Her answer was immediate. She was certain in every cell of her body. Graham loved her. No amount of money could convince him to leave her.

"He won't have to leave you now," Quinn said. "Think about that."

Standing alone on the saddest day of her life, another answer to Quinn's question came to her. She was stunned. And her mind immediately protested. It was impossible, it couldn't be, she would never love someone capable of that. She recognized the words for what they were, a refusal to accept a reprehensible idea that, if it were true, would ruin her life. There was no way for her to know for sure, at least not right now. Was it possible? She didn't want to think about it.

A strange combination of emotions coursed through her body—fear and thrill and boldness. Like the times Cody tempted her—coke and booze and weed—all mixed up, exhausted and wired.

Her body registered the biting cold. When she followed Graham out to the truck, she went out without a coat on. Now she stood shivering in the snowy driveway, her hands and face numb, her feet freezing in her fancy dress boots.

She didn't want to die. Her next thought freed her from paralysis. She would live like her grandmother; she would be a rock, she would go on, nothing would take her.

She turned and ran back to the warmth and safety of the house filled with sorrow and shame and the unexpected thrill of sexual excitement. Her parents were dead. Her boyfriend might be a murderer.

CHAPTER 39

It felt important to say good-bye to Quinn in person, to make it real. I fell asleep without setting the alarm on my phone and almost missed him.

I splashed cold water on my face, pulled my hair into a bun, put on perfume and lipstick. In five minutes, I was dressed and in the Jeep. I called his cell to tell him I was on the way, but it went to voicemail. Quinn knew of my lifelong chronic lateness. He also knew I made it a point to never be late when it mattered.

I drove the quarter mile to College Hill, turned left onto Elk Street, and pulled into the parking lot of the Outlaw Inn as Quinn came out the front door of the lobby carrying his suitcase and a backpack he'd bought to carry home all the new western clothes he'd acquired. He scowled when he saw me and kept walking.

I added up all the reasons why being here was a mistake. Quinn was a morning person; he was spoiled and overreacted when slighted, a drama queen who nursed a grudge.

I parked and walked over to him. He kept his back turned to me while he took his time to arrange his things in the trunk.

"Quinn," I said.

He slammed the trunk and turned to look at me. Some people's faces hold the power to disarm anything negative coming their way. His charm was of the wounded type, and it made you want to hold and comfort him, make up for any prior hurts and sorrows, be the one who came through. He had pulled me into that dance so many times. Not the slightest tug this time.

"Still not a morning person."

He was fresh from a shower, and the smell of his aftershave lotion lit up my hormones before my rational brain had a chance to talk some sense into them.

"I'm glad I caught up with you," I said.

"You didn't need to come."

"I said I would."

"I thought you might come early, but I've been wrong about a lot of things," he said.

"This is good-bye. No confusion this time."

"I'm not as clueless as you think," he said.

"No one planned for things to go the way they did. Take care of yourself. Don't let fear stop you from having a life with someone you love," I said.

"Do me a favor, keep an eye on Paige. She's got nobody now. I have my doubts about her boyfriend. If it turns out he had anything to do with this, I'll be back here to take care of him myself."

"She has you. You'll stay in touch with her?"

"I'll do what I can from two thousand miles away. My life's about to get busy. Jessica called last night. The DNA results came back. It's mine."

"Congratulations."

"I got to admit the whole thing scares the shit out of me. Families are crazy. I can't see how any family I make is going to be any different."

"It will be what you make it."

"She might never forgive me for asking for the test."

"If she knows you at all, she knows you have a problem with trust."

"Tell me why I should bring a kid into this sick world?"

"We need more players on our team, keep the bad guys in check," I said.

"You think I'm a good guy?"

"You have potential," I said.

"It sucks what happened to Dan. Keep working the case, OK?"

"OK."

"You're really OK out here? This is what you want?"

"This is where I want to be. You should get on the road."

"I wish you guys had an airport here. I have to drive five hours to get on a plane."

"Good-bye, Quinn."

"I held it against you all that time because you didn't say good-bye when you left. Now hearing you say it—it was never what I wanted to hear. Be careful what you wish for, right?"

CHAPTER 40

Ice formed a lacy mosaic on the window of Antelope's office in the old county building on C Street. The new heating system installed during the recent rehab project didn't service the old structure well.

Steam and the aroma of his favorite espresso beans warmed the air and lightened his mood. The copper and brass beauty had cost him a week's salary but was worth it. The storm that came through on the day of the funerals had left the desert coated with snow.

Antelope waited for Amber Delman to show up. The night before, she'd left a voicemail message and asked to meet with him. The caller ID showed the number for Days Inn in Rock Springs. They had agreed to meet at the office at ten the following morning. Unlike most people he dealt with in murder investigations, she seemed eager to talk with him.

Where was she? It was ten thirty, a half hour past the time they'd agreed to meet. He called the cell number he tried before and got the same response—no answer, no voicemail.

At eleven o'clock there was still no sign of her. He called the motel and asked to be connected to her room. The phone rang on and on.

A chill ran through him that he couldn't shake off as he drove to the Days Inn in search of Amber Delman.

Jonah, the intern, who was on the phone at the front desk, held up his index finger and mouthed "one minute." He ended the call and for the first time in their brief acquaintance, smiled.

"Good morning, Detective."

"Hello, Jonah."

"Mr. Hastings isn't here, Detective. Can I help you with something?"

"I've been trying to reach one of your guests through the main switchboard, but there's no answer. I wonder if I got it wrong. Could you check for me?"

"What's the name of the guest? I'll check for you."

"Amber Delman."

Antelope noticed the shift in Jonah's energy.

"Spell the last name, please," Jonah said.

"D E L M A N, Amber Delman."

He watched Jonah's face and there it was—the eyes widened, the intake of breath, the recognition.

"OK, I have her, room one oh eight."

"You recognize the name. Were you here when she checked in?"

"It was last night."

"Call the room."

"Sure, but do you want to call? I can hand you the phone."

"You call, Jonah."

Nervous, a tremble in the fingers, holding his breath, Jonah dialed the extension, put the phone on speaker, and listened to the ringing.

After a minute, Antelope said, "That's enough."

Jonah hung up the phone.

"Did she check out?"

"Checkout's at eleven. I came in at eight. I haven't checked anyone out. I'll look. She might have left real early."

After a minute, Jonah said, "She hasn't checked out."

"I need the key to the room."

"Do you want to wait a few minutes? People don't always check out right on time. We have a grace period."

"Give me the key, Jonah."

He handed over the keycard. "Take a left, it's the first room after the door for the pool area."

A white Honda Civic with Fremont County plates was parked in front of Room 108. He knocked on the door, waited, knocked twice more.

"Open up, Sweetwater County Sheriff."

No sound or movement from within Room 108. The blinds in the window to his right shifted, fell back into place.

He slid the keycard into the door, paused, found the light switch, and stepped inside. The bed looked slept in, pillows and blankets on the floor. In the closet, high heel boots and a black dress, her funeral clothes; in the bathroom, a purple sequined makeup bag. Car keys on the dresser, no sign of a purse or phone.

He took the keys and checked the car, which she kept clean, no belongings or trash. The trunk held a spare, winter hazard gear, blankets, flares, energy bars. Prepared to be stranded, but this other thing, whatever happened to her, she didn't know it was coming, met it without preparation.

For the second time in a week, he used crime scene tape to close off a room at the Days Inn. He returned the keycard to Jonah and gave instructions to keep the room off limits.

He sat in the parking lot of the Days Inn and thought about what to do next. He could go back to his office and brew a fresh espresso. And after that he'd have to call Craig Delman, and he wasn't ready to do that. He decided to call Pepper Hunt instead.

"Do you have some time to catch up today? There's been a new development."

"I'm on my way to Farson to meet with Bella. What's up?"

"Amber called me last night and asked to meet with me this morning. She didn't show and when I went to her hotel, she wasn't there, but her car was. I've got a bad feeling."

"That doesn't sound good."

"Did you talk to her yesterday?"

"Briefly."

"What did you think?"

"She has a kind of spacey vibe. I wonder why she wanted to see you."

"I should have pushed her to tell me last night."

"What should I tell Bella about Amber?"

"Nothing yet. She could show up. She might have just hooked up with someone. She's a sex addict under stress. That could happen."

"What are you going to do?"

"Call her husband. I've been putting it off; that's why I called you first."

"Come for dinner. I'll put some steaks on the barbecue, and you can fill me in."

"I'll be there."

"Eight o'clock."

He took a deep breath and prepared to call Craig Delman. He'd start by asking if Amber was at home. It was a strategy to buy time, ease into a conversation he didn't want to have.

He dialed the number of the landline in Riverton and for the fourth time that morning listened as the phone rang on and on.

CHAPTER 41

I already felt apprehensive about questioning a woman who'd just buried her son the day before. Knowing that Amber could be missing didn't make me feel any better about seeing Bella.

Bella was on the porch, a cup of coffee in her hand, her posture still statuesque.

Each time I entered the Sanderson ranch house, it was like going back in time. The kitchen still had the original wide plank floorboards. An ancient wood stove stoked high with logs heated the room like a sauna.

"Let's sit here in the kitchen. Nicole's coming over later to pick up the things from yesterday's gathering. I haven't got the strength to do it."

The aroma of strong coffee mixed with the smell of wood-smoke. I longed to curl up on the sinking cushions of the old sofa under the window that framed the Wind River Mountains and spend the rest of the day slumbering under the afghan that covered it.

We sat at the large wooden kitchen table that held the marks of a century of family dinners and art projects. Bella poured coffee into heavy mugs, dark blue with small white flowers at the rim. I was reminded again of the ways of the wealthy of the old

West, those who had gained their fortunes from true hard work, held onto things until their usefulness expired.

"These were my mother's. It's amazing they've lasted all this time. It makes me happy to think about the way our things outlast us. They just go on without us. It shouldn't be so, but it is," she said.

"They're lovely. I imagine it's like having a part of her with you."

"It is, actually. I cherish them. But that's not what you came here to talk about, is it? I was glad when you called this morning," Bella added. "There's something I want to tell you, but first I need to promise you won't tell anyone in my family. I don't want to burden them. I'll understand if you have to tell Detective Antelope."

"Of course, what you tell me is confidential."

"A month ago, I received some very bad news. I have brain cancer. The kind that doesn't give you very much time. It's not too bad yet. I have headaches, I'm tired a lot. The memory problems were the first sign. I'm surprised they didn't show up on your tests. There'll be more symptoms as the tumor grows."

"Your scores on the tests were all in the normal range, only the slightest cognitive decline, consistent with your age. I'm amazed at your resilience. You have so much strength. The day I saw you in the hospital, your doctor encouraged you to follow up with treatment. Are you doing that?"

"I chose to do it my way. Accept what is and make the best of the days I have left. I've known so many people who chose treatment, and I know it's not for me."

"That feels like a very brave decision to me. I admire your courage."

"I think of it more as a matter of choice. Having the option to choose has always been important to me. This is one of those situations in life where none of the options are without pain or complication. I have a low tolerance for pain, especially pain that's not of my own making," Bella said.

"So many situations in life come with their own brand of pain. It then becomes a matter of knowing yourself well enough to know how much pain you can carry."

"We make the best decision we can based on the information we know. And many times, there are consequences that we could never have anticipated."

"I think you're saying that we might be fooling ourselves thinking that we have control over these things."

"I think we control the choice. We make decisions. We commit to an action. Beyond that we don't have control of what happens."

"That's why it's so important to know what you can live with and not make decisions that you can't survive."

"I don't like having situations put on me and having to do what's expected. This ranch would have gone to my brother in the normal chain of inheritance, father to oldest son. When Eric died at twelve years old, I was told the ranch was now mine. I didn't want it, I didn't want this life, but I felt obligated to accept the responsibility. That's why I considered leaving it to the Nature Conservancy, so no one else would have to carry it and be shackled by it the way I've been."

"That's one of the things I wanted to ask about. We recently learned that Dan had a problem with gambling. I've known him for years and it came as a surprise to me."

"To me as well. He lived away for so long. I really didn't know anything about his life. I thought things were fine with him and Heather, and they weren't. I think they got worse when they moved out here. She was so unhappy, a fish out of water. The same was true for Dan, though he would never admit it."

"He owed a lot of money. I understand you helped him pay it off."

"Ten thousand dollars. He didn't ask for my help. That was Heather's doing. She wanted to help him, but it backfired, and it was just another thing they fought about. To him it was more proof he couldn't trust her, because she went behind his back and came to me. She intended to pay me back. I told her that wasn't necessary."

"Did she actually start to pay you back?"

"A check was issued to the casino from my trust account. I told her if she ever had any extra money, she could always send it to my lawyer; he's handling all my financial affairs now.

"I'm grateful I got to see Amber again, even if only for a few hours. I called her and asked her to come to the funeral. I doubt she would have come on her own. I so regret all the years I wasted being angry with her, all the lost time.

"The last time, the big break, she stopped coming because I sent her away. She confronted me with something from my past, something I was still ashamed of and didn't want to acknowledge."

"What was that?"

"I've never told anyone about that. I hoped that by never speaking about it, I could somehow make it not true. When I found out I was pregnant after the rape, I reacted the same way. Someone else's action threatened to change my life in a way I didn't want. I refused to let that happen."

"At the time there was no safe and legal way for me to have my first choice. Roe v. Wade happened the following year. Even then, legal abortions didn't become immediately available everywhere. Women had abortions before then, many with bad outcomes. I chose to place the child for adoption."

"It must have given you peace of mind, knowing the child would go to a family who wanted a baby."

"That's what I intended. But that's not what happened. The adoption law requires posting a notice in the local paper as a way of notifying a father. The man who raped me, I never knew his name, I never wanted to know. The hospital told me that his family saw the notice and stopped the adoption process. He took the baby. I just didn't have the strength to do anything about it. There's been no peace of mind."

Amber took a DNA test and learned I'd had a child out of wedlock and given it up for adoption. She shared that information in a contemptuous way. I think it gave her pleasure to have proof that I was in no position to judge her. And I did judge her for so many things. She wanted to tell me his name, but I stopped her. I didn't want to know. I told her to leave and she hasn't been back until yesterday.

We have a lot of healing to do. She's my last living child. She left before we had a chance to talk yesterday and anyway, it wasn't the right day to have that conversation. I just hope it's not too late.

■ ■ ■

On the drive back to Rock Springs big lazy snowflakes fell slowly, drifting and twirling. As a small child, I pretended snowflakes were tiny ghosts falling from heaven to visit the people they left behind.

I've always loved snowstorms. My mind turned a traumatic experience into an enduring connection.

My parents died together when their car went off the road in one of the biggest snowstorms to ever hit New England---the Blizzard of 1978.

I have some things in common with Bella Sanderson that I would never be able to tell her. That's the thing about the work I do. So much must remain private and contained within the self. It's work that honors secrets.

But in the quiet space left by these untold stories, our unconscious, shared experiences resonate and a bond is created.

CHAPTER 42

Cody woke to darkness and silence and heat, T-shirt soaked and stuck to his chest, slick with foul-smelling perspiration, his mouth and nose so dry he could barely breathe. He thought of the last time he tried to sit up. Then he slowly pushed himself onto his elbows and lowered his socks onto the cool tile floor. His head spun. He needed fluids. The urge to empty his bladder was strong.

He hated everyone who worked in this hell hole. There was no other way; he was too uncomfortable.

The hallway was empty as he made his way silently past the deserted nurses' station. The clock showed a few minutes past eleven. There was a window in the door to the staff room, and he could see some people seated around a table.

He used the bathroom and ran the water to ice cold, splashed his face and hair, and began to feel his temperature return to normal. He bent and swallowed gulps of water straight from the faucet. He drank until his stomach hurt.

On the way back he stopped in the patient kitchen and grabbed an armload of water bottles from the refrigerator. Their chill was a balm against the heat of his body. He remembered he needed food. He put the water bottles on a tray and added a few bags of chips and cookies, an apple and a banana. He returned to his room without anyone taking any notice; the staff were still in the meeting room. He heard laughter and chairs scraping on the tile floor as he slipped into his room and closed the door behind him.

Back in his bed, he finished off the fruit in seconds. His stomach began a series of sickening flips. He slid the tray under the bed and lay on his side on the hard mattress. He kept his face turned away from the door, hoping any staff person doing checks would read his body language as that of someone asleep. He wanted to be left alone, and he didn't want to chance doing anything that would put him on their radar.

He lay very still and listened to the accelerated beating of his heart, the churning sounds of digestion, acid released to attack the food. The heat enveloped him like a heavy blanket, sweat rose from his pores, and he shivered. What the hell? It occurred to him that he might be sick, his body assaulted by something as ordinary as the winter flu and not the toxic shit they'd pumped into his system.

The last time he was sick like this he'd missed a week of school. His mother had tended to him, a cold cloth on his forehead, chicken soup and Jell-O. He jerked his head to throw off the image. That was all a lie. She was an evil bitch. He knew the truth about her now. His hurting gut cramped harder.

He swallowed the bitter bile in his throat. He wouldn't be sick. That's all they'd need, another reason for them to decide to keep him even longer.

The idea came to him like a light bulb turning on, bright yellow spokes flaring out, a cartoon.

The way he was feeling, it was tempting to let himself surrender to the sweet escape of sleep. The silent ward stretched out around him to lull him into that escape. He needed a plan to get himself out of the eerie suspended reality of the mental patient in captivity.

He'd been in the day room and witnessed the activity at the time of the shift changes that occurred every eight hours at seven and three and eleven o'clock. The action started about fifteen minutes before as staff members entered the unit through the main door. The door remained locked at all times, and staff members would manually open it with a key carried on a lanyard they wore around their necks. They would direct the visitor to the sign-in sheet at the nurses' station and escort them into either the day room for an unsupervised visit or to one of the small private rooms designated for meetings between clinical staff members and patients' families. While the doors opened manually, they locked automatically on closure. He pictured the layout of the room near the main door. He couldn't figure out a way to hide that would allow him to quickly access the door before it swung closed.

The heating system malfunctioned throughout the day, alternating between unbearable levels of sauna-like heat and meat-locker cold. The staff complained that the maintenance department ran a skeleton crew on the weekend, and no one was certified in heating and ventilation. The malfunction affected the psychiatric unit, which had low status compared to the medical units. A window in the dayroom was propped open. Someone must have figured it was safe to leave it open when all the patients were in bed asleep.

The discomforts of his fevered body helped to keep him awake. He developed a plan.

At the next shift change he would make his escape.

And then it hit him. He wasn't going anywhere. It was fucking December, and he'd freeze his ass off out there. This must have been what his mother meant when she called him manic.

CHAPTER 43

After the psychologist left, Bella made herself another cup of tea and sat by the window as the afternoon light left the sky. A low bank of bruised clouds hovered over the shadowed fields. She sat alone in the dark with her thoughts. A killer targeted her family. She looked at the house where Dan and Heather were murdered and knew that their killer could be watching her now. She wasn't afraid. Eventually, she knew it would be her turn to die. She felt the impending threat move closer every day.

As always after talking with the doctor, she felt calmer, her thoughts clearer. They'd talked about a lot of things which at the time didn't seem connected. And then she saw what she'd been blind to, what she hadn't wanted to see, what she didn't understand at the time.

It was amazing to Bella how the idea formed in her mind, like two separate puzzle pieces, fitting perfectly together to form a new image.

If only she'd paid more attention, been more discerning, she would have seen what was right in front of her eyes.

Now that she knew, she had to do something. Though her greatest wish was to deny it, deny the truth of his existence and what it might mean for her, she needed to face it. She needed a plan.

She turned the lights off and walked out into the December night. She could feel the beginning of a storm in the turning air, and big white flakes moved on the currents of air, gathering force.

She dressed in several warm, light layers. She wanted to avoid any physical discomfort. It was important to be free of distraction, the annoyance of small discomforts. The night required her full concentration. The crowded sky was filled with close stars, old friends. Whenever she felt lost or afraid and all alone in the world, she'd look up at the night sky and find a star to fix on.

She'd imagine her mother existing out there in the far-flung reaches of the galaxy, one of the solitary stars. It made her own loneliness bearable. Whenever she needed the strength, she thought of her parents. Her mother had died in childbirth on a snowy night in a farmhouse. She had given birth at home. She'd been young, twenty years old, and no one ever imagined there would be any complications.

All these years Bella had kept the rape a secret. It was a sordid, shameful event for her, and it changed who she was in her own eyes. She'd stayed late at the library and walked home alone in the mild weather. The next morning the campus was bright with yellow buds of forsythia bushes. She'd pushed the thoughts of the attack out of her mind and focused on the beauty of the yellow flowers and the idea that one small spot of beauty changes the landscape.

Each year in March she experienced an anniversary reaction; a coldness filled her body. While everyone else was getting cheerful, enjoying the end of snow, the returning green of the earth, she bundled up but could never fully drive out the chill. By June she would be OK again. She hated the claim of her body, its memory of that night.

She never saw his face and was glad of that. He came up behind her, grabbed her, and slammed her hard to the ground. There wouldn't have been anything to describe if she had gone to the police. It would have been harder to forget. Forgetting was what she needed. But the memory remained, under the surface, a small humming electrical charge that now was cut loose from its grounding wires and all the current freed and jolting through her veins.

She felt so alive as she reached the grove of pine trees. It was a favorite place, and she hadn't made the long walk out there in a while. She walked into the dark woods and felt the safety of the surrounding trees so steady and close in, so different from the openness of the ranch.

As she got closer, she heard the river currents, as steady as a heartbeat, rising and falling, rushing along, alive and cold and certain. And in that moment, she knew what she had to do.

CHAPTER 44

I was on the deck setting up things for the barbecue. Antelope was due to arrive any minute. The sound of a jet flying east out of Salt Lake City got me thinking about Quinn for the second time that day. His plane would be landing soon at Logan Airport. I smiled thinking of him back on his home turf.

We'd said good-bye with both of us knowing it would be the last time. A somber feeling had settled over me as I watched him drive away.

I didn't love him anymore, but I had loved him. So it mattered that it was over.

As the day went on my troubled feelings lifted, and a gentle calm set in, like stillness after a storm. I was free to love again if I wanted. At some level, I must have thought that part of life was over for me.

From time to time in solitary moments, I wondered about Antelope in that way, considered saying yes to his invitations, fantasized on more than one lonely night about having him in my bed.

The unfinished business with Quinn had stopped me. I didn't know how it would finally end because I never intended to return to Cambridge, and I never imagined Quinn would come to Wyoming. And then he had come here, and it was over, and with that the last of my former life was in the past.

There'd been a different dynamic between me and Antelope with Jimmy Quinn in town. Antelope didn't like him sniffing around a case of his, but I suspected it was especially annoying to have someone from my past whom he hadn't quite figured out.

I was still trying to figure out what, if anything, to tell him about Quinn. My relationship with Antelope had some traction. I didn't want to sabotage it with too much information.

After years of listening to love stories gone bad in my therapy practice, I'd developed my own philosophy in this area: the less said, the better. It's a bad idea to reveal the details of old lovers. Once something is heard, it can't be unheard. People embellished with their own fantasies and meanings.

I was suspicious of people who wanted to know the whole story. They were often the same people who wanted to erase the story. Because of their own insecurities, they were threatened by the presence of others, even those who existed in memory.

The thing with me and Jimmy Quinn turned complicated in a way neither one of us anticipated. If he hadn't come to Wyoming, I would never have told anyone about him.

What did that say about me? I was capable of being secretive about important experiences in my life. I was sure Antelope had his own secrets. I hoped he'd keep them where they belonged: in his heart and in his past.

■ ■ ■

I carried the marinated elk steaks to the back deck, turned on the gas grill, and opened a bottle of Cabernet. I pulled a pashmina shawl around my shoulders. The fine wool was as soft as cashmere but gave little protection against the night's frozen grip.

The sky was clear. A creamy slice of the waxing crescent moon outlined the spine of White Mountain.

Headlights in the driveway lit up the looming skeletons of the bare winter birches surrounding the house and turned their swaying branches bright silver.

I heard a car door close, followed by a loud knock, and I went to let Antelope in.

I sensed something different between us. We looked at each other, and neither of us spoke. He tilted his head slightly, and we looked into each other's eyes for a long time. The air was charged like the live field around a sparking, downed wire.

He unzipped his soft leather jacket, and the night's cold came off him. With another step he closed the last inches of distance between us. He smelled of sage and earth and his own maleness.

His cell phone rang.

"Antelope, here. Where, exactly? OK, I got it. I know the place. Keep them there, I want to talk to them myself. I'm on my way now."

"What is it?"

"Green River dispatch. Search and rescue pulled a body out of the water at Expedition Island—a woman."

"Do you think it could be—"

"Amber? That was my first thought," Antelope said.

"Are you going there now?"

"Want to take a ride?"

It was a clear, cold night. The interstate was empty except for long-haul semis carrying cargo from east to west, and we made good time on the way to Green River.

The mood had shifted between us; the playful intimacy was gone. We were back on the case in work mode. I remembered the reason we planned to see each other tonight.

"How did it go when you talked to Craig Delman?"

"I didn't. I called him a few times, but he didn't pick up. Answering machine's full," he said.

"So they're both missing in action."

"I've got a bad feeling about the body in the water."

"What if it is Amber? What will that mean?"

"Hold that thought," Antelope said.

My questions distracted him from his process; I'd never been with him at this point in an investigation. I stopped talking, and we rode in silence the rest of the way.

We arrived at the site the same time as the county medical examiner's van.

"Are you ready for this? I don't know what we're going to see. Depending how long the body was in the water, it can get gruesome."

"I'm here. Let's go."

Expedition Island is located in the Green River, which flows through the town of Green River. It was originally one large island, but over time erosion divided it into two smaller islands. The northern one remains undeveloped, but the southern island is a public park with a recreation center and parking areas at the southern end, and a tree-lined, grassy expanse to the north.

It's accessible by a road bridge from the north bank of the river and by a pedestrian bridge from the south.

A van and two patrol cars were parked at the entrance to the pedestrian bridge.

The man and woman who discovered the body stood huddled together, their arms around each other, shaking.

While Antelope questioned them, I stood quietly wondering if I'd made the right decision by agreeing to come along. The coroner's van was parked at the riverbank, and two men in wetsuits slipped into the water and swam toward the bridge and out of sight. It didn't take long to free the body. A few minutes later I watched their slow movements, a peaceful synchronization, towing the inert body between them, the black dress billowing in the swirling current, the long gold strands of her hair fanned across the surface of the icy water.

Now all of Bella Sanderson's children are dead, I thought, and we still don't have any idea why.

"When will you notify the family members?"

"I'll make the rounds in the morning. Can I let them know you're available if they need support? I'm thinking mostly of Bella and Paige."

"Of course."

It was Antelope's idea to take a raincheck on dinner, and I agreed. I had no appetite at all.

We were silent the rest of the ride back to Rock Springs. All I could think about was Bella and the devastation she would feel when she learned about the death of her last living child. Just the day before I had seen Amber so alive and vibrant, felt the force of her even in grief. The contrast was chilling and sobering and left me without words. I figured it was the same for Antelope.

I took a long, hot shower, turned my phone off, and went to bed.

■ ■ ■

In the morning, I had a voicemail from Aubrey Hiller. He had information about Mark Kastle.

"I'll tell you whatever you want to know about Kastle. Don't tell me you're interested in this guy."

"I'm not, but I need you to tell me why I shouldn't be."

"Mysterious as always. All right, here goes. We go way back. We went to law school together in Laramie. Our professional lives have taken pretty much the same course, personal lives too. You know, we both make big bucks, both married and divorced too many times. We've never been friends. He's a hard guy to get to know. One time at some dinner we were both at, he said something that stuck with me, took things to a whole different level.

"You know me, I'm not the nicest guy, but Mark Kastle is in an entirely different league."

"I'm following. What did he say?"

"He pointed out the similarities in our lives, the success we both enjoyed. He bragged about how he had ended up with most of the assets his ex-wives brought into the marriage. I thought he was kidding at first. That's not how it went for me. Not that I'm complaining. I make enough money for me and all the exes.

"I love money, and I don't care about money at the same time. Easy come, easy go. But I'm a sucker for love. I fall hard and give a hundred percent, and it breaks me every time. And here's a thing about me: If I loved you once, I'm always going to take care of you.

"That's what I told him, and he told me I was doing it all wrong. He offered to teach me some of his tricks, if I was interested. If I played it right, I could actually make money on women. Here's a direct quote: 'The love business can be lucrative, better than flipping houses.'

"That was the last time I talked to the guy, until he barged into our lunch that day."

"This is very interesting."

"What's he up to that caught your attention?"

"I'm helping out on the investigation of the shootings up in Farson. He's the attorney for one of the persons of interest. We're talking to everyone involved."

"I can tell you this. If there's a woman with money involved, she won't have it when Mark Kastle is done with her."

CHAPTER 45

On Wednesday morning, Antelope took his time before starting the serious work of notifying Amber's family of her death. It was definitely a double-espresso morning. He gave it his full attention, letting himself take in all the sensual satisfaction of the strong brew—the aroma, the deep taste, even the feel of the thick white cup in his palm, the glowing beauty of the apparatus of the coffee maker, the sweetness of the steamed milk, the slightest sweep of it across the surface that erased the harshness.

He planned to tell Paige first about Amber's murder and then head up to Farson where he'd meet with Nicole and Bella. It felt like one of the worst days of his work life. He could have handed the job off to other officers, but it felt wrong, the coward's way out.

This was a highly traumatized family, and he and Pepper Hunt together had managed to keep them open and cooperative with the investigation. Sometimes in murder cases, the family will turn against the investigators, accusing them of not giving the case enough attention. He attributed the good relationship with the family to the support they'd been given every step of the way.

After talking with the family, he'd try reaching Delman again. He started to wonder if his disappearance was related to Amber. He had the sense when he saw them together that whatever deviant forces had originally brought them together, somehow the two of them had found value in each other, a saving grace that allowed them to lean on each other in the hard life they had.

He recognized the sentimentality in his thinking. It was a weakness of his, this desire to see things in their purest form. He was right some of the time.

Yesterday he had made a request to the Lincoln County Sheriff's Department to do a wellness check and heard back that no one had answered the door at the house in Riverton and there were no cars parked in the driveway. He didn't know where or if Delman worked. It occurred to him that Cass might have that in her files, but it didn't seem critical enough to play that card.

■ ■ ■

He headed south back to Rock Springs and the Days Inn to talk with Jonah.

There was a different intern at work who told him Jonah had come in for his shift but had gone home sick with a stomach bug. Derek Hastings provided Jonah's address and phone number.

He tried the cell phone a few times with no luck and drove up the hill past the turnoff to the hospital and the community college to a modest neighborhood of townhouses where Jonah lived with his family.

A tired-looking woman in hospital scrubs answered the door. Unmistakably Jonah's mother. Short red hair, buzzed on the side, spiked on top, the same open, trusting smile as her son.

"Good morning, you almost missed me. I'm usually in bed by now. I work the night shift at the hospital. What is it?"

"Sorry to bother you. I'm Detective Antelope, here to speak with your son, Jonah."

She took the county ID card in her hand and gave it a close look.

"He's just come home sick from work; that's why I'm late getting to bed. Is there something wrong?"

"A woman drowned near Expedition Island. She stayed at the Days Inn the night before the body was found. Jonah checked her in."

"Oh dear, that's terrible. He's got the stomach bug. You sure you want to risk it?"

"It won't take long, if he's up to it."

"Come on in, I'll check. Have a seat in the family room. It's the most presentable room in the house."

The family room took up the entire lower floor of the house. Every wall was hung with hunting trophies, the heads of dead animals. A few minutes later Jonah joined him, a washcloth draped over his head, carrying a plastic bucket. He sprawled in the middle of the giant U-shaped sofa and placed the bucket on his chest.

"I could puke at any moment."

"It came on fast, I heard."

"I know why you're here. It was on the news that woman drowned."

Jonah bent over, grabbed his stomach, and heaved but nothing came up.

"I've got nothing left, but I still feel like shit."

"You told me you checked her in. The guest registers show it at 7:08 p.m. Did you see her or speak to her at any other time that night?"

Jonah sat up, He wiped his eyes and face with the washcloth. "I might as well tell you. You'll find out anyway. My fingerprints are in my HR file."

"What happened?"

"Promise you won't tell my mother?"

"Tell me what happened Jonah."

"I'll get fired if work finds out."

"You went into her room?"

"She asked me to come. She said there was a problem with the television."

"And you went to her room to check it out. Wouldn't that be a job for maintenance?"

"They leave at five. We handle those things if we can."

"So far you haven't done anything wrong. Why would you get fired?"

"Other stuff happened. Stuff that could maybe be traced to me."

"Did you hurt Amber Delman, Jonah?"

He doubled over, in the grip of another stomach cramp. "Ahh, that hurts. It feels like someone's clawing my guts out."

"Jonah, did you hurt Amber?"

"God, no. It wasn't like that. I'd never hurt a girl."

"What happened in that room, Jonah?"

"I have to tell you something else first, and you have to believe me. I'm not lying about this."

"OK."

"I wasn't the last person to see her alive. She went off in a truck with somebody."

"What time was this?"

"Not that late, like nine o'clock, I guess."

"Describe the truck."

"One of the big ones, dark, black, I think. I couldn't tell for sure. I'm not a truck guy."

"License plate?"

"No. I was looking at her."

"What did you see?"

"She kept shaking her head, no."

"OK, this is helpful, Jonah. You're doing good."

"I really need to sleep. I feel like crap."

"We're not done yet. Let's go back to what happened in the room."

Jonah closed his eyes. "I don't know if I can do this."

"You can do it, Jonah. Take your time."

"I guess you could say she seduced me. I've never been with anyone like her. We did it. We had sex. A lot. It was the best thing that ever happened to me."

CHAPTER 46

Antelope was asleep on the couch when the call came in from the hospital about Paige. After a day giving death notifications, he wanted to turn off his brain, check out from the world. He ate the two cheeseburgers he'd brought home from the burger place in Farson paired with two beers. Then he fed his dog, Domino, and let her out in the backyard. The last thing he remembered was her barking to come in. The empty wrappers and bottles were on coffee table. The dog was asleep on the floor beside the empty bag of French fries he was too full to eat. He didn't have anything left to give to anyone, so it was a good thing that Paige didn't need his skills. She needed Pepper Hunt.

He called Pepper and told her Paige was in the Emergency Department of Sweetwater Hospital, in stable condition after a suicide attempt. The doctor who treated Paige recommended an overnight admission for observation, but she wanted to discharge AMA. They requested a psych consult ASAP.

He got off the phone with Pepper and was instantly asleep.

■ ■ ■

Paige looked better than she should have given the amount of Xanax she'd ingested.

"They said you'd come. I want to get out of here. Can you please tell them it's OK for me to go home?"

"If I'm going to give a professional opinion, we need to talk first. I can't say you're safe to go until I do my assessment. Can you be patient, hang in there with me for a while?"

"Can we fast-track this? You have no idea how much I hate hospitals." She lifted the arm attached to the IV pole and shook it. "I'm trapped! There must still be some Xanax in my system, or I'd be having a panic attack."

"You need that. You lost a lot of fluids when they pumped your stomach."

"That was truly disgusting."

"It's the only way to stop the drugs from being absorbed into your system. It saved your life."

"Is that a tough love thing? It works! I'll never try it again."

"Last week when I asked you, you told me you'd never commit suicide. Do you remember?"

"And I didn't. That's not what this is."

"Tell me what happened, Paige. How did you end up here?"

"It was stupid and I overreacted. I didn't want to die. I just didn't want to feel what I was feeling any more. It hurt too much. I couldn't stand it. Too much has happened to me, my parents are dead and Amber, and what's going on?"

"Tell me about those feelings. Sometimes it helps to tell someone else."

"I'm afraid to be alone. I don't know if I should be worried that someone's going to kill me too. Graham doesn't understand, he doesn't get it. He keeps going on with his life like the world is normal. It's not for me. Graham finally came home for like a minute and said he was going back to work, they needed him. What the hell! *I* need him. He's so stubborn, and he can't deal with me when I get emotional, and that's all I've been."

"I made him lie down with me. We haven't been together since my parents died. I wanted to feel close to him; sometimes that's the only way he can be sweet. I fell asleep, and when I woke up, he was gone.

"I told him, don't ever leave me without turning a light on. I'm afraid of the dark. I always have been since I was a little kid. It makes me think of death. It scared me even when it wasn't real, and now it is. I was all jittery with nothing to do. I took some of the Xanax, and it calmed me down enough that I started thinking. All the people I love are dead or gone, even Cody's in the hospital. All I have is Graham!

"But do I have him? Is he there for me? I called him, and he didn't answer. I texted him like a hundred times, and he didn't text me back."

For someone who didn't want to talk about her feelings, Paige did a good job once she got started.

"I started wondering where he was and who he was with. I get that way sometimes, insecure and jealous if he even talks to another girl. I made him set his phone so I can check his location. I promised I wouldn't use it unless he made me feel unsafe.

"So I checked and he was where he told me—at work at the gas station. I called him there, and he picked right up. I yelled at him, I couldn't help it, why didn't he answer my calls?

"Turns out he forgot his phone charger and the phone died. A part of me was so relieved, but then, I was still mad. How can he be so careless! Especially now when I need him so much! He was like he gets when he's at work, all business and no time for me, like I don't even exist for him.

"After we hung up, I was still miserable. I took a few more Xanax and just wanted to zone out. I opened the location tracker and scrolled through it, not to check up on him, I didn't have anything else to do. And then the worst thing happened."

She stopped for a breath, and her eyes filled with tears.

"What is it Paige? You can tell me."

"Maybe it doesn't mean anything. I hope it doesn't mean anything. He always tells me I should trust him. But I didn't. I couldn't figure out why he went there, you know? I didn't know what to do. I couldn't call him again. I went to the bathroom. I almost threw up."

"What did you see that upset you so much, Paige?"

"I don't want him to get in trouble. He'll be so mad if I get him in trouble."

"It depends what you tell me. You're not thinking clearly right now; there's no way you could. You have to trust that I am."

"The night my parents died, Graham was there at the ranch, twice! Once early, like around six o'clock and then later after ten, that's the time he gets off work. That's like close to the time they died."

"It's worth finding out why he was there. There could be a good reason, and then you wouldn't have to worry."

"I don't know."

"You don't think that's possible?"

"There's something else. I'm afraid to say it out loud. I love him so much."

"What is it, Paige?"

"Last week Detective Antelope asked if we found money, two thousand dollars, in my parents' house or anywhere on the property. He said he wasn't even sure the money was there, but he asked us to look. We searched everywhere and didn't find it.

"Oh God, I can't believe this is happening. It was cold in the trailer, it's always so cold there. I went looking in Graham's closet for one of his sweatshirts. I like wearing his stuff. He's such a neat freak, he keeps them all folded on the top shelf.

"When I reached for it, the whole pile of them tumbled out. I started to refold them and there it was. A bag full of cash. My heart was beating so fast. I took it in the bathroom and locked the door. I was so nervous I kept miscounting. I don't know how many times I restarted. Finally, I got it right. I was holding two thousand dollars that Graham probably stole from my parents!

"I sat there for a while, so calm. I was there but I wasn't. I put the money back in the closet and folded the sweatshirts.

"I texted Graham and told him I wouldn't be there when he got home. I needed to be home at the ranch.

"As soon as I drove away, all the feelings came back, I started shaking so bad I couldn't drive. Then I took some more Xanax to try to calm down. I took the rest that was in the bottle. And then I panicked. I knew I'd taken too much. I didn't want to die. So I came here and passed out in the ER before I could even tell them what I did."

By the time she finished telling me everything that happened, Paige was exhausted. She agreed to stay overnight in the hospital and have the doctor evaluate her condition in the morning.

They wouldn't discharge her until she was medically stable, but I was even more concerned about her mental stability. If Graham murdered her parents, she would have lost the three most important people in her world.

CHAPTER 47

Graham clocked out at ten and headed straight home. He thought about what he could say to Paige so she wouldn't freak out. She'd be pissed he'd turned his phone off. It was her own fault. She kept calling. He didn't want to deal with her when he was at work. He'd told her that.

He turned his phone on, and what the hell! She'd called eight times! She needed to chill the fuck out. He wasn't going to deal with this.

A text came through, and he began to calm down. She must have figured out she'd gone too far. She'd left to go to the ranch for the night. Good choice, Paige. She needed her family more than she needed him right now.

He made a quick pit stop at home to change clothes and pick up the cash, and by eleven o'clock he was on the road again headed north to Casper. Graham looked forward to the long trip alone; ten hours roundtrip to Casper, but it was worth it. He got a better deal for his money.

A half hour north of the Eden Valley, the cloud cover lifted, and the road was lit by moonlight for the rest of the trip. The road was a mix of black ice and packed snow.

Four hours later, a few miles west of Independence Rock, he started to nod off and veered off the road. He pulled into the state rest stop and parked at the farthest end of the lot away from other vehicles. It was three in the morning, and he needed to sleep.

. . .

He woke to lights flashing and the scraping sound of plows. When he opened his eyes, the bright snow light made him squint. The truck windows were covered in snow. His head and neck hurt from sleeping against the ice-cold window. Cold air had seeped in through the heavy quilt, through his Carhartt jacket. Miserable and hungry, he needed to pee.

Just what he needed. A fucking snowstorm to screw up his life even more.

He reached for his phone to check the time. The cheap piece of shit was dead again; it couldn't hold a charge. He needed a new one. He checked his pocket to make sure the envelope was safe where he put it. That's all he needed. If he lost that money, he might as well just keep on driving.

Damn! He couldn't call Paige with a dead phone! Even if he found an old school phone somewhere, he didn't know her number. It was in his contacts. What a dummy! He didn't know his own girlfriend's phone number! Like most people in the modern world. But Paige wouldn't care about anybody else.

Time to get the show on the road. He cleaned the snow from the truck and drove over to the restrooms. It was coming down hard, and the wind made it worse, mixed it up and multiplied it by a million. So much snow, like walking through a shifting wall of cold pellets. The tires slid as he pulled out of the rest area.

He knew the road well and five miles later took the exit for the Sunset Bar and Grill, an old-school place with red-and-white checked tablecloths and curtains, it reminded him of Paige's grandmother's kitchen. Back when Cody first introduced him to Paige, the three of them would hang out there, talking and drinking coffee for hours. Sometimes Bella would sit with them, and sometimes they could hear her moving through the rooms, doing her own thing.

Simple times, laughing and talking with friends, good times. And good feelings, weightless and floating, but not alone, tethered to a mother ship, safe. Would that ever happen again for the three of them? Probably not. Too much had happened already. The two times she took him home, she made coffee for him. They sat and talked and drank coffee for a long time. Then he met her parents, and that was the end of his visits to the ranch.

He ordered a cheeseburger and two coffees and took his time getting warmed up.

The rest of the trip east to Casper on US-20 was a slow crawl. He passed a few vehicles stuck on the shoulder. The wind started up for real, and snow flew crosswise in front of him; the wipers barely kept a clear space.

By the time he got to the Eastridge Mall two hours later, he wasn't surprised to find an empty parking lot and every store closed.

He punched the steering wheel hard five times. Then he yelled, roared, cussed. Damn his fucking luck!

No way would he freeze his ass off another night in the truck. He drove around in search of a motel he could afford for one night. He checked into the Rodeway Inn.

He locked the door behind him. No one in the world knew where he was. He took a hot shower, turned the heat up to eighty, and slept for the rest of the day.

CHAPTER 48

The room was filled with light; he pulled the covers over his head to block it out.

"Cody, time to get up. You're about to miss breakfast."

She was in the doorway. The pretty nurse with the kind eyes.

"You *are* alive. I was starting to get worried. You've been out a long time. How do you feel? You're not going to lose it are you? I heard you gave them a hard time yesterday, cowboy."

"I'm OK," he said.

He threw off the thin blanket and sat up, embarrassed to have her see him in the grimy T-shirt and gray sweatpants. His hair fell over his eyes. With both hands he combed it back and tucked the long oily strands behind his ears.

"I'm hungry," he said.

He couldn't remember when he'd eaten a real meal. He shook his head. Nothing felt right. He'd lost track of time And probably missed the funeral. It was all Mark Kastle's fault.

"Buffet breakfast today. Anything you want, but hurry up, or you'll miss out. They're about to start the cleanup," she said.

"Anything? How about McDonald's eggs and sausage?"

"The cowboy has a sense of humor. Must be time for discharge," she said.

"Today?"

"The hearing starts at noon," she said.

"Good. I won't have to execute my escape plan."

"That kind of talk isn't going to get you discharged," she said.

"Did I blow it yesterday?"

"Clean up and don't lose it with the judge. You should be all right. You're not the worst case we've seen, believe me."

"That's some strong shit you guys use. What is it?"

"Haldol, an antipsychotic. It works fast when injected into muscle," she said.

"Antipsychotic? I'm not crazy. That's a bunch of bullshit lies in the chart."

"That's what they all say."

Anger flared up again, his neck and face burned. When he looked at her, she smiled. She did have kind eyes.

"Is that what set you off?" she said.

"Damn right," he said. "Everything in that police report came from him, and none of it is true."

"Who lied?"

"My mother's boyfriend, Mark Kastle," he said.

"Why would he lie?"

"I know something he doesn't want anyone else to know," he said.

■ ■ ■

It wasn't a real courtroom, and the judge wore a suit with a white shirt and a red bolo tie instead of a robe. The pretty nurse unlocked the door to the unit and walked with him to the elevator. She was smaller than she looked on the unit, about the same height as his mother, her head barely reaching his shoulder. She pressed the button, and the elevator began a slow descent to the basement. It was the two of them. He could smell her perfume, a clean grassy smell. It occurred to him how easy it would be for him to overpower her. It was the epitome of poor judgement that they let this small woman be the one to escort him alone.

The elevator door opened, and his mother rushed toward him, her hands reaching for his face, and he instinctively stepped backwards into the safety of the elevator.

The nurse was between them, her hand up to stop his mother from coming any closer and the other arm in front of him, a signal to him to stay put. It would be useless if he wanted to charge. But he didn't. The surprise of seeing his mother there left him feeling small and defenseless.

As if she were the all-knowing and all-powerful mother again, like when he was a little kid, and she knew what he was up to and could tell when he was lying.

He didn't want her there. She was the enemy now. She made her choice, and that choice was Mark Kastle. She had chosen Mark Kastle over him. She was no longer on his side. He shouldn't have asked her to come.

A door opened, and a security guard took a quick scan of the group and gestured for them to enter the room.

His mother turned away and walked into the room. The nurse gave him a quick assessment, her kind eyes took on a calculating look, focused and serious. It made him want to grab her, but he didn't. His breath came fast, and the sound of his heart was loud in his ears. His body was a machine that turned itself on, and all he could do was try to slow it. Sometimes that worked.

Time to get control of himself, knock this shit off, or they'd lock him up for good.

He looked at the nurse and gave her his best smile, the one that always worked to disarm his mother.

"I'm good," he said.

"OK, cowboy, let's do this," she said.

He walked in front and her fingers grazed his back, the touch so light and so quick. But it made a difference. He wasn't alone. She was on his side. Or was it his imagination?

■ ■ ■

Cody left the hospital parking lot and turned left in the direction of Dewar Drive and the on-ramp to I-80 West. She came in his truck like he asked her to, which was smart of her. He needed to feel free and in control after being locked up for three days.

"Where are you going?" she said.

There was a hint of panic in her voice. He got it. Five minutes before, he'd been locked in a psych ward. Good. She deserved it. She had screwed up big time.

"The place we need to be when we have this conversation."

"Stop talking crazy. Drive home."

"I'm not going back there."

"Of course, you are; you need to come home. You need to get on a good routine to go back to school. Hanging out at Graham's drinking and drugging and not sleeping is what got you so messed up."

"That's what you think? It didn't have anything to do with two more people in my family getting shot? Have you ever heard of triggers? I got triggered by Dan and Heather dying! They died by gunshot. Just like my dad!"

"Calm down! You're going to make yourself all upset again."

"I am upset! I have a right to be upset."

"I can't handle you when you're like this. I can't handle you alone."

"Is he there? I'm not going back if he's there."

"Don't blame Mark. You were in a bad way, we were worried."

"You have to get rid of him. He's got to go. I mean it."

"He's good to me. He's good to our family."

Cody laughed from deep inside. Nicole stared at him, fear and confusion in her eyes.

"What's wrong with you?" she said.

They entered the Green River Tunnel. A slight turn of the wheel, meet the concrete wall, and it would be over. A chill ran through him, his face dripped sweat. When he wiped his palms on his jeans, his hands trembled.

"Really? He's got you so fucking fooled."

"I hate it when you talk like that."

"Give me a break. I've been locked in a psych ward for three days. You know he lied to the sheriff? That's why they took me in."

"They shouldn't have let you out."

"That's the fucking point! He lied! He told them I did shit that I never did! He's trying to make me look crazy so no one will believe me. Because I know stuff he doesn't want people to know!"

"He didn't need to lie. Do you remember what you did?"

He got quiet. She had a point. He'd been so mad, and he'd lost it. He'd put his hands on her. That was wrong.

"The things you were saying! You needed help. That's why Mark called the sheriff; you weren't in your right mind. Mark's a lawyer. He knows how these things work. You don't know the things he's done for our family."

She didn't say anything when he took the exit and turned onto the road toward the hotel.

"Like what? What has he done for our family?"

"He helped Bella with her will."

"That's his job, right? He gets paid for that."

"He helped Heather when she left Dan."

"Really? A lot of good that did! She's dead."

"He told her how to get a restraining order and how to get Dan's gun into custody. But she didn't follow through with it."

"Good work, Mark, big help there."

"You can't blame him for that. It happens all the time. Women ask the court for protection from abusive husbands and then they change their minds and call it all off. Stop trying to make me think he's not a good person."

"He's a psychopath."

"He told me you'd do this, try to turn me against him."

"Did you ever get a restraining order?"

"Against your dad?"

"Did you?"

"Why would I do that?"

Was she really going to lie about this too? He was burning up, so mad. He didn't want to yell. It made things worse, but what the fuck?

He swiveled in the seat and the force of his voice pushed her back and away from him.

He drove with his left hand on the steering wheel and pointed to his chest. "Look at me! It's me! Cody! I was there with you! I saw everything! I remember. Do you?"

"Why do you want to think about that now?"

"I can't stop thinking about it. And it's all right here!"

He pushed his index finger hard into his temple.

He pulled into the slow lane, getting ready for the exit.

"That was a long time ago."

Nicole sat so still beside him; her voice had a dreamy whisper.

"Not for me! Every day it's right here! Here! In my head!"

His head throbbed and pounded.

"It stopped a long time ago. He stopped."

"So you stayed."

"I stayed for you."

"No you didn't."

"You think you know everything, Cody, and you don't."

"You'd be surprised what I know."

He pulled off the road and parked the truck at the very edge of the gravel road. If he opened the passenger door and gave a light shove, his mother would fall, arms flailing, feet slipping on loose and shifting rocks, unable to break her fall, dead within minutes.

For the first time, Nicole took note of the surroundings. Her eyes widened and her cheeks lost their color; the flush of her anger drained away. She pulled the collar of her suede jacket tight at her neck.

"Cody, why did you bring us here?"

Wind tore through the canyon and buffeted the truck. Straight ahead the mountain fell away in a dizzy tumble of jagged boulders.

It was a day much like this one when they found his father's body at the bottom of the ravine.

"Is that why you cheated on him?"

"You can't ask me that."

"I just did."

"That's not your business."

"Really? Not my business. You cheated. He caught you. That's why he killed himself. It's all my business!"

"Mark was right. You're paranoid."

"If paranoid means I don't trust anybody, then he's right. I don't trust him, and I don't trust you."

"And I don't trust you right now. I don't like it here."

"It freaks you out being this close to where he died. He did it because he found out about you and Mark Kastle."

"I want to go, Cody."

"Are you afraid of me?"

"Please, let's get out of here."

"I wanted your attention, that's why I brought you here. You need to listen to me. Ever since he came into your life everything started falling apart. Do you trust this guy?"

"He warned me. Mark said you'd do this, try to turn me against him."

He should just drive the truck off the cliff right now. There was no hope for her. Which meant he was on his own. Just like Paige. The woman beside him was still breathing, but as far as he was concerned, she was as good as dead.

He shifted into reverse and hit the gas. The truck bucked and screeched through the gravel. He turned the wheel hard and bumped up onto the hard surface of the road. Nicole's head bounced and hit the window as he made the turn.

"Ow, Cody, slow down! Are you trying to kill me?"

He increased his speed and played the curve, letting the tires slide. Each time he looked over at her, all the way down the mountain, her eyes were still on him, wide with fear. A small satisfaction, she was afraid of him.

CHAPTER 49

I was alone in the office finishing up some notes when someone knocked on the front door. I checked the security camera at the front of the house. There was no vehicle in my driveway or on the street. The knocking continued as I walked to the door and heard a woman call my name.

I opened the door and Nicole walked in, wild-eyed and hyperventilating, makeup washed away by tears, eyes red and swollen. Her right eye and forehead were swollen in a dark bruise, She'd been crying, and now she was afraid. She turned her head back and forth, scanned the room behind me, checked the porch behind her.

"Nicole, what happened? How did you get here?"

"I ran over from the hospital. I don't want him to know where I am. I'm sorry to bother you, Doctor. I don't have anywhere else to go. Please!" she said.

"Yes, of course, come in."

"Everything's getting to me. Maybe I'm the paranoid one now."

I led her through the small entryway and pointed to one of the two leather chairs that faced each other in front of the small gas stove. I got two water bottles from the mini-fridge and handed one to her and sat in the other chair facing her. "Drink this. I'll make us some coffee. You need to warm up."

I gave her the warmest blanket I own, a sherpa backed with pink suede.

"Cover up. I'll be right back."

"Do you have any ice? The hospital, they said to put ice on it."

"I'll be right back. There's ice in the that small refrigerator over there."

When I came back with the coffee a few minutes later, both water bottles were empty, and Nicole was slouched into a comfortable chair, her head tilted over her shoulder, the plastic bag full of ice cubes balanced on her forehead. She startled at the sound of the serving tray on the table.

"It's OK. Take a minute, breathe," I said.

She closed her eyes and put her right hand on her heart. Her lips moved as she slowly counted to ten, once and again.

"I don't know what to do or where to go. Cody needs to go back into the hospital again. Can you help me?"

"One thing at a time. What happened there?"

She lifted her head to answer but tears came instead. She squeezed her eyes closed and shook her head from side to side.

"Did Cody do this to you?"

She cried harder and nodded yes and gave in to sobs.

I put the tissue box on the chair arm. "Take all the time you need. I'm not in a hurry."

A few minutes later, she was quiet. She opened her eyes and found the tissues and the ice bag.

"God, my head hurts like crazy."

"Can you tell me what happened?"

"My son is out of control. He was driving like crazy. He almost drove off the mountain and got us killed. I hit my head on the window when he swerved the truck. I was about to say it was an accident. But I'm not really sure."

"The last thing I knew, he was in the hospital. When was he discharged?"

"This afternoon. The three days were up. They had a hearing and said he could go. They didn't have a reason to commit him. They asked him, and he said he didn't have any plans to kill himself or anyone else. An hour later, this is what he did!"

"Were you at the hearing?"

She started to shake her head and winced. "Cody wanted me there. He wanted someone to tell them he had a safe place to go home to and someone to look out for him. I should have told him no. I told him I'd think about it. Honestly, I wanted to run it by Mark. I know I'm too soft when it comes to him. My son asked me to speak on his behalf. What was I supposed to do? I don't want him locked up in that place. And he needed a ride. I told him I'd be there for him. Then he started demanding I bring his truck. And I should have known then, he wasn't OK. I do it every time. He always breaks me down.

"Mark warned me, he told me not to do it. He's not Cody's parent so he can see things better. He could see how Cody turned on me. He doesn't want me to be happy. Mark said it's not normal the way Cody feels about me, it's too extreme, it's like he's paranoid.

"I didn't want to see it. But I know he's right. Cody's been mad at me for a long time. It got worse after his dad died, but if I'm honest, he's been angry with me for a very long time. I assumed he was calm and in control when they discharged him. He was perfect. The best! I haven't seen Cody like that in a long time."

"How did things get bad again?"

"You're going to think I'm a terrible person. The things I'm thinking."

"I'm sure that's not true."

"But I might be. I'm just not sure anymore. He drove us to the place where Jack killed himself, and then he told me it was my fault.

"I'm really worried about Cody. He's not thinking right. He's got everything twisted. I'm afraid, Doctor. I'm having these terrible thoughts that maybe Cody did kill Dan and Heather. Tell me I'm wrong."

Her phone vibrated.

"Oh, that's Mark. I'm going to take it, I'll just be a minute.

"Mark, thank God. Did you listen to my messages? I had an emergency with Cody. I'm all right. No, he's not here. I don't know where he is. It's a long story, I'll tell you when I see you. I need you to pick me up in Rock Springs."

I brought the coffee things into the kitchen to give Nicole some privacy. When I came back into the office, she was applying makeup.

"Nothing's going to cover this," she said, and made a face in the small hand mirror.

"It'll take at least a week and probably look worse before it starts to turn."

"Mark's on his way. I'm so lucky to have him. I can't imagine going through this alone. He's so supportive, and he agrees with me. Cody isn't stable, and he could be a danger especially to me, the way he feels about me. Mark invited me to stay with him in Green River until things calm down. But first we have to pick up my truck and some clothes. It's been a long day. I'll be glad when it's over."

CHAPTER 50

I woke in the night to sounds in the house. Random night noises? Maybe. My heart was beating fast. The room was bright. A big white moon sat low on the horizon. Someone was knocking on a window. Louder, in the sunroom. Shaking the door.

I sat up in bed, put on my robe, and dropped my cell phone in the pocket. I was at the door before I remembered to take my gun. I almost walked off without it.

I lived in Wyoming now, but that's not the only reason I own a gun. I took it from the top drawer in my bedside table, retrieved the round from the box on the bottom shelf. Sound of the door shaking in the frame. I felt a little better with a loaded Beretta in my pocket.

Silhouette of a man outside my office, his hand on the doorknob, his shoulder on the frame.

I walked into the office, and he turned when he heard me.

The moonlight saved things from going further in a bad direction.

Cody looked as freaked out as I felt. I called his name and turned on the overhead light.

"Cody, you scared me. What are you doing here? It's the middle of the night."

"I'm sorry. I kind of lost track of time. I know some things I wish I didn't know," Cody began.

He sat in the same chair his mother had sat in just hours before. I felt better knowing I didn't have to face down an unknown intruder. But Nicole's report of Cody's behavior and mental state didn't mean I could relax. I put my hands in my pockets, cell phone in one, gun in the other. My resources, ready when needed.

"Tell me."

"OK, here goes.

"A few months after we buried my dad, my mom started talking about this new friend she'd met at her job at the Mercantile. She wanted me to meet him, like it was supposed to be important to me, like I even cared.

"I read the dude on the first look—slimeball con man. I don't get how everybody doesn't see it. She wanted to know what I thought, so I told her. Things haven't been right with us since. She chose him, that's how I see it. I told her to ditch him and she won't. My dad found out about it. That's why he killed himself."

"How do you know this?"

"My cousin Paige needed someone to talk to about all the crazy stuff with her parents, how her mom was never home, and how it made her dad crazy jealous. It hit me how similar things were. I started digging to see what I could find. I guess it got to me. I probably needed those days in the hospital. It gave me a chance to clear my mind. And I remembered stuff from before he died, the way things were with my parents.

"My mom's social, she likes going out and being with people, not just men. She gets a lot of attention from men. I guess she's attractive, that's what my friends say. I can't even think about that.

"My dad was kind of a loner. He never went out with her, and he hated when other dudes talked to her. Sometimes he accused her of cheating on him. She'd get all upset and deny it. That shit happened a lot.

"The last fight I remember was right before he died. They said all the same stuff and when it got to the part of him calling her a slut and a whore, she took off. He opened the door and yelled out, 'I'm not stupid. I know where you're going!'

"He took his time and got himself together, got in his truck and drove off.

"I didn't put it together then. But I found the proof on my dad's laptop. He'd put a tracker on her phone. All the records are there. She went to Green River a lot.

"The night he killed himself, my mother was at the Hampton Inn in Green River probably hooking up with Mark Kastle. The place where my dad killed himself is just a few miles up the mountain road behind that hotel."

That's when I flipped out. I got crazy drunk and confronted Mark. He twisted it into me being psychotic and got me locked up.

I thought about what Quinn said—that's exactly how he'd called it.

"It really hurt, making that connection. It fucking gutted me. I hate them both."

"It took courage to do this, Cody, I know it wasn't easy. Your instincts were right. Studying psychology would be a good fit, I think."

He looked like a sad little boy, no victory at all in being right in this case.

CHAPTER 51

Antelope came to my office with triple-strength espresso from home. It worked to wake me up and focus my mind. I wasn't able to sleep again after Cody left.

"I thought we'd have a leisurely morning, but I got a call on the way over that changed things."

"Why do you do that?"

He tilted his head and gave me a quizzical look.

"You're not fooling me; you know what I mean. You give a little information and stop before you've told the whole story."

"Suspense. Everything's better when you have to wait for it."

"That's a provocative thought. What was that call about?"

"Craig Delman got picked up on a DUI last night. He's in lock-up now. He went off the wagon when Amber left for the funeral and was drunk and off the grid for a few days. He'd finally sobered up, and someone told him his wife was dead in the Green River morgue. He bought another bottle and started driving down here. He's sober now and needs a psych clearance to stay in the Detention Center. According to the clerk he's pretty distraught. They need to know if he's going to cause a problem with suicide or self-harm."

"Do you think he had anything to do with Amber's death?"

"I'd guess not. But you still have to ask the questions."

"I'm not looking forward to it. Everyone we talk to is in the throes of grief. Does it get to you?"

"It drains me, body and soul. The night Paige went to the ER? I fell asleep at seven o'clock. They woke me out of a dead sleep, I called you, and zoned out again. I woke up on the couch the next morning at seven. Best sleep I've had in a long time, not one damn dream. I spent all day yesterday doing mind-numbing paperwork, and then I took Domino for a walk at Flaming Gorge. I feel much better."

"Sleep and nature, they're the best."

"And dogs."

"Animals of all kinds. I haven't been riding once since this case started. Speaking of sleep, I had an unexpected, middle-of-the-night visitor last night."

Antelope gave me a mischievous look. "Someone related to the case?"

"This high-grade espresso keeps your mind sharp."

"I've got a reputation to protect. I have the highest solve rate in the county. Not doing so well on this one, though."

"Paige is in a bad state. The deaths alone were enough to do it, but now she suspects Graham murdered her parents. I managed to convince them to hold her in the hospital for a while, and she's not fighting it. She's afraid to be alone, and I can't blame her."

"I authorized one of our guys to be outside her door. If he shows up there, I want her safe. She agreed to call you if he gets in touch with her, right?"

"That's the plan."

"Who showed up at your place last night?"

"Cody Petrangelo. He thinks Nicole and Mark Kastle were seeing each other while his father was alive, and that's the reason he killed himself. Apparently, Jack put a tracker on Nicole's phone. Cody found the tracking data saved on an old computer."

"Why would that matter for our case?"

"I don't know, other than they both work hard at being evasive. It makes you wonder if there is something relevant."

"He went to a lot of trouble. What's his angle?"

"I think he just wanted to know the truth."

"Not trying to deflect our interest away from him?"

"I didn't know we were interested in him."

"You have a high tolerance for psychological abnormality. I see a guy like Cody, close relative of the murder victims, spent the last week in jail or the psych ward, it makes me interested."

"I'm curious why you're having a hard time taking Cody's thoughts seriously?"

"He's unstable. Everything he says is self-serving, gives him reason to go on resenting his mother and hating Kastle. Even if it's true they got together before her husband died, what does that prove?"

"Maybe we should look closer at Nicole as a suspect. She has reason to resent Dan and Heather. She lost her home to them."

"I could argue Cody's our killer."

"He was in jail the night of the murders. And what motivation does he having for killing Dan and Heather?"

"The arrest report said psychotic and paranoid."

"I haven't heard or seen anything that supports a diagnosis of psychosis or paranoia. He has a lot going on mental health-wise. But his problems are not at that level of pathology."

"Grief, depression, trauma—any of those can distort reality."

"That's right."

"Let me turn the question around. Why aren't you questioning his thinking and credibility?"

My phone vibrated on the table beside me. The screen read Paige Petrangelo.

"Hello, Paige."

"Dr. Hunt? Graham just called. He's back. I told him to wait for me at his place. Oh, this is so hard. I want to see him."

"Thank you for letting me know. You did the right thing, Paige. Be strong. Everything will be OK."

"Graham Douglas is back. He's at his place."

Antelope sent officers to the Elk Street Mobile Home Park to apprehend Graham and have him transported to the Detention Center.

"Between the two of us, we're going to get some answers. Let's drive down there together," Antelope said. "I'll interview Douglas while you're in with Delman. Between the two of them, we have to shake something loose. Too many people are dead. We need to stop this killer."

CHAPTER 52

On the way back from Casper, Graham worked out how he'd make it up to Paige, all of it—going missing, not charging his phone, leaving her alone to deal with her grief by herself. Maybe her parents and Cody and that detective were right, maybe he didn't deserve her.

Bullshit, he loved the girl and all she wanted was for him to love her and stay with her. Done deal. He had the ring to prove it. The ring would make everything right for both of them.

She had shown it to him months before in the catalogue. And he'd made it happen. Went all the way to Casper to the closest store that carried the ring she wanted. He'd tell her the story of all the hours he worked overtime to get enough money and how he'd driven through a blizzard and slept in his truck so he could get her the ring she wanted.

As he came into the trailer court, his heart started to race. He was about to do the most important thing he'd ever done in his life. Again, like the night he had tucked her into bed, he was overcome with a feeling of love for Paige, for the woman he was about to propose to. For the first time, he was afraid. What would he do if she didn't say yes?

Paige must feel the same panic every time he left her alone, and she didn't know where he was or whether he'd come back to her. He promised himself if Paige agreed to marry him, she'd never have to worry about his love again.

When he rounded the corner of the last lane, his heart sank. The trailer looked deserted, no lights on, blinds closed, Paige's battered old Toyota nowhere in sight.

All the long drive home he imagined her here, waiting for him. But she hated being alone, especially being alone in the dark. He'd been driving five straight hours. The thought of driving another hour up to the ranch turned him in a dark direction.

Tired, hungry, thirsty, cold. Might as well stretch his legs, use the bathroom, charge his phone, feel human again before getting back in the truck.

In the half light of late afternoon, the small, shadowed rooms looked shabby and lonely. No wonder Paige never wanted to be here alone. He turned on the heat and all the lights and plugged in his phone. Beer and bottled water in the refrigerator. He took one of each and turned on his phone. There were so many missed calls and texts from Paige, it'd take him all night to go through them. After two days of being out of contact, he was smart enough to know he couldn't text her.

He found her name in his contacts and called her.

She should have answered immediately. The phone rang on. What the fuck? Don't play this fucking game, please.

It went to voicemail and he pressed stop and called her again. Same thing. One more time and then he'd get in the truck and head to the ranch.

On the third ring she answered.

"Where the hell are you, Graham? What makes you think you can do this to me?"

"Don't be mad, I had a reason. I can explain."

"Like I even care. I hate you for this."

"You'll forgive me when you find out what I did."

"Maybe. Maybe not. Where are you anyway?"

"At my place. Where are you?"

"Why does it matter?"

"You sound really weird, Paige. What's going on? You want me to come get you? Is that what you want? Look, I know I screwed up, but I promise it's going to be OK."

"No. Stay there. I'll come to you. Give me a few minutes to say good-bye, and I'll be there. OK? Just stay there and wait for me. I love you, Graham."

"Paige?"

He heard car doors closing. Pounding on the door.

"Graham Douglas, open up, Sweetwater County Sheriff."

CHAPTER 53

The Rock Springs Judicial Complex is a ten-minute drive down Highway 191, to a turnoff that leads to a two-lane road that cuts through open desert with a raw, wild feel to it. The 58,000-square-foot glass-and-steel complex resembles an upscale resort in design. The only manmade structure in the remote landscape, it has a chilly aura that brings to mind aliens or mad scientists, both preferable alternatives to murderers in my mind.

As we drove the lonely road, a chill ran through me, and I shivered to shake it off.

It was late afternoon when we arrived at the Detention Center. Soon the sun would go down, and the desert would turn dark and desolate.

We walked through the screening area and into the part of the complex that held the sheriff's offices. Antelope would interview Graham Douglas in a standard interview room, and I would meet with Craig Delman in a softer setting that was more conducive to doing a psychological screening.

"Whoever finishes first, we'll hang out in the family room and wait for the other. Good luck to us, I guess. We need something to break on this case." Antelope said.

Graham Douglas looked angry. His jaw was tight, his face expressionless. Most people revert to the usual customs of social etiquette even in the highly charged environment of being questioned by police. Most people wanted to give a good impression, appear compliant and cooperative. Most people, but not Graham Douglas.

He gave a wary look, his left eyebrow raised slightly, his head cocked to the left, appraising and waiting, trying not to give anything away.

"Ask me anything you want. I've got nothing to hide."

"For the record I will be reading you the Miranda warning before we proceed any further this morning," Antelope said.

"There was no love lost between you and Paige's parents. They didn't like you, Graham. They didn't think you were good enough for Paige. Is that why you killed them? They were messing up your plans."

"You're crazy. You're playing some mind-game shit on me. That's it, I'm done. You get nothing more out of me without a lawyer."

"We can continue to dick around here with your attitude and my intimidation techniques and waste a lot of time and cost you and the county a lot of money, or you can drop your adolescent bullshit posturing and get to answering the questions I need to ask you in order to do my job effectively.

"How would Paige feel if she knew you were obstructing justice in our attempts to identify and apprehend the person or persons who shot her parents in cold blood? Would she still think you're awesome?"

"What do you want to know?" Graham said.

"We know you were at the Sanderson Ranch the night of the murders. Why?"

"You don't know anything."

"Your girlfriend has an app on her phone. She tracks you. You were there."

"Paige told you I was there? This is bullshit."

"Are you denying you went to the Sanderson Ranch the night Paige's parents were killed?"

"I took a drive. Driving relaxes me. There's no crime in that."

"Why there?"

"Me and Cody were at the Saddle Lite. He got on my nerves, and I left. I drove up there, turned around and drove home and went to bed with Paige. She already told you that."

"Where's the money?"

"What money?"

"The two thousand dollars you took from her parents after you shot them."

"Hold on! I didn't shoot anybody. And I didn't take any money. I work for my money. Anyone will tell you that. Ask Paige, I bust my balls working."

"It was Paige who found the money."

"What?"

"She found the cash you stashed in the closet. Where is it?"

Graham smiled, shook his head from side to side.

"I can't fucking believe it. Paige told you this? What did you do, torture her? She's my girl, and she's not going to set me up for something I didn't do."

"You had her fooled. I guess losing her parents put some things in perspective for her. They always said you weren't good enough for her. But you took care of that. You even told your pal Cody you had a plan for dealing with her parents."

"Here's the plan."

Graham reached into his pocket and placed a small blue velvet box on the table. When he opened the box, the overhead light picked up the points of light from the diamond.

"I've been working overtime for months, saving up for this. Don't believe me, check with the boss at the Get and Go.

"I paid nineteen-hundred seventy-five dollars cash money for it. That's more money than I've had at one time in my whole life. Maybe some guys would go to all that trouble to buy a ring for the girl they want to marry and still be able to pull the trigger on her parents. But that's not me. I didn't kill Paige's parents."

"I wonder how much you'll get for that when you try to sell it secondhand? A diamond that another woman refused. Proposing to a woman who thinks you killed her parents is going to be a hard sell. Don't forget it was Paige who told us you went to the ranch that night. Why?"

"You think I'm a joke. Here's another laugh for you. When Cody said Paige's parents would never accept me, it made me mad. I already had the plan to do this. I decided to step it up, do it the right way, be the man they wanted for her. I drove out to the ranch to ask her father for permission to marry her. Real old-school stuff. And here's the joke. I lost my nerve. I was at the house, and I couldn't get the nerve to walk up to the door. I turned around and got out of there.

"By the time I got to Highway 191 I was hating myself for backing down. I told myself if I didn't have the guts to ask if I could marry his daughter, maybe I really wasn't good enough for Paige.

"But when I got back there, someone else was there, there was a truck parked in front of the house. I needed them alone for the conversation I wanted. I threw my truck in reverse and got the hell out of there."

"You have any idea who it was?"

"I know who it was."

"Who was there?"

"Cody's mom's boyfriend. The lawyer, Mark Kastle."

CHAPTER 54

I met with Craig Delman in a room reserved for social work visits. The intention was to have him relax, let his guard down, not feel like he was being interrogated. The heating system had malfunctioned, and the air conditioning was blasting cold air. The chill came in through my down jacket.

He might have been the most sorrowful-looking human I have ever encountered. Everything about him—his face, his posture, his presence—appeared flattened, knocked down and run over by high-velocity grief.

"Mr. Delman, I'm Doctor Hunt. I'm so sorry for your loss. I met Amber at her brother's funeral. She was lovely and so alive. This is such a shock."

"She shouldn't have gone to that damn funeral. She'd be alive now if she'd kept away from those people. I told her not to go, but she wouldn't listen to me."

"Were you angry that she went even though you told her not to?"

"I was worried. She always gets hurt when she's around them. I guess I was right again."

"Did you think about going with her?"

"That wouldn't work. We both knew that. It never came up. They hate my guts."

"When was the last time you spoke to Amber?"

"Why does that matter?"

"We're trying to figure out what happened, if Amber had plans to meet with anyone. She may have said something that could help with that, something you're not even aware is significant. I know it's hard, but I need your help."

"I wanted her to come home that night. But she packed a bag anyway. 'Just in case,' she said. In case what, Amber? She didn't know how it would go, maybe she could patch things up with her mother. She told me not to worry, she'd probably be home that same afternoon, but she wanted the option to stay down there. That's when we argued. I was totally against her being away overnight."

"And that was the last time you talked to her, when she left for the funeral?"

"Sorry . . . no, I lost track. It was in the afternoon, late. She called to tell me she was staying. She wanted to see her niece for lunch and then she'd be back. I had a hard time with it. I imagined all kinds of things, things that happened in the past. There was nothing I could do about it.

"I needed something to calm my nerves, just a few drinks, that's all. Well, you know how that goes. How does that happen, one day to the next? Your life is one way and then it's completely changed. We were doing good. Both of us clean and sober. Both of us working. And now it's all gone. Why? That's what I want to know. I never should have let her come here alone. This place, her family, there was nothing and nobody here who ever gave her the love and respect she deserved. And now this is how it ends? She mysteriously drowns in a river? Why?"

"I wish I could help make some sense of this tragedy for you. I know you want to go home and be left alone to grieve. The reason you're still here is we very much want answers to the question you're asking. We want to know why."

"I don't know anything that's going to help you. Me and Amber left this area in disgrace twenty years ago. I'm sure you heard all about us. We were the big news, the bad news for a long time. That's why we settled in Riverton. We'd never be able to move past how we started."

"That's exactly why I want to talk with you. You have a different perspective than anyone here. You might be right, but I'd like to give it a try. I promise I won't take long. Can I ask you a few questions?"

"I'll do my best. I'll do it for Amber."

"Why don't you start by telling me about Amber. Anything that you think is important, especially as it relates to the family. I appreciate you doing this."

"She was the best of them. She didn't see it, but I did. She had a soft nature, very forgiving, not like the rest of them, especially her mother. She set the tone, and the brothers followed along. It wasn't Amber who broke the connection, it was her mother.

"You know the story, I don't have to go through the whole thing for you, do I?"

"You do. If I have a question about anything, I'll stop you and ask you to tell me more. How does that sound?"

"OK. Basically, there'd been no contact, not even when Annabella was born. That was Amber's choice, who knows if it might have made a difference. Lots of times people get over things when a grandchild comes along."

"We know she talked to her brother Dan."

"I think that started around the time Annabella was born. Before that he sent her pictures of his girl, and Amber would send things, cards and little presents, when she was doing good. The kids were a safe subject. I think little by little things got better between them. They talked about once a month, again when Amber was OK. Then he moved out here. He came up to see her once a week. That made her happy."

"We've been told Dan had a gambling problem and might have owed money at the time he was murdered. Did Amber say anything about that?"

"I think that's what softened his heart toward her. He had his own thing, and he learned for himself how hard it can be to stop."

"Tell me about Amber's sex addiction."

"It was bad. We broke up a few times. She got it under control, though."

"When she didn't have it under control, how did she act out?"

"One way, always the same. She'd pick a guy, hook up with him, it would last as long as one of them wanted it to. Sometimes she got bored in a day, sometimes it went on for months. It wasn't like she'd start a new relationship. It was all sex. She'd go off with one guy and maybe add in a few more before she got tired of it. Then she'd come home to me."

"That must have been hard."

"It was. Finally, I stopped being there when she got home. I think that got to her. Let's face it, we were all the family either one of us had. She didn't want to lose me. She was locked up for a while. Drug court gave her a chance, and she took it. We've been good since then."

"In spite of all the shame and distance, Amber wanted to go to the funeral. I imagine it took a lot for her to face everyone. How did she seem to you before she left?"

"Strong. She loved her brother and wanted to be there. I think she would have gone even if her mother hadn't called her. I'm sure that helped a lot. She was the one who'd pushed Amber away. It was like being welcomed home."

"Her mother couldn't accept her and judged her for her choices and mistakes. Is that what happened?"

"That pretty much sums it up. I was the first bad choice, the big mistake. I've had a lot of guilt about that over the years. It gave me a good excuse to keep drinking. I'm working on that now. The thing that closed the door, though, didn't have anything to do with me."

"What was it?"

"A few years ago, she got interested in genealogy, so for Christmas that year I bought her one of those DNA test kits. She got a surprise when it came back and didn't know what to do with it. It turned her world upside down. She'd spent so many years feeling bad about herself, like the worst person in the world. Then she finds out that the person who judged her the most wasn't so perfect. She couldn't wait to talk to her mother about what she'd learned. I warned her. I said, 'How is this going to make anything better?' She wanted the satisfaction of confronting her mother."

"What was it that she found in the DNA report?"

"A half-brother on the maternal side, born a year before her parents married."

"It didn't go well when she confronted Bella?"

"She denied it. She refused to look at the proof in the report. And she told Amber to leave and never come back again."

"How did Amber handle that?"

"It crushed her. She relapsed. She couldn't let it go. She got the idea she'd fix it by meeting him. He'd be happy to meet her, the other child her mother had thrown away, and in her mind that gave them something in common they could bond over."

"Is that how it went? This person was receptive?"

"We never talked about it. She came back from meeting up with him and went into a full-blown depression. The next thing I know, she's busted for possession. I never asked her about it. One more thing that didn't work out for Amber, and I didn't want to make her sad again."

"Do you still have the DNA report?"

"Why, do you think it had something to do with Amber dying?"

"I don't know. I'd like to see it."

"It's gone. She burned it when she got back from that trip. She said she wished she could get rid of other family members that easily."

"She never told you his name?"

"She might have. This was three years ago. Back then I got high every day. If I ever knew it, I don't know it now."

"Where did she go to meet him?"

"Green River."

"She met him in Green River?"

"He's a lawyer there. We both laughed about that, her having a lawyer in the family, after all the money we spent on lawyers, he could have helped out. It's not funny really. He rejected her just like the rest of her family. I was the only one who ever really loved her and accepted her for who she was."

CHAPTER 55

We came out of the interviews at the same time and looked at each other and knew without saying anything that we had the truth, we were at the end. And then we spoke at once, and the same words came out of our mouths: "Mark Kastle."

My phone buzzed in my jacket pocket.

"I think I should take this," I said, and showed him the name on the screen.

He nodded, "Put it on speaker."

"Hi, Nicole, I'm here with Detective Antelope. I'm going to put you on speaker phone."

"Oh, OK, that's fine. Remember I told you, Cody asked me if I could trust Mark?"

"Yes. What's going on?"

"I've been staying at his place."

"Yes."

"I probably shouldn't have, but I couldn't help myself. I went snooping in his stuff."

"Were you looking for something in particular?"

"I get insecure sometimes and worry he might be seeing someone else. I've done it before. I know it's not right. It didn't help that I kept hearing Cody saying, 'Can you trust him?'"

"What did you find?"

"I might have it wrong. It might be a mistake. I hope it's a mistake."

"What did you find, Nicole?"

"The weekend Dan and Heather got killed, I was supposed to be with him in Laramie. Then Cody came home early for Thanksgiving break, and Mark said I should stay home and spend the time with him. I started to think Mark told me to stay home so he could go with someone else.

"I found the credit card receipt from the hotel. The conference started on Saturday. Mark didn't check in until Sunday. So now I'm wondering where he was on Saturday. I'm starting to feel really afraid. I don't know what to do. What should I do?"

"Are you at Mark's place now?"

"Yes, he's not here."

"If you're feeling uncomfortable, why not go home?"

"What's going to happen? Will he find out I told you this?"

"We're piecing things together right now. Like I said, if you're feeling unsafe, why don't you pack up and go home?"

"I don't want to be anywhere near Farson. Mark's there right now. He has a meeting with Bella."

Antelope took the phone from me.

"This is Detective Antelope, Nicole. Get in your truck and call Cody. I want the two of you to stick together. Get over to the hospital and stay with Paige. We've got an officer posted at her door. I don't want to take any chances with your family's safety.

"Let's go," he said to me. "I'll call for backup when we're on the road."

We started for the door, but Antelope stopped suddenly and said, "Hold up."

He ran back to the room where he had interviewed Graham Douglas and opened the door.

"I'll tell them up front you're free to go. Paige is at Sweetwater Hospital. She's OK, but she'll be better when she sees that ring. Go get engaged."

CHAPTER 56

On I-80, Mark overtook the semi's, driving fast on his way to meet Bella Sanderson, the speed an expression of his anger. She had called and summoned him to come to the ranch like he was hired help. He was getting tired of her entitlement.

He felt confident and powerful. Sex always did that for him. Minutes before, he had left Nicole lying naked on the carpet in his office. He liked having sex in the daylight with the curtains open. Sometimes hikers would pass by on the trail that ran behind his house. It gave him an extra thrill to think of people watching him in the act. It was an effort to get up from his place at the window, but he sensed that something was up with Bella, and he was curious to know what it was.

As he drove away from the house, the cliffs along the Green River were falling in shadow and darkening to a deep blue. The crevasses in the rock turned blacker, a perfect place to hide a body, he thought.

Now that he was out of the house, he realized how good it felt to be alone and how he'd missed it. Having Nicole in the house was making him claustrophobic. That situation needed to settle; she had to go home soon and resume her regular life, get Cody under control and back to school. He wasn't going to be able to stay with her if her son was going to be the center of her attention.

He didn't like leaving her alone in his house. He knew she went through his things. His level of organization and need for precision meant that he picked up the smallest signs of disturbance. He wondered what she was looking for. Signs of another woman, no doubt. That's what they were all concerned about. That obnoxious behavior would have to stop, too. He had no tolerance for violations of his privacy.

Something was going on with Nicole. She was getting insecure, losing her trust in him. He needed her to believe in him, see him as the savior she once did, way back when she was desperate to escape her boring marriage.

He'd fallen into the same pattern as Jack, not giving her enough attention. It was Nicole's fault. She wanted too much and had a way of devouring men. She loved hard, and at first it felt good to have a woman crave sex and never be able to get enough of him. Then he started to feel like nothing more than an object of her pleasure. He thought the same thing had played out with Jack.

He'd done the man a favor when he put a bullet in his head. The night Jack came looking for him, he had wanted revenge or an explanation or murder, maybe all three. Mark didn't want to take a chance and wait for Jack to pull the trigger.

First, he had to deal with Bella. He had to convince Bella not to change her will. Lately, she had seemed less trusting, skittish, and ill at ease. Well, there was a lot going on. She was a strong woman, and he expected more from her.

She wanted to finalize the new will before anything else happened. She had finally made a decision to donate the ranch to the Nature Conservancy. That wouldn't do. Not now. Not after everything he had done to get to this point. If he couldn't convince her to trust him and take his advice, he'd have to do something else.

CHAPTER 57

Bella waited outside at the edge of the pasture and leaned against the fence post. The weather was a sturdy, hard-edged presence all around her, but the cold didn't penetrate. The land stretched out behind her; she felt the weight of it, and the support, her land.

She was thankful for the brief time with Amber. They hardly spoke at the funeral or the dinner after. Bella slept through most of the gathering, exhausted by grief and a headache that wouldn't stop. When she joined the others after her nap, she looked for her daughter. Amber stood at the western window and behind her white lightning flared and skipped across the ground. When the rogue electrical storm shut down the power, her face was a shocking, ghostly white in the candlelight.

She watched the Suburban come slowly down the ranch road. Mark parked and called out to her.

"Hello, there! I didn't see you out here!"

She stared in silence. Let him feel discomfort when she didn't do the expected thing. She had a pass now. Everyone agreed she was experiencing some cognitive decline. Words formed in her brain that she would never speak.

This man is your son.

It could have been a heartwarming moment—he wasn't responsible for the event that had changed her life so many years before. It wasn't inevitable that he would become a psychopath like his father, or was it? She hadn't thought so at the time or she would have done the other thing.

He was gathering his things, opening the door when he saw her come toward him.

"I want to take one last ride around the property before I sign the papers. I hope you'll indulge me."

They left the ranch road and drove a mile east to the boundary road where the Big Sandy River ran along the property line.

She watched him as they drove. It amazed her that they were related. She looked at him, her only living child.

He stopped where she asked him to so she could have a final look at the sun setting over the fields and the river.

"It's beautiful land isn't it?"

"I still don't understand why you want to let it go. It's your birthright, your legacy. It should go to your family."

"But they're all gone now, all my children. I think they died because of this land and because of me."

"What do you mean?"

"I know who you are. Why did you kill my children?"

"I'm your child, your first-born son. Why did you abandon me? You let a monster raise me. This is all your fault."

She looked at Mark and tried to understand. In all the time she spent with him, there was never a hint of their connection. She felt nothing. There was no reason to think he was her son. It seemed strange to her that there would be no sense or intuition.

Even now that she knew, she could find nothing familiar in his face.

"You must look like your father. There's nothing of me in you."

"I do look like him. The only good thing the bastard ever gave me, a face that people trust. I worried you'd see the resemblance."

"I never saw his face. Did he tell you he raped me?"

Mark was a skillful liar, but she saw her words register in his cold eyes, the rape was news to him. But there was no softening of his manner, no empathy for her. The way he was conceived, the crime that brought him into the world, changed nothing.

"I'd believe anything of him, there's no pain he's not capable of inflicting. But you're probably lying. He told me not to look for you because you didn't want me then so why would anything be different?"

"But you didn't take his advice. You came looking for me."

"I couldn't be bothered looking for a cold bitch like you."

"Then how are you here?"

"Your drug addict daughter found me. She was hungry for another family because the one she had rejected her. You rejected her because she didn't live up to your standards. Kind of a pattern for you, throwing your kids away."

She wanted to be away from him, away from his malice that filled the space between them like toxic gas. She leaned back, her head against the hard glass, felt the clean, cold air pressing in.

"I know you killed Dan and Heather and Amber. Did you kill Jack, too?

"Of course. I killed all of them. They were all in my way. They all had what I didn't have, money and family. And none of them did anything with it. You made the wrong choice. You should have chosen me. I made it without you, but I could have done so much more. It's my turn now."

"You have rights of inheritance under Wyoming law. I've always known that. This was all so unnecessary. All you had to do was produce your birth certificate after my death. You would have shared equally in the assets."

"I deserve so much more than that and I'm going to have it. That's the real reason you wanted the ranch to go to the Nature Conservancy, isn't it? You didn't want to take a chance I'd show up."

"Was your father a highly intelligent man or did you get your fine strategic mind from me?"

"He was a brutal dummy. So thank you for your contribution there. It was the least you could do for me. I was able to outwit him by the time I was 7."

"I never meant for you to be with him. He stopped the adoption plans I made."

"There's nothing you can say that will change anything. You made the wrong choice and we both have to live with it."

His handsome face was hardened by hatred. She felt the coldness in his heart, colder than the winter night outside. It was just the two of them enclosed in the dark, shrouded, evening forest, and only one of them would leave.

"You're right," she said, "I made the wrong choice."

It happened fast.

Her hand on the gun, the pressure, the release.

Short sliver of time, the flash of surprise in his eyes, the certainty, before the bullet hit.

The sound, so loud in the small space, jolted and frightened her. She dropped the gun.

It rested on the seat between them. She felt revolted by it, her stomach roiled with acid. She'd carried it for so long, so close to her body, but now she was sickened by it's evil purpose. She had to get the gun into his hand. She didn't want to touch it. She didn't want to touch him. Her head hurt from the sound of the shot.

It would only get harder to do, and the night would get darker and colder.

She wiped the gun and placed it on the seat close to where his right hand rested.

The gun could never be traced to her. She had bought it the week after she was attacked and raped in Laramie from a student who needed the money. There'd been no record of the sale, and she had never registered it or gotten a license. It was part of the secret she'd carried all those years.

She entered the darkness and shelter of the pines and started the slow walk home to the ranch.

CHAPTER 58

There were no streetlights this far out of town, leaving the Jeep's headlights to cut through the encroaching presence of the black night. We entered another world, away from conveniences and comforts, and surrendered to a place where anything could happen. We arrived at the ranch a little before five o'clock. The dying sunset flared in the western sky, dragging long tails of red and purple.

We both noticed at the same time. The dark house was the first sign of trouble. We walked the short distance to the house and knocked on the door. From the porch we could see into the kitchen and the great room beyond, not a light on, no sound or movement.

Antelope knocked again and called Bella's name.

"I'm going in. Wait here."

I waited on the porch. The cold weight of the Beretta at my waist reminded me of the reason we were here.

The sound reverberated across the fields, shattering the silent evening.

I jumped and Antelope startled me again when he appeared in the door with his weapon drawn.

"Get in the truck. It came from over there, behind the trees, near the river."

Antelope drove off-road over the snow-covered ranch fields. We raced toward the pine forest straight ahead, a black fortress rising from the land.

A figure stepped out of the trees and headed for us.

Bella Sanderson looked like the walking dead with her pale face and dark circles accentuated by the flashlight held under her chin.

Antelope hit the brakes and the big Chevy engine stopped and stalled.

"Can I get a ride back with you?"

Bella was silent on the ride back to the house. By the time we got inside it was clear there was something wrong. She tried to talk and couldn't find the words. She became agitated with the effort to speak. She agreed to go to the hospital, and Antelope called for an ambulance.

The three of us sat together and waited. Bella looked distressed, her eyes wide and brimming with tears, filled with intensity. Her gaze moved back and forth between me and Antelope.

"Did Mark Kastle come here?" Antelope asked.

She nodded yes.

"It's over," she said.

When the ambulance had taken Bella away, we drove again across the fields following Bella's footprints until we came to the pine forest that made it impossible to proceed in the vehicle.

The moon had come up, and shafts of pure white light lit our way through the dense grove.

When we came out the other side, we were on the bank of the Big Sandy River where dark fast waters churned and coursed through the steep banks.

We surveyed the scene from the shelter of the trees. A dark vehicle was parked at the headland, its windows glinting silver. The passenger door was open. We saw the deep impressions of Bella's boots, the place where she landed when she jumped out of the vehicle, and the long strides she took away from what happened and back to the safety of the ranch.

Antelope put his left arm out to signal me to stay in place. He drew his weapon and walked away from me, holding the weapon with both hands, arms straight, careful steps, crouched low.

My heart was pounding fast in my chest with memory of the gunshot that had surely come from this spot. I held my breath, waiting.

A light wind stirred the air. My breath was another sound in the night alongside the rumbling river, the gently tossing pine boughs.

I jumped back when Antelope stood straight, his weapon at his side. He leaned into the cab of the truck for just a minute and then he turned and looked at me.

"Kastle's dead. Looks like a suicide."

CHAPTER 59

Bella remained in the hospital for a month. In that time she regained her speech and strength. She was discharged home with the plan that Paige would stay with her. The hospital had recommended she consider moving into an assisted living facility because of the high likelihood of similar incidents occurring in the future.

I visited her in the hospital once a week, and each time I was amazed at her progress. When she'd recovered to her former functioning, I asked what happened the night Mark Kastle died. But the memory problems, a common symptom of the brain tumor, had worsened. It's also possible that the trauma she'd experienced had caused her to dissociate. Bella said she had no memory of that night.

CHAPTER 60

The weather on the first day of spring surprised everyone in Sweetwater County. The balmy sixty degrees put everyone in town instantly in a better mood after one of the longest and coldest winters on record. The soft air and bright sun gave a hint of the seasonal changes underway. As I walked into the Deer Trails Assisted Living Center, the desert breeze carried the scent of sage.

The night before, Paige called me with an update on Bella's medical status. When she moved into the apartment at the start of the new year, her medical condition improved; she regained some strength and mental clarity. For the first time in her life, she enjoyed being cared for and having the leisure time to socialize.

Last week, she began to decline, and some symptoms started that she recognized as the last stages of her illness. Her doctor recommended hospice services, and Paige had moved into the apartment to be with her grandmother. She remained comfortable in her bed at home, conscious and alert, but that could change at any time. Bella wanted to see me, how soon could I come? Paige let me into the apartment and left for a quick shopping trip to give Bella privacy for our visit.

The display of spring blooms at Albertsons Market had lightened my mood, and I had bought two bundles of forsythia stems,

one for Bella and one for myself. In the kitchen, I unwrapped the
flowers and filled the vase I'd brought with warm water and the
packet of plant food that came with the bouquet.

■ ■ ■

Her eyes were closed when I entered the room. I placed the flowers
on the oak table at the window. Sunlight spread the golden color
of the blooms onto the walls and ceiling, and the room glowed.
Bella opened her eyes, took in the flowers, smiled, and closed them
again, I sat in a pink velvet wing chair beside her bed. Every piece
of furniture in the apartment had come from the ranch. At the
time, I'd commented that it must be hard to choose from all the
possessions gathered over a lifetime, especially the things passed
down from her parents and grandparents. Bella had disagreed.

She'd been preparing for this moment for a long time.
The pieces from her family would be divided among her three
grandchildren. She would hold onto only things that held good
memories, items she loved, and gifts.

The first day in my office, sitting at the table, about to begin
testing, Bella had admired the view of the desert and White
Mountain and told me how she began every day at a table in
her kitchen, looking out at the Wind River Mountains. Now that
same table faced the sunny southwest corner of her room at the
foothills of White Mountain.

When I reached out and touched her hand, she stirred and
opened her eyes. "I'm so glad you've come to see me. Will you
adjust these pillows, please? I'd like to sit up for our visit. Perfect,
thank you. You remembered the forsythia. They make the room
so much cheerier. Whenever I open my eyes, the sun is shining.
Are we having a real spring?"

"It seems that way. How are you feeling today?"

"I'm as good as I can be, I suppose. Paige has been staying
with me. That's a comfort."

"Yes, she said you wanted to see me. I came as soon as I could."

"I wanted to see you while I still know what's going on. You know how this process goes. At some point my mind will not be focused here."

"It means a lot to have this time with you."

"It's strange . . . we've only met a handful of times and yet, you know so much about my life, more than anyone else alive. You came in at the end, but you know the whole story. I want you to know, that day in your office when you asked all those questions, that was the first time I told anyone about what happened to me. It wasn't easy to do. I was so ashamed when it happened. But that went away, and as terrible and heartbreaking as these last months have been, I haven't felt ashamed. Was it always that easy, just tell the story?"

"You must have been ready to let it go."

"I think so. I'm making it sound like you waved a magic wand, and the shame instantly disappeared. I left your office feeling terrible, just exhausted and so sad. For the next few weeks, I'd break down in tears for no reason. And then I got the news about the cancer and figured that's what caused the mood swings.

"The crying jags stopped. I felt better than ever, stronger without the shame. Even with this terrible diagnosis and with so little time left."

"I'm glad it helped you to talk about it."

"Do you want to know the real reason I changed my mind about bequeathing the ranch to the Nature Conservancy?"

"Besides wanting to provide financially for your grandchildren?"

"I felt an obligation to do that and, of course, I care about them and won't be around to know what they need. They all lost parents, which is such a hard thing for young people. I lost my own mother before I met her. I think it must have made a difference, growing up without a mother's love. I imagine I would have told her what happened in Laramie. It's interesting, isn't it? To think I might have lived an entirely different life if just that one thing had been different.

"I'm happy with the way things turned out. The ranch was an extension of me, and anything related to me was tainted with my shame. I didn't want to pass that shame on to my heirs. If I separated my family from the ranch, I'd protect them from carrying my shame, and at the same time, I could feel proud of being a generous donor to a very worthy cause. It was a pretty clever plan, though I didn't understand it all at the time."

"Our unconscious minds do their work undercover."

CHAPTER 61

If I'm being honest, I knew it would happen that night. But that knowledge was burrowed into the folds of my limbic brain, the core survival site where impulses for sex and aggression hide out, their primal energies coiled and ready. And the limbic brain is famous for keeping secrets and the resulting surprise attack.

I invited Antelope to come for dinner. He'd just returned from his annual two week trip to Mexico. We were on the deck, enjoying the last hours of the spring equinox. I pulled the orange and red cotton blanket tighter around my shoulders as the wind picked up.

We watched the bright orange-and-purple twilight deepen as the red sun slowly left the western sky.

"These were such a good idea. Thank you for getting them for me."

"I was at the outdoor market, in shorts and a T-shirt, and I pictured you back here in the cold under one of these."

"And you bought two."

"Good thing I did, or one of us would be freezing our ass off right now."

"Probably you."

"That's what I figured."

We sipped the sangria he'd made with the Tequila he brought back from his annual trip to Los Cabos.

"This is good. I'm feeling very relaxed."

"Can I ask you a personal question?"

"Sure, you're allowed a personal question, at this point," I said.

"We're at a point?"

"The point where you know you can ask me anything and I'll be comfortable telling you. What do you want to know, Antelope?"

"Who was there for you when Zeke was killed?"

"It wasn't Quinn, if that's what you're wondering."

"OK."

"My parents died when I was young. That's a story for another time, OK? I need to trust someone before I can share my pain. That person didn't exist at the time."

"Will you let me be that person?"

"It would help if you kissed me."

He reached for my hand and pulled me toward him. I swayed and leaned against his chest, solid as granite, grounded as a boulder against me. We stopped to take a breath. I rested in his arms, lightheaded and dazed with pleasure.

He spread the blankets on the floor of the deck, in a corner out of the wind.

"Come here," he said and held out a hand to me.

"You sure about this?" he said, with the intensity he showed when interrogating murder suspects.

I wanted him to touch me again.

"I'm sure," I said. There was nothing standing in the way of this moment.

Some of my hair had come loose; I brushed it off my face.

"Take your hair down," he said.

I reached back to remove the tortoiseshell combs and shook my head. My hair fell down and over my chest. He ran his fingers through the curls.

"I like this, all loose and wild."

"I'm a loose woman," I said.

"That works."

"I'm a wild woman."

"Even better."

I took his face in my hands and brought him to me. His long fingers worked the pearl buttons of my shirt and slipped it over my shoulders. I took off the lace camisole underneath. His hands cupped my freed breasts.

His mouth on me was gentle at first, then hungry, insistent, and stirred a deep longing that turned me wild with wanting him.

I undid his belt buckle. He unzipped my jeans.

We undressed with an easy grace savoring this turn into new territory. The first touch, a surprise and a wonder. Our slow hands surveyed the novelty of skin.

I lay down, and he got on top of me, his long body a warm shield over mine. Our bodies found their rhythm and settled in it as if returning to a known place.

The world around us went away, the cold, the dying light, the wooden deck. The only thing that mattered, our raw desire, was alive between us. A rogue wave of pleasure coursed through me searching for its own way home.

And the sweetness at the end when I opened my eyes and found him there, each of us returned to our separate selves again, changed by what had happened between us.

We lay with hips touching, skin slick with sweat. The sounds of our breath coming fast, my heartbeat loud in my chest, the body's reverb after sex. For a long time, I drifted in a satisfied daze. Antelope rested with one arm over closed eyes, the other at rest on my thigh.

Without moving he said, "That was something. I didn't see that coming."

"You've thought about it, though," I said.

"Us like this? All the time."

"How long?"

"Right from the start."

In the silence a phone rang.

"That's me. I'm on call," I said.

"I'll get us some more of this," he said and went into the house.

A cold wind started, and I pulled the blanket around me. In the light from the candles, I found my phone. It was Paige.

As we talked, a gust of wind moved across the deck and knocked over the forsythia vase, blew out the candle flames, and scattered the tea lights across the deck. The pillar candle remained upright.

We said good-bye as Antelope came back with the drinks, a silhouette in the doorway, backlit by the moving light from the gas fireplace.

The flame from the center candle flared up.

"That's better, now I can see you," he said.

"You have hidden talents."

"Thank you. There might be trouble if word got out."

"I like what you do with Tequila, and other things."

"Mixing drinks is an art. I tended bar to pay room and board in college. Your call—do you have to leave?"

"No, I'm not leaving. That was Paige calling. Bella died tonight."

"She said Bella's last words were a message for us. She remembered what happened the night we found her wandering in the snow. She said it felt good to finish what she started."

ACKNOWLEDGMENTS

This book began as a Nanowrimo 50,000 word draft and was completed during the lockdown and isolation of the pandemic. While writing a novel is an inherently solitary process, it has been even more so this year, with fewer opportunities to meet with others for discussion and feedback. I am grateful to those who spent time reading and sharing their thoughts as the work evolved, for caring about the story and about me—Todd Bontecou, Rain Chippewa, Rob Hanson, Judy Jamieson, Stephanie Lottridge, Stephen Lottridge, and Pat Martin.

Special thanks to the editorial team at She Writes Press and Sparkpoint Studio for careful attention to the final process.

ABOUT THE AUTHOR

J. L. Doucette lives in Rhode Island where she has a private practice in psychology. She lived in Rock Springs and Jackson Hole, Wyoming. The landscape and wild spirit of the high desert became her muse and the setting for her mystery novels.

Author photo by Staceydoyle.com

SELECTED TITLES FROM SHE WRITES PRESS

She Writes Press is an independent publishing company founded to serve women writers everywhere. Visit us at www.shewritespress.com.

Last Seen by J. L. Doucette. $16.95, 978-1-63152-202-4. When a traumatized reporter goes missing in the Wyoming wilderness, the therapist who knows her secrets is drawn into the investigation— and she comes face-to-face with terrifying answers regarding her own difficult past.

On a Quiet Street: A Dr. Pepper Hunt Mystery by J. L. Doucette. $16.95, 978- 163152-537-7. A funeral takes the place of a wedding when a woman is strangled just days before her wedding to a district attorney—and Pepper, whose former patient happens to be the brother of the victim, is soon drawn into the investigation.

Del Rio: A Novel by Jane Rosenthal. $16.95, 978-1-64742-055-0. District Attorney Callie McCall is on a mission to solve the murder of a migrant teen, but what is she to do when her search for the killer leads her straight to the most powerful family in town—her own?

Glass Shatters by Michelle Meyers. $16.95, 978-1-63152-018-1. Following the mysterious disappearance of his wife and daughter, scientist Charles Lang goes to desperate lengths to escape his past and reinvent himself.

Water On the Moon by Jean P. Moore. $16.95, 978-1-938314-61-2. When her home is destroyed in a freak accident, Lidia Raven, a divorced mother of two, is plunged into a mystery that involves her entire family.

TRAGEDY TO

Restore,
Recover,
Rebuild

TOAN NGUYEN

BALBOA.
PRESS

A DIVISION OF HAY HOUSE

Balboa Press books may be ordered through booksellers or by contacting:

Balboa Press
A Division of Hay House
1663 Liberty Drive
Bloomington, IN 47403
www.balboapress.com.au
1 (877) 407-4847

Print information available on the last page.

ISBN: 978-1-5043-1023-9 (sc)
ISBN: 978-1-5043-1022-2 (e)

Balboa Press rev. date: 11/29/2017

Contents

"There's only so much you can do with blood and bone and heart."
                                    -Diane Esmond

Introduction

For anyone who cannot fathom or envision the devastation a flood can inflict,

- Imagine World War Three. Imagine everything in the aftermath of a global war; buildings—timber, brick, and steel—everything twisted, wrecked, and torn.
- Imagine your home ruined, a mud swamp, every single item destroyed.
- Imagine having the heart to put in the time and effort to bring your house back to the point you will be permitted to step back inside.

And now imagine you are an old man or woman alone, or a young couple, a small family, a young adult living by yourself with little money and few resources because the flood has taken everything except your humanity.

Imagine that, and you might better understand what happened to my community. And what happens to other disaster-ravaged communities.

Chapter 1

CELEBRATING AUSTRALIA DAY

The beginnings of 2013 had not been particularly auspicious. For those who believed in bad luck, these first days were the beginning of a whole year featuring bad luck related to the number 13.

On January 20, a low-pressure system in the far north, over the Gulf of Carpentaria, became a tropical cyclone and began dumping water down the east coast of Queensland. For the last couple of days before Australia Day, the weather had been pretty much rain, rain, and more rain. At my home in North Bundaberg, six adults were stuck inside, as well as my four-year-old daughter, Ruby. I had been working in the office, so it didn't really bother me so much.

It is also true that we are a large family and used to each other's company. So no one was really getting on anybody's nerves. Instead, the family was able to fill the time by cooking, cleaning, and watching television. Other family members dropped by, too. Everybody was pretty happy, considering nobody could get outside much because of the rain.

The rain was all a result of that tropical cyclone, which was now called Oswald. Oswald seemed to be the usual sort of cyclone; nothing special. As usual for a cyclone, it started up north and headed our way—south. We're used to expecting rain from these cyclones, and sometimes they come close enough that we get some big winds. Sometimes we have a flood.

There were many warnings, of course, on radio and television. But Bundaberg had its once-in-a-century flood two years previously, so I don't think anybody thought we should be seriously worried about Oswald.

We'd only had rain for a short time, and it didn't seem so heavy, but it was constant over several days. Everything felt damp. The heaviest rain, the news services told us, was out west, over towns like Gayndah and Mundubbera. That meant it was raining heavily in the catchment area of the Burnett River, which flows through Bundaberg. It also meant that while we hadn't had a heavy downpour of rain here, the river was filling up fast.

People didn't seem too worried, but I went to bed that night concerned. It was still raining outside, and I had a feeling I can't describe—a bad energy that I couldn't explain at the time.

The next morning, I woke up and learned the bad energy probably wasn't from the cyclone. I had other things to worry about.

I went down to the office, which is at the front of the house and quite a distance from where everybody had been sleeping. It was only because we slept some distance off, and because of the rain, perhaps, that it could have happened.

We'd been robbed!

I saw the office had been ransacked as soon as I opened the door. The room was a total mess.

That was a big surprise. I couldn't think. Someone had been in our house. I stood there for a moment, unable to do anything.

Then came the biggest surprise.

The thieves had actually stolen our safe. I couldn't see it anywhere.

What do you do when something like this happens?

I couldn't believe we'd been burgled. I didn't think of ringing the police straightaway. I was so shocked. I couldn't get my head around what happened.

There was a sense of it all being not quite real. Not as if it were unreal, like a dream, but perhaps as if it were happening to someone else. You see and hear about crime all the time on the news, but I could never believe that it could happen to me.

So I didn't call the police. Instead, I ran to tell my wife, Gina, who was still half asleep. "Honey, we've been robbed," I said. I remember the look on her face. The surprise. Then the dawning shock that people had been in our home while we slept.

Only then did I think of the safety of the rest of the family and ran to tell them about the intruders. BM, Trinity, and Ruby had been sleeping nearby. Gem, my mother-in-law, and Uncle 7 were on the other side of the house.

At least everybody in the house was safe, but all of us—the whole family—were completely stunned. How could we not have heard anything? Not when they searched the office desk. Not even when they took the safe.

My wallet was gone. So was the rent money. They'd also taken Gem's and Gina's wallets. These items had been stored in the office drawers.

We had stored our passports in the safe, so they had disappeared with it. In total, someone had taken almost $10,000!

That's how the situation slowly became real to us all. Thinking about it now, it didn't really take long to come to grips with what happened, but time seemed to have slowed. Hours seemed to have passed after I first walked in that office door before I called triple zero.

This is where Cyclone Oswald began to trouble us. First, I was put on hold for quite a long time. When the call was finally answered, the woman I spoke with could only take down the details because no police were available. All the police were out preparing for the flood they believed was about to hit.

Instead of worrying about that, the family spent the whole day, Australia Day, playing detective, trying to track what had happened, maybe discover some suspects. But there wasn't a single footprint inside the house, which was odd considering it had rained all night. We had no luck.

Instead, we were completely distracted from what everybody else was worrying about.

There are no accidents in life. Everything happens for a reason, whether it is good or bad. If it's good, learn to be grateful for it, and if it's bad, learn to forgive. Understanding this gives me a new perspective on life, and I can have a more peaceful life.

Chapter 2

GETTING READY
FOR THE FLOOD

It rained even more heavily that night.

The next morning, we drove around a bit to get an idea of what was going on. Listening to the news and weather warnings can give you only so much information, and that is probably out of date by the time it's put on the air. We wanted to see for ourselves what was happening after the heavy rain. We wanted to know exactly how worried we should be. Trinity thought she might go back to her home at Bargara.

We drove towards the river only to find it was flooding *again*. (I say "again" because the river had flooded as recently as New Year's

2010–2011). We came to a place where people were dragging their caravans up to the side of the road. Gina asked if they needed help, but the caravan park manager had flood emergency plans in place, and they seemed sure they'd be all right.

To be honest, we thought nothing of the rain and the potential for flooding until we heard the State Emergency Service (SES) announcement that everybody should start preparing for another disaster, and everyone in the area might need to evacuate.

The SES couldn't tell us how high the river might peak, but the considered opinion of the SES and other emergency service channels was that it might reach 8.5 metres. The previous flood peak had been more than half a metre lower, at 7.92 metres.

With that in mind, we knew the water would reach the prayer hall (in-house temple) in our home, so we prepared to lay sandbags. Our prayer hall had started life as a garage. Outside, it hadn't changed much, but we had replaced the usual garage door with sliding-glass doors.

Our family practises Tao, a philosophy teaching the way of life. As you can imagine, there are not many of our faith in this area, so we felt we needed a place we could come together as a family to celebrate our festivals and our learnings. It's true that we could have chosen to have a special place set aside in the house, just as other faiths might. But we are such a large family that we thought it would be better to make our garage into a small temple, our prayer hall.

We knew that we could do nothing if the flood rose as people were saying it would. At the same time, we knew we had to do everything we could to save our home, especially our prayer hall.

Gina and I immediately set off, driving around to find some sandbags. There were none available on our side of the river, and as evidence of how cautious the authorities were, we were unable to get across to the other side of the river because the bridges had been closed.

I started to realise just how much trouble this Cyclone Oswald was creating and how dangerous it might be. Gina, at the time, was thirty-six weeks pregnant with our second child, and as we rushed back home, I felt the first stirrings of panic. In my head, I began listing all the what-ifs and all the maybes that Oswald might bring with the rain—and how it could affect our family.

At home, Mum was the centre of calm. She suggested an obvious solution—that we make our own sandbags. So we pulled out dozens of pillowcases, found empty rice bags, and filled them with sand from a nearby children's playground.

We had enough bags to protect the prayer hall if the water rose by the extra half metre being predicted. After placing the sandbags, we took the precaution of lifting everything inside the prayer hall up as high as we could.

Then news came that the river would keep rising as water flowed down from Gayndah and the Burnett catchment. We were told Paradise Dam would overflow. As before, nobody was offering precise numbers or heights, but they did agree the water was expected to arrive sometime on Monday, January 28.

That was our signal to start shifting everything again. We thought of it as a precaution only because how could the river rise so far? But we put everything in the living room and kitchen onto a higher level again. Small items, like electrical appliances and anything we wanted to save, went on tables.

Then there was nothing we could do but watch, and wait … Watch and wait … And boy the water came up fast.

By 5 p.m. Sunday, the floodwaters had reached our 2010–2011 flood level and was halfway up our driveway. Only an hour later, the water had made it inside the prayer hall.

We all panicked. For a third time, we went around the house, moving as much as we could up, up, up. That was a real workout. We moved all the little things as well as big things like beds, mattresses, desks, tables, and couches.

Even though it was raining on and off, the weather was hot and very humid. We were all so drained and very tired, especially Gina, who was carrying our baby and was due to give birth in only four weeks. She hadn't stopped all day. We had all, me especially, pushed ourselves harder knowing that.

It was time for us to decide what we were going to do next. Should we stay in the house until morning? Or evacuate now.

When SES first started talking about the need to evacuate, we thought we might move next door, where the house was on stumps and sat much higher than our own. The house belonged to relatives, and they were out of town. Naturally, they were concerned to know about the flood, but we had agreed that, if the worst came to worst, we could evacuate to their house. I'm pretty sure we were all joking at that point. None of us really expected we might have to move next door to their place.

Uncle 7 and I went over next door, wading through water that by this time was just below our knees. We checked the back door and front door, and both were locked. A front window was ajar just a little, but it was too high up for us to get to.

We could have gotten a ladder from our shed, climbed in through the window, and opened the house right then and there. It seemed such a big step to take, going into another person's home, especially when we weren't even sure we'd have to.

So we decided to just stay the night and wait and see what happened next. Nobody could sleep that night. Outside was silent. It had stopped raining, and the sky was clear. I could see the full moon. We had all been too busy preparing for the flood that we had forgotten how quiet it was without the rain. I could feel the anxiousness and worry of everyone. We all had this eerie feeling ... waiting to see what happened next.

At 9 p.m., I started marking some measurements—ten centimetres, twenty centimetres, thirty centimetres, forty centimetres, and fifty centimetres—on the house wall near the driveway. I knew that once it reached the forty-centimetre mark, we needed to leave the house.

I hoped it wouldn't come to that. I knew the water was rising, but I didn't really know how fast. So I stayed there and watched the water level.

By 10 p.m., the water had only risen by about five centimetres. *That's not so bad,* I thought. I did a few quick calculations. At that rate, say two hours per ten centimetres, it would take the river seven hours to reach the forty-centimetre mark, which would put it just at our front door.

That meant we wouldn't have to decide about leaving until five the next morning.

But I like to be safe so, just to make sure, I stayed to watch the water rise for another hour.

And yes, it rose only another five centimetres in an hour. It had reached the ten-centimetre mark and confirmed my prediction. Feeling safer, and a little more secure that I had a plan to deal with this disaster, I went to bed.

Not that I slept much. But I was aware, no matter what, that we all needed to rest as much as we could. It had been a hard day for us all, moving everything up to safety and sandbagging. Those sandbags weighed about thirty to forty kilograms each.

We were all tired. Gina especially. There was a very real possibility Gina would need all our strength to help her, pregnant as she was, get through the next couple days.

Knowing how important it would be for Gina to be rested, I went in with her and tried to rest, too. But all through the night, we could hear Mum and Uncle 7 going outside. We knew they were checking the water level. Knowing they were on watch should have meant we could sleep, but Gina and I spent the night drowsing, half asleep and half awake.

At 4 a.m., Mum called to us from the hallway, saying it had reached the forty-centimetre mark. So the river was at our front door an hour earlier than I'd calculated. That meant the river was rising faster. It also meant that, as we'd feared, the prayer hall, our laundry, bathroom, and library were completely flooded.

It was time to move.

Our first plan had always been the house next door. Moving there might have been a bit of a joke at the beginning, but the joke had turned into truth. Surely we would be safe in that house. It was up on stumps, and quite a bit higher than our own home. We knew it was locked tight except for that window.

The water at the top of our front steps mocked me. Rain had stopped falling, and the water was smooth and featureless. If there hadn't been so much of it, it could almost have been a tranquil pond at the bottom of the garden. But it was floodwater, and no matter how peaceful above, beneath the surface were unknowns, perhaps dangerous unknowns.

With 20/20 hindsight, I saw now that Uncle 7 or BM or I should have taken the ladder and gone across and opened that window earlier. But earlier, none of us had quite believed that we couldn't ride out the flood in our own home. Now, not only did we have to move, but I felt it was up to me to get the ladder out of the shed at the back of our house, and it, too, might be flooded.

I wished I had thought to get the ladder out of the shed earlier, even if we hadn't intended using it straight away; just to be better prepared. All the time we'd been sandbagging, and I'd been watching the water rise slowly past the measurements on the house, all that time passing, and I hadn't thought to get the ladder out of the shed just in case it was needed.

I guess in all that time I hadn't faced the

truth of the situation. Maybe I had hoped, deep inside, that the flood might not be as bad as people were saying. Wishful thinking.

Dawn wasn't far off, but it was still very dark looking out at the water. We had no power at all across North Bundaberg by that time. Quite correctly, the authorities had disconnected the electricity at the first sign of floodwaters. It was eerie to look out, see no lights at all, and remember how many people lived nearby.

Faced with the prospect of wading through that black, silent water in the dark, I began to accept the enormity of what was happening. This wasn't something just happening to my family. In homes all over north Bundaberg, people would be looking out at the water, wondering why they'd decided to stay, why they hadn't been a little better prepared or reacted sooner to the call to evacuate.

At that time, standing on my top step, what I really didn't understand was that for some people, their homes were already completely lost, and they would wake up, wondering what their future would be from this morning onward. My family still had our future to make, and I was determined that it would see all of us happy and safe again, even if we had to walk away from our house.

But first I had to get the ladder.

It is during our darkest moments that
we must focus to see the light.
　　　　　　　　　—Aristotle Onassis

Trying not to think of all the animals—
snakes particularly are what I thought of—that
might be taking refuge in the shed or might
be carried along by the flood, I stepped into
the water. Driving me past my primal fear of
reptiles with fangs was the thought of Gina,
and how much she and my little girl, Ruby,
had to rely on me. In fact, I felt like the whole
family was relying on me. But, of course, the
truth was we were all relying on each other.

With the torch in my mouth, I felt my way
through the cold water along the side wall
of the house and then struck out across the
water-filled space that should have been our
backyard to the shed. The water was waist
deep across the yard, but it was still a surprise
when I rolled the door up and got inside to find
everything afloat.

The ladder was long and awkward to carry,
a heavy-duty piece of equipment. I managed to
carry it to the neighbour's fence and use it to
help climb over. Again, a spike of fear caught

me. I didn't really know what was on the other side of the fence, hidden under the water. Any minute I expected to trip over something or put my foot in a hole. And if anything had floated by and touched me then, I'm not sure what I would have done.

It seems like a scene out a movie when I try to imagine it. There I was, carrying this heavy ladder over my head, my only light a torch held in my mouth, with floodwater dripping off the ladder into my eyes, probably getting into my mouth. I remember praying to God to help us all get through this—to help me get through this for the family's sake.

Until you've tried to extend a ladder in the dark, waist deep in floodwater, I don't think you can actually understand how difficult such a simple job can be. It was a heavy-duty ladder and difficult to manoeuvre at the best of times, so I virtually had no control over it. I couldn't be certain of my footing, and the water made it difficult to balance.

In fact, I was concentrating so much on trying to get the ladder up that when it swung around and hit me on the head, I actually forgot I had the torch in my mouth long enough to yelp. And that's how I lost the torch in the water.

A full moon was pushing a weak light through the clouds, just enough light to help me open the ladder and get it up against the wall of the house.

I just couldn't get it to sit firmly enough feel safe using it. I didn't want to be halfway up the ladder and find myself dropped in the water, perhaps carried away. The dilemma, I discovered, was due to a thick shrubbery against the front of the house. Rather than the weight of the ladder resting against the wall, the springy branches of the bushes were taking the weight, as well as moving in response to the water and to every movement the ladder made.

In the end, there was nothing I could do. All the time I spent trying to make it safer I was thinking of the water, of how it was rising and rising, and how it wasn't going to stop just because I couldn't get a ladder safely against a wall. I worried for all my family, but the strongest thoughts in my mind were for Gina and Ruby.

Gina was heavily pregnant, and Ruby was only a little girl, so I think I was right to worry more about them. They had to be my most important personal responsibility, but everybody had to be moved as soon as possible. I had to take a chance. I just had to push as hard as I could against the bushes and hope the ladder stayed in position long enough for me to get in through that window.

> *If it can be solved, there's no need to worry, and if can't be solved, worry is of no use.*
>
> —Dalai Lama

Chapter 3

THE FIRST EVACUATION

When you think back on times like these, you realise that your mind works in very different ways when you're stressed.

I had been so worried about getting up the ladder the thoughts had slowed me down. But after I managed to get into the house and opened the front door, climbing the ladder seemed so easy. In fact, in my mind I started to think how simple a job it really had been, and I obviously had secret reserves I could call on when disaster struck. Maybe I could think of myself as a bit of a hero, sort of like Spider-Man—only without his webs—climbing the ladder so fast it felt like I was running up the rungs and sneaking though the window, opening the front door to safety.

Then I looked out at the dirty swirling water and realised climbing the ladder had been the simplest thing to do compared with getting the family, little Ruby, and especially Gina across the water safely.

So I was a different man who went back to the fence to climb back over to my own yard. Not so cocky or sure of myself. Worried about what still had to be done.

What I saw on the fence gave me something to think about, stopping me for a moment.

The top of the fence was alive with ants desperately clambering on top of each other to reach the highest point of the fence to keep out of the water.

Learning from the Buddhist teaching, I am taught to revere all life, but I don't think my faith is necessarily the reason I suddenly saw our situation differently. Watching the ants climb over each other, carrying their eggs, it came home to me that, at times like these, we humans are no different than other living creatures—just as desperate to survive. The only difference is that humans can make choices about what actions they take.

Those ants helped me look outwards to what everyone was facing rather than inwards to me and my family. Sure, there might be people like the ants, who would climb over other people in their panic to stay safe, but I had faith that most of the community I knew and was part of would reach out to help, and together, we would survive.

This understanding did a lot to free my thinking. Thoughts had been going around and around in my head: *What will we do? How will we all be safe? How could we keep Ruby safe? Gina cannot possibly walk through this water.*

I had been unable to make any real progress solving that immediate problem, which was getting Gina across to the house.

It seems that life is a lot more like a movie script than we believe possible. Just when you're most desperate and almost out of ideas, no options left, the miracle happens.

The lesson of the ants was still in my head, and that encouraged me. But how to translate the lesson into the reality of safety was a concern that really discouraged me. Then, just as I got to the house, I saw Gina. She was smiling so sweetly and with such pride that I immediately stopped worrying, and the miracle happened.

We can use mattresses, I thought, *to get Gina and the family across to the house.* We would take Gina first, then Ruby, then Mum. The visualisation of us riding on mattresses like rafts struck me with the realisation that here we were, like refugees all over again.

Well, we'd done it once. We could do it again.

I remember especially the smile on Gina's face as she climbed onto the raft mattress. To this day, I don't know if she was smiling at using a mattress as a raft, or because she was enjoying the experience. All I know was it gave me such confidence that we would be all right. She was handling it well. Ruby thought it was fun. "Daddy made a nice boat," she said, which made us all laugh even though the water was up to my waist.

Mum was a bit frightened by the experience. She didn't see how the mattress could float with the weight on it. But she was strong and composed herself. By the time she was halfway across, she was smiling, too.

Uncle 7 stayed on one side of the raft, and I stayed on the other, steadying it as we navigated towards the fence. We then used the ladder to make a bridge from the fence to the house.

Then we couldn't put it off any longer. It was time for us to say a final farewell to our home. Uncle 7, BM, and I went around shutting all the windows and moving some of our belongings even higher. Perhaps something might be saved.

It was a shock to see the prayer hall. Water had risen to the point where the table was almost underwater. We moved everything from the table—our lamps, Buddha statue, vases, prayer mats, everything we could move—to higher places in the house. While we worked, I couldn't help wondering how high the water would rise, even though I realised there was no point worrying because it was out of our hands entirely. All we could do was the best we could do … and hope.

We worked as fast as we could.

After all that hard work and feeling we were making a difference, suddenly we had nothing to do but try to rest in a strange house and gather our physical resources.

My mind wouldn't let that happen. We were resting, of course. What else could we do? But our minds were on full alert. Gina and I talked about the flood and the impossible amount of water that had come and was still coming towards us. Nothing anybody had said prepared us for the reality of this flood. Do you think if we'd known or could imagine it that we would have stuck around just for the thrill of floating around on mattresses? Of course not.

But, of course, people sometimes don't want to hear the truth.

Gina's younger brother, Tam, had been calling non-stop, begging us to just go. Mum had tried to get Gina and Ruby and me to go, saying she would stay to look after things. Had we listened to their concerns and all the family had left, we wouldn't now be trying to rest in the next-door house while our own home slowly went underwater.

So the sorry truth was that maybe we had been told but just hadn't been able to believe. Whatever the case, we soon learned there were a lot more people in the same boat.

As it grew closer to dawn, more and more sounds came from outside. We could hear voices, shouting and calling. And vibrating through the air was the sound of boat engines. At about 5 a.m., I tried to get some information off the radio. We needed to know what was happening to work out what to do next. All I could get was music. Gina and Ruby were drowsing on the floor, and nearby, Mum, Uncle 7, and BM were trying to do the same thing.

At last, I decided to use my phone to try to get some news off the Internet radio. We had been a long time without power by that time. The phone was dangerously low on power, and I wanted to make it last until we were all safe.

The news was not good. First, they told me how the water had risen past 8.5.

I wanted to swear. I wanted up-to-date news. I had almost no power, and it was being wasted on somebody telling me—and everybody else waiting for up-to-date information—what I already knew.

But then they said the water was at 8.73 metres and was continuing to rise.

I jumped up; 8.73 metres!

Too bad if everybody needed more rest. We had to get out. And we had to do it now.

> *Knowing is not enough, we must apply. Willing is not enough, we must do.*
>
> —Bruce Lee

> *I always like to look on the optimistic side of life, but I am realistic enough to know that life is a complex matter.*
> —Walt Disney

Chapter 4

THE SECOND EVACUATION

We all heard the sounds coming from outside. We all knew there were boats outside, moving along the streets, and that they carried people.

Knowing is different than believing. Seeing is believing.

The street had become a river. The houses formed the "riverbanks." If you stayed in the middle, between the houses, you were in the main channel—the centre of the street.

Everything ... all we'd had the day before to remind us that we lived in the midst of houses and shops and parks, farmlands, and shopping centres had disappeared. We were a community of lake houses and of boats.

Lots of water. Lots and lots of water. I remember looking around and being stopped by the realisation of just how much water there was.

Gina flashed her torch, and I shouted for help. We had no boat, and the fact remained that the water was still rising.

Two men on a boat came close by us. One of them pointed to another boat coming into view around a corner. We understood that boat would pick us up.

We came to know the man in that second boat as Darren, but all we could do at first was watch as this young stranger, dressed only in shorts, tried to manoeuvre his boat as close as he could to the front stairs of the house. The problem for him was the fence and the shrubs, all hidden underwater and ready to foul his engine.

We didn't care that he was young. Or that he was barely dressed. He had a quiet calmness about him that was extraordinary in the circumstances. He gave the impression of an old soul. Whatever the case, we understood he would do his best job and that his job would be saving us. He gave us hope and confidence for the future.

Looking back, I realise I had, for a moment,

wondered if it might have been just too early in the morning for such a young man to be full of chat and energy. More kindly, I thought that perhaps he was weary from a night rescuing people and had no energy left for chat. I wondered if the calm competence that gave us confidence was nothing more than exhaustion of one sort or another.

The thoughts were fleeting. Watching him manoeuvre his boat, I was sure he would see us safely away. Indeed, I learnt later that part of his quietness might have been exhaustion. He had been up all night, ferrying people to safety. He and his boat were there for us and for so many other people.

Once we were all on board, Darren turned the boat towards the highest point of the street nearby, which was the Liberty Petrol Station. As the morning sky lightened, we could see in the distance people standing around at the petrol station. If the water had seemed calm and there'd been no boat, perhaps one of us might even have tried to walk or swim there for help. But it soon became obvious any attempt of that sort would have been doomed from the start.

The water raged against us. We were heading directly against it by trying to get to the petrol station. The river pushed back as hard as we pushed forward, swinging us off course a couple of times. Changing direction in the little boat was not easy, but Darren had to navigate his way, and course changes were necessary. A couple of times we were pushed into signposts as we were moved sideways, but Darren finally got us to the petrol station.

Or as close as he could get. He had to drop us off with a good hundred-metre walk through fast-moving water to reach dry land. The water was only knee deep, but I was particularly worried, of course, about the smallest people, Gina and Ruby.

At times like this, you have to put everything aside and do what you must do. Darren knew what he had to do. We watched him get back in his boat and go back out onto the water.

Now it's up to us to help ourselves, I thought.

I went out first to see what the conditions were like underfoot. If Gina or Ruby fell, the water could carry them away before we could catch them. It seemed that it was flat underfoot, as long as we stuck near a fence line.

In the end, we set off with Uncle 7 in the lead, carrying Ruby. I followed, holding on to the fence with one hand and to Gina with the other, staying close to Uncle 7. Then Mum and BM.

When we made to the end of the road, we realised we had another problem—an underwater roundabout. Somehow, we had to get across the space, and we knew the levels would be changing underfoot because of the roundabout. Not only that, but the wide area meant the current was very strong and the water very turbulent. Even though the water wasn't as deep, it was more dangerous.

Mum suggested Chu Bay and I take them across one by one. We should leave her and Gina behind, first taking the littlest, Ruby. Then we could come back for Gina and last of all, for Mum.

We thought about that for some time. Neither Uncle 7 nor I liked the idea of leaving anybody behind, but we also thought we would be stronger if we stood together. Finally, we linked arms and set out across the flow of the water, fearful of what the roundabout might bring.

That's when we met our second saviour of the day.

A Land Cruiser ute left the station and came slowly across the water toward us. The driver was an older man called Scott. Like Darren, he had been playing a big part in rescuing people, using his four-wheel drive.

About fifty people were waiting at the petrol station for the SES. Looking at their lost and fearful faces, we caught a glimpse of what our own faces must have looked like to them.

The men and women sat with their belongings, mostly a small backpack, though some had their dogs. I had carried my laptop over one shoulder, and we all carried a small bundle of things we'd need.

The sun was now well up. We had left the neighbour's house at about 5:30 a.m., and it was now about 7 a.m. We had the small sense of relief that we would soon be taken from our little dry island that was the petrol station. But time passed, and the water continued to rise. Dry spaces became harder to find.

One man insisted he had been given permission to do whatever was necessary to keep people dry, so he and a few other men broke into an abandoned building next door and moved some of the woman and children—including Ruby, Gina, and Mum—into the house. That wasn't such a good idea, as it turned out, because the balcony collapsed a bit later. The building was unsafe, and hence, it had been abandoned!

Everybody scurried back out, but before we had time to stop being surprised about the collapse and begin worrying again about the rising river, we learned the SES boat was nearby. So we started readying ourselves to be evacuated.

By that time, our fifty evacuees had turned into between seventy and eighty people thanks to Darren and his other boat rescuers. From where we were, we could see other people being rescued from the roofs of their houses by helicopters. Soon it would be our turn to be taken somewhere safe.

Space was tight. Everyone needed to be dryer than they were. We were tired, hungry, shocked, hopeful, and grateful at the same time. And we couldn't wait to be somewhere else.

It was time to begin the next leg of our journey.

> *Sometimes life hits you in the head with a brick. Don't lose faith.*
> —Steve Jobs

Chapter 5

THIRD EVACUATION

Word came that the SES was going to be evacuating us soon and were busy planning how to get us out. Helicopters were busy everywhere. Perhaps we would be taken out by helicopter.

Then we learned the SES was down the "road" and around the corner, nearly a hundred metres away, and we would have to go to them. No helicopter for us.

The SES plan seemed unreasonable until I realised the helicopters would have been reserved for the truly desperate. We weren't at that stage yet. But surely we shouldn't have to go back out though the water to get to the SES.

Then we saw one of the boat rescuers dragging his dinghy through the water. The water was too shallow to be safe, but deep enough to be dangerous. We would use the dinghy to ferry older people across the street, closer to the SES boats.

We would have to use four or five men to haul the dinghy carrying only one or two people at a time. More people would make the dinghy too heavy. Once everybody had been ferried across the street, they would have to walk around the corner some fifty metres to the SES.

I must admit, by this stage I felt completely used up emotionally and physically. I was ready to let the rescuers take control of everything. *Just tell me where to go and what to do, and I'll do it,* I thought. But Gina, my beautiful pregnant wife, had other ideas.

She wanted to help. Gina is always looking for ways to help, to add value to people's lives. Being pregnant is a glorious state, but I'm sure it can feel limiting sometimes. Gina was in no position to be towing dinghies about, rescuing people. But she thought it was something I could do. And so I became both rescued and rescuer.

To be sure, having something to do that made a difference to people's lives did more to make me feel better than sitting about waiting could have. I had more left physically than I thought, and mentally, I found being able to help empowering. And, of course, Gina's proud smile was a big encouragement.

I remember one elderly woman in particular. She was still in her nightgown. Sometime during the night, she injured her shin. The bleeding had stopped, and the cut was quite dry but looked painful. The dirty river water would have infected an open wound. I helped put her in the boat, and we dragged her around the corner. Then I set off to carry her to the SES boats.

It's not that she weighed so much, really. But gee, after a while, she started to get heavy. I was pushing against the muddy water, holding her out of it, and by halfway to the SES, I thought my arms surely had to be about to fall off.

I was starting to regret volunteering to carry her, thinking that I wasn't so big a man and that someone larger and stronger would have done a better job. But by that stage, I couldn't just let go, or she'd fall into the water. Somehow, I kept my grip. Eventually, it did become too much, and I had to ask a man just ahead of me for a hand. My muscles really thanked me when he took some of the weight.

That was when she cracked a joke to let

me know she'd seen the agony I was going through.

Luckily, she told me, she hadn't had breakfast yet.

Her appreciation for what we were doing for her and her implied understanding of what we, her rescuers, were going through, actually helped me recover my energy for the second time! I actually felt pretty good that I had been the one to volunteer to help her.

And every time I headed back toward the dinghy and helped another elderly person, child, or animal into the boats, I could see Gina, smiling and encouraging me with all her positive energy, not at all worried about our baby and how vulnerable being pregnant made her in these dangerous times.

I am so proud of her. And I realised how right she was to have pushed me into volunteering to help—and how often women are right when they push their men to do things. I love her, so I usually end up doing what she wants. I might grump a bit, but as soon as I start doing whatever it is, I usually feel really great about doing it.

Then it was our time to go.

When we climbed into the SES boats and put the life jackets on, I finally felt like we were truly in safe hands. These were people trained for emergencies like this. I had confidence in all the other people who already helped us and felt very grateful they had helped. But they had been working on good intentions and instinct, and I now realised how much safer I felt in the hands of trained people.

We went into different boats. Ruby, Gina, and I smiled and waved to Mum, Uncle 7, and BM like we were all going off on a cruise down the river. For a moment, the experience felt so lighthearted.

Then we went past our house.

The water had reached our bedroom window. I felt my smile suddenly disappear, and I saw the same thing happening on the faces of Gina, BM, Mum, and Uncle 7. Looking at our home made me feel sick deep inside.

Gina picked up her phone just then. I saw her put a big smile on her face. My mother from Perth was calling, wanting to know what was happening with us as she had been watching the news. Gina told her not to worry, that everything was fine, we were all okay, and the water wasn't really troubling us. My mum thought we were out in the car, and that's why there was a lot of noise.

That's Gina, who doesn't like to worry people unnecessarily.

I was thinking if Mum had called me, I wouldn't have thought at all and would have blurted out the news. Mum would have panicked and worried herself to death. Luckily, my phone was dead. The universe plans well. All things happen for a reason.

We travelled down the other side of the road—well, really the other side of a river—past the IGA shopping centre, car park completely under, and on down Queen Street, which reminded me more of the Mekong River than a Bundaberg street. Everywhere I looked was water. Eight in the morning, the sun shining, clear visibility all around, and the only thing to see was water and half-submerged houses.

Trees floated by like twigs. Skip bins bounced along in the current.

Yet again, I upgraded my idea of how vast this flood was. It was beyond "the big wet." This was a true inundation.

We were headed towards North Primary School, high up off the river's flood plain and the primary evacuation point in North Bundaberg for disasters like this flood. There were hundreds of people there, more than I thought possible, and more boats were arriving by the minute. More people had been rescued during the night by boat and helicopter. Thousands were without homes.

We landed at North Primary, and a policeman told us we had to keep going to North Bundaberg High School, where there was an evacuation centre. He was trying to find a ride for us when a man with a ute offered us a lift.

The boys all sat in the back, and the girls got to ride in the cab, which was a bit of a tight fit. We drove past numbers of weary police and fire and rescue, people you don't often see groups of in Queensland and a sure sign the flood was considered a true disaster.

The evacuation centre was not as I imagined it would be. It was full of people, that's true, but nothing much seemed to be happening. It was as if once rescued, the people had been dumped. People lay on mattress, stood around talking, or just seemed in a daze, unfocussed.

We settled in, and I set off wondering what could be done to help. A truck full of fruit and veggies was waiting to be unloaded, so I did that.

The Red Cross and Salvation Army said there were shortages of bread and mattresses. Paul, my friend over the river, might have been able to do something about mattresses, so I found a phone and rang him. Then I met a nice woman, Jenny, who was waiting for her husband to arrive at the evacuation centre, and asked her to take me to the BP service station to look for bread.

Everybody had the same idea. There was hardly anything left.

Gina tried to donate some money to help buy supplies but was told there were no supplies to be bought. It really brought home the idea that sometimes, money just doesn't have any value at all. Personal effort is all that counts. But there's only so much you can do with blood and bone and heart.

Soon after that, I ran into Trevor, one of my employees. Gina's brother, Victor, had asked him to come and find us. Trevor took me out to the farm, and suddenly, I felt like I was a little in charge again. There was my own ute, and I could charge my phone. Of course, I could only drive between the evacuation centre and the farm thanks to water across the roads, but I felt I could at least do something.

I drove the ute back to the evacuation centre to pick up Mum and Uncle 7 and drop them at the farm, where they felt more comfortable. But Gina wanted to stay back to see how she could help. I later joined her after dropping Mum and Uncle 7 off.

> *You cannot escape the responsibility*
> *of tomorrow by evading it today.*
> —Abraham Lincoln

> *Try not to become a man of success,*
> *but rather try to become a man of*
> *value.*
> —Albert Einstein

Chapter 6

THE FINAL EVACUATION

In total, we evacuated four times: from our house to the neighbour's, to the Liberty Petrol Station, to the evacuation centre at North Bundaberg State High School, and finally to our farm, SSS Strawberries.

When Gina and I chose to stay back at the high school evacuation centre, we didn't know that a little later, we'd be helping evacuate the high school as the river continued to rise.

As Gina said, this would be the only time Australian police were okay allowing a run-down ute to be on the road, especially a ute with a trailer filled with people. When I got to the new evacuation centre, Oakwood School, near our farm, we found cars parked everywhere. I offered drivers of cars with caravans a spot at the farm's car park, so we had two evacuation centres at Oakwood.

On late Monday afternoon, I had a call to help evacuate the elderly in the retirement village.

One of the policemen helping people at the village was called Mark. Exhausted, he sat there in my old, rusty, barely legal ute and told me he had been waist deep for eight hours, helping the evacuation. What a hero!

About eighty to ninety people ended up staying on our farm. We could provide fresh drinking water, some food, power to charge their phones, and a roof over their head. Oakwood School had thousands of people, and supplies there were hard to find.

As you can imagine, we made many friends and heard many stories while Oswald's flood ruled our lives.

> *Don't walk behind me; I may not lead.*
> *Don't walk in front of me; I may not*
> *follow. Just walk beside me and be my*
> *friend.*
>
> —Albert Camus

Chapter 7

THE CLEANUP

It wasn't till about five days later that we and the people of North Bundaberg were allowed to return to our homes. As you can imagine, after the water receded, everything was a wreck. Roads were torn apart; houses removed off their stumps, some were even washed away down the road; cars turned upside down; and fallen trees everywhere. It was just like a war zone. The disaster management people needed to check everything to make sure it was safe for people to return to their homes. The authorities, especially police, monitored the bridge as they didn't want tourists nosing around while the residents faced the agony of seeing their devastated homes.

As I got to my house, I could see the

aftermath of the flood on my house. There was sand and mud across my front lawn. The letter box had fallen over, and the air-condition units once sitting nicely against the side wall of the house were washed away and lying next to the fence line. As I walked up the front steps, I could see the sand and mud on the front veranda and the water stain on the front window.

Inside, I could hear the smoke alarm going off as Uncle 7, Mum, and I tried to open our front door. The door was jammed due to a thick layer of mud inside the house, and a piece of furniture had pushed against the door, making it very difficult to open. After many pushes and shoves and kicking, we managed to open the door just enough to squeeze inside. The first thing that hit me was the smell of the mud. How can I describe it … imagine urine mixed with human waste, dead animals, dead fish, rotten food all mixed together. Thick, thick mud was everywhere.

As I walked through the house, going through the hallway, past the bedrooms, into the kitchen, past the living room, down the library, and into the prayer hall, I was emotionally overwhelmed. At that moment I thought, *What a mammoth task this will be.* I just didn't know where to begin. Everything was everywhere. Whatever we had stacked up or placed up high on tables or desks was now scattered everywhere on the floor, in the mud. The water had gone up to my head inside, so you can imagine everything we moved up was now covered in mud. Nothing was worth saving.

Chapter 8

CASE STUDY

Keith Iseppi
Bundaberg Outdoor Power Centre

If you ever wanted to know what it is like to have all your hard work covered in muddy water up to the rooftop of your shop, Keith is truly the man to talk to. His business did not only flood once, twice, three times, but numerous times not just in 2013 but also in 2011 as well.

The shop that he leases is right on the lowest point of the town centre. And every time it rains we all cross our fingers as the first place to flood will be his business. The building is two stories high, and it was built up after the 1942 flood. He thought the second level was his haven and that no water would ever reach that high. So he shifted his entire inventory to the second level. Well, not only did the water reach the first level, it ended up being 1.6 metres high into the second level. Everything that he and his staff shifted up there to prepare for the flood is now gone.

What's funny was that the day the flood came, Keith was enjoying his holiday with his daughter in Tasmania. When he was finally able to answer his phone, he had like a thousand messages. Everybody was looking for him and asking him for advice. Having experienced the 2011 flood, he stayed calm and told his staff to shift everything up to the second level, and he would jump onto the next flight back home.

Another dilemma Keith encountered was that his car was parked at the Brisbane airport, and he couldn't drive home because the roads were blocked due to the flooding. Anxious as he was, he made it as far as Hervey Bay and had to charter a plane to Bundaberg.

Through perseverance and experience, as soon as the water receded, he and his staff were able to quickly get into the shop and start the cleaning process. As a business owner, time was at the essence for Keith. The quicker he could get his shop repaired, the sooner he could start trading, and that was exactly what they did. Within a matter of weeks, they could start trading again. It couldn't come at a better time because their business had so much to offer the community, especially to those who were still cleaning up.

From a financial side, Keith was able to claim a lot back from the insurance company. Again, because of the experience he had in the 2011 flood, he made sure that his business was covered in the case of another natural disaster.

One advice that Keith was able to offer is to look at your insurance policy and make sure that it covers whatever you need. There is nothing worse than assuming that because you have insurance, whether for your house or business, that it will cover for any natural disaster. Again, it's all about being prepared, especially if you are living in a natural disaster–prone area.

Dion Taylor
Tasty Food Creator

I can recall being one of the first people to
return to the North side of town when the old
bridge was formally re-opened to pedestrians
and my business was literally one of the first you
could see on the right hand side of the bridge.
Mixed emotions pulsed through my body as
we had been relying on the local news footage
and after seeing what I thought a helicopter
view of our building being virtually engulfed
by water just days before, relief genuinely set
in when I first handily saw the damage.

It's a strange experience to recall, but I
vividly remember the sense of community and
in the same breath, helplessness.

You see, when I walked over that bridge
my first desire was to make sure everything
was ok, but in realising that most possessions,
excepting some heavy timber furniture and the
fortunate paperwork in the top drawer of a 4
drawer filing cabinet that hadn't been moisture
affected or directly washed, it fast became
apparent that there were many; many others,
particularly residents that had lost belongings,
pets, homes and much loved memories.

Fortunately within what seemed like hours,

there was a fleet of organisations setting up in the immediate area to offer general cleaning assistance, rubbish pile creators and refreshments to keep us nourished.

I don't recall knowing many of the volunteers and yet there was a genuine need to help out a total stranger in what was evidently a time of need for so many of us to try and restore what had previously been some kind of normality in our suburb.

During the following days, building were emptied of debris, the streets started to look like what I can only imagine a war zone of kinds with a feeling if senseless loss and heart ache. At the time I wasn't aware, but looking back, many of us were dealing with shock, mental & physical fatigue and the million dollar question of when will life return to normal.

Rebuilding did come. Whilst slow at first, it seemed that as our minds changed focus from destruction to survival, our instincts were to rebuild with what we have and look for alternative sources of space. We were fortunate to have access to another business premise in the short term that one of our clients offered us and for this we are eternally grateful.

In summary, we had some lessons I would rather not experience ever again, though in the same instance, I now know the level of resilience & determination that is needed to recover both professionally and personally when something like a natural disaster is upon you.

- PREPARE for disasters to occur. They may not ever happen in your lifetime, but not knowing what to do is not an option.
- Have a PLAN. When the disaster occurs, ask yourself who goes where, what happens to the business, your staff, your home, and your family?
- HELP. How can you help out? Once you have assessed your own situation, are there others that need help more than you? The sense of community is restored by everyone getting back on top of things.
- ASK. Don't forget yourself when helping others. It's imperative to keep on top of nutrition, rest and mental health. Any level of involvement during disaster management can be tiresome and there is no benefit if you also go down in the storm- so to speak.

OFFICE OF THE MAYOR

JACK DEMPSEY
T: 07 4130 4264   W: 1300 883 699
E: mayor@bundaberg.qld.gov.au
facebook.com/BundabergRegionalCouncil
bundaberg.qld.gov.au

BUNDABERG
REGIONAL COUNCIL

A tumultuous time

The worst of times so often brings out the very best in people. The floods and tornadoes that created such destruction to the Bundaberg Region in January 2013 may have shattered our homes, our possessions but never the unshakeable faith we, as a community, have in each other.

Our region is no stranger to adversity. We have endured natural disasters of every kind, and every tumultuous event has simply strengthened the bonds of mateship on which we have forged our community spirit.

People helped simply because they could. They wanted to. The lending hand that genuine communities extend to those in need was there for all to see. While that initial level of help to victims of the disaster was delivered in an ad hoc yet genuinely responsive manner, some priceless moments were forever etched into the memories of those who received the organised assistance of the Mud Army.

Community volunteers in their hundreds – the Mud Army · swarmed across the flood and tornado ravaged areas and assisted in a clean-up that otherwise may have taken authorities weeks to effect.

In the final damage analysis, the financial cost was in the tens of millions of dollars. The level of community care, the value of what we gave to each other – simply priceless.

Jack Dempsey
Mayor - Bundaberg Regional Council

Chapter 9

WHAT I LEARNED FROM OSWALD'S FLOOD

While we were at the evacuation centre, sitting there, waiting for someone to come and register us, I realised something. At that moment, people are just like all other people, with the same needs and fears.

It didn't matter where we had come from, what status we had achieved, how much money we had. Rich or poor, we were all the same.

Money was not an issue.

Even if you had it, there was nowhere to spend it and nothing to spend it on. Even if you wanted to spend your money for the benefit of all evacuees, there was still nothing to spend it on: no food, no dry clothes, no beds to be paid for.

I saw a man I knew who was very wealthy. He drove an expensive car, always wore the best clothes, and lived in a very prestigious area. When I saw him, he looked exactly like everybody else, dressed in shorts and the T-shirt he'd grabbed before being evacuated.

I learned that at a time of disaster, the only thing you have of any value is your ability to give of yourself.

Times like this are about people helping people. Strangers helping strangers. It's a time to take whatever resources you have—your hands, legs, energy, or your car or boat—and share what you have. Make someone else's life a little better and safer.

Gina, my wife, and Mum did a lot to help me understand this. They are always looking for ways to help people. They have a mindset that doesn't allow them to rely too much on other people but gives them the strength and ability to be helpful to people who might need a little help. In times of adversity, if you focus on serving other people first, it will give you strength to overcome any obstacle.

> *In times of adversity and change, we really discover who we are and what we're made of.*
>
> —Howard Schultz

For instance, we had the option of being choppered across the river. Victor, Gina's older brother, was waiting to take us to Bargara, where our lives could get back to normal, and we would leave the drama of North Bundaberg behind.

But we decided to stay where we could help. With our access to the farm, there was so much we could do in North Bundaberg to help. In Bargara, we would have just been sitting in a comfortable home, being a little selfish.

That was never an option we could consider.

I also learned resilience is very important. Having the courage to get back up and get going after being knocked down numerous times shows how strong the human spirit can be. Don't let anyone tell you otherwise. Stand up for what you believe in, and don't ever give up.

> *Don't ever let somebody tell you, you can't do something ... you got a dream, you gotta protect it. People*

*can't do something themselves they
wanna tell you that you can't do it.
You want something, go get it. Period!*
—Chris Gardner, *The Pursuit of
Happyness*

For me, being robbed, getting evacuated four times, moving three times, and cleaning our homes and friend's business made me and my family stronger. With the persistence and work ethic, my family and I were able to overcome those hurdles. I believe if you can embrace the resilience and persistence, you can overcome any adversity in your life.

*Nothing is impossible, the word itself
says "I'm possible"!*
—Audrey Hepburn

(L–R) BM, Uncle 7, Mum, and Gina, sandbagging.

Sandbags in front of our prayer hall. We used
rice bags and pillowcases as sandbags.

Sitting in our front driveway, waiting. The water level was the same as in the 2011 flood.

Me walking up the neighbour's front stairs. These are the mattresses we used to carry the family across to the neighbour's house.

Riding past our house and seeing the water level.

The facial expression says everything.
Taken around 5:30 a.m.

Evacuating from the Liberty Petrol Station to the SES.

On the SES boats.

Riding past our house again.

The evacuation centre on our farm.

Coming back to our house for the first time after the flood.

Air-conditioning unit washed away.

The front porch, mud and sand everywhere.

How high the water got inside our prayer hall.

Damage everywhere inside the house.

Me standing there. What a mess! Where to start?

Gina assessing the damage. The water
level was well above her head.

Start cleaning.

Because of contamination, we had
to throw everything out.

The rubbish we threw out covers our front lawn.

Printed in the United States
By Bookmasters